Just One Life

Pat Abercromby

London | New York

Published by Clink Street Publishing 2017

Copyright © 2017

First edition.

ISBN:
978-1-911525-53-0 - paperback
978-1-911525-54-7 - ebook

Plaisir d'amour ne dure qu'un moment.

Chagrin d'amour dure toute la vie.

The joy of love is but a moment long.
The pain of love endures for a lifetime.

Music by Jean-Paul Egide Martini (1741–1816)
Lyrics by Jean Pierre Claris de Florian (1755–1794)

This story is dedicated to all the lives affected by events that leave in their wake, total dependency on others. But particularly, for the ordinary and often extraordinary lives of carers; young, old, male or female, whose hopes, dreams and ambitions for their futures are snatched away from them, often in a heartbeat. Carers who find themselves sublimating their own needs and frequently their physical and mental health to look after a dependent family member. Without proper support or understanding from their community, nobody fully appreciates how difficult a task they have. They all have a story and should be heard.

Prologue

'Has your husband signed a DNR?'

DNR? Fran's brain could not make any sense of his words.

'Does -he -want -to -be -resuscitated?' He pronounced each word carefully, as if he were talking to someone with little understanding of English.

He had not even bothered to sit down beside her as she sat numbly, waiting outside the side ward. Instead he stood, impatiently waiting for her to answer, his arms hanging oddly limp at his sides, the sleeves of his white coat, incongruously too long. Why did she notice such a trivial detail when Rob's life was hanging in the balance?

'I don't know,' she replied, stunned, looking up at him. 'Is he that ill? We never discussed it.'

'Yes, he is quite unwell, he has pneumonia and sepsis and if we can stabilise him here, he will be transferred to the Intensive Care Unit.' The doctor was impatient for a specific response and kept glancing back through the small window of the side ward.

'Well yes, I think he would want to be resuscitated.' The words slipped out of her mouth unbidden and before she could elaborate or ask any questions the doctor shot back into the room slamming the door behind him. Through the small window, all she could see were the backs of gowned and gloved minders wielding tubes and fluids, forcing life back into her husband's inert body.

She sat for hours in the hospital's I.C.U. family waiting room, staring at the eponymous hospital copy of *Country Life*. Balm for the souls of the distressed and grieving she thought, wryly leafing unseeingly through the pages. It all seemed so unreal. She felt very disassociated from it all, as if it were happening to somebody else. She almost felt like laughing, as if this unfolding drama were some sort of joke. What was wrong with her? For once he was out of control and had no say in the outcome. In that moment, she had held his life in her hands. Then reality set in. What if they could not resuscitate him? What if he were to survive this latest assault on his being? He might end up even more dependent. How would she react? Random thoughts and possible outcomes swirled around in her mind. How had it all come to this? How had she become caught up in this hopeless dynamic of life-time carer? For the first time in her life, she gave herself permission for introspection, without judgement. She had never wanted to examine her life choices, or her motives, so closely before. It was too uncomfortable.

It had started at an early age she realised now. She remembered hearing as a three-year-old, that Mr Potter across the road had died. Everybody drew their blinds on the day of the funeral and spoke in sombre tones. Fran had somehow escaped from her house and marched across the road with a dustpan and brush to sweep Mrs Potter's doorstep, quite sure that this would be a comfort. Mrs Potter had opened her door and looked down in astonishment at the wee girl.

'I'm sorry Mr Potter's gone to heaven,' she had lisped. Even at that tender age, wanting to rescue. For most of her childhood though, she remained invisible. Fran was, after all, the third, unplanned child born to a mother unprepared, and edging towards an eventual nervous breakdown.

'Mrs Patterson?'

Fran looked up, startled out of her reverie as the I.C.U. nurse crossed the room and sat beside her. The nurse laid her hand on Fran's arm. 'We have managed to stabilise your husband, but he is not out of the woods yet. Just to warn you,

2

the doctor has had to insert a tube into his neck vein so that we can deliver antibiotics and other medications directly into his bloodstream. It looks a bit horrific, but we are keeping him comfortable.'

Fran thought this might be a euphemism for, 'We might still lose him but we are doing our best.'

'You can come and sit with him if you want,' the nurse encouraged kindly.

'Is he conscious?' Fran asked anxiously, reluctant to keep vigil with him otherwise.

The nurse hesitated. 'He is slipping in and out of consciousness, but it might help him if he hears your voice.'

My voice is not necessarily the voice he would prefer to hear, Fran thought to herself, but she nodded her head and obediently started to follow the nurse through to the ward. She was vaguely aware that some of the other relatives in the family room were looking at her as she left, but she could not bear to make eye contact with them, they all had their own traumas to process.

The I.C.U. ward felt like a space station. Each bed was surrounded by a variety of robotic-looking machines and monitors bleeping and clicking away, guarding the occupants with lines attached to exposed chests and tubes inserted into orifices and veins. She glanced fearfully at each patient as she passed their beds. Who would be claiming their broken bodies with their failing organs she wondered? Mercifully their eyes were closed, either because they were unconscious or because of the glaring lights. She searched out her husband. His bed was in an L-shaped part of the room, away from the main ward and he too was hooked up to the robots. Sure enough a tube, held in place by tape, was sticking out of his neck. She had the irreverent thought that if he had a matching tube sticking out the other side, he would have looked like Frankenstein.

The nurse brought a chair over for Fran. 'Rob, your wife's here to see you.' She spoke loudly into his ear, perhaps thinking that Fran might be incapable of speech at that moment. His eyes fluttered open for a second, squinting against the harsh brightness of the overhead light. She had visions of the neck tube popping out if he turned his head. She quickly stood up and leaned over him so that he could see her face, and to block out some of the light, allowing him to keep his eyes open for longer than a nanosecond.

'Hey, it's me, Fran.' His eyes cracked open again, at the sound of her voice. 'You didn't have to go to these lengths to get a fix.' She smiled, wondering if he understood her joke. His dark eyes focussed briefly onto hers, but he didn't respond, other than to squeeze her hand feebly, before closing his eyes again. He still clutched her fingers, but now in a tighter grip. She sat back down beside him, imprisoned once more, and gazed at his rugged features. He was still a handsome man, everybody said so. His face, normally tanned, was drained of colour, glistening with fever, the flesh under the high cheekbones sunk in, giving him a skeletal appearance. For the second time in the five years since his devastating stroke, she held his hand and silently prayed that he would let go of whatever was holding him on the planet, keeping them both in bondage. The minutes ticked by with no further reaction from Rob and she found herself drifting back to her memories, some unbearably painful and others mystifying, lulled into introspection by the rhythmic clicking of the monitors.

Beginnings

'Iona? What kind of name is that to give anybody?' Which was her mother's first response when Fran came hurtling into the house to show off her scraped knee. She had been pushed off her bike by Billy Robson, the street bully, who lived further up the road. Her mum was standing at the deep kitchen sink scrubbing a towel up and down a ribbed washboard, her hands red and wrinkled from the hot, soapy water. She didn't turn around to look at Fran.

Fran had been breathless with the pain from her knee, but more from excitement and astonishment that someone had stood up for her. The first time that had happened in her first seven years of playing with the other children in her street. She had spent the first few years of her life, after being allowed out to play, trying to avoid the jostling for power that went on amongst the children. Frequently she was the quiet victim of the Robson family. Billy's big sister Marion, once trailed the four-year-old Fran, fully clothed in her new winter coat, through the boating pond at the park. She was chest high in the murky water. Perhaps her mum or dad had had a word with Mr and Mrs Robson, but after that the Robson children never missed an opportunity to bully Fran. Seeing Fran proudly riding her newly acquired handed-down bike had been like a red rag to a bull to the troubled Billy Robson.

'But Mum, Iona pushed Billy Robson over and asked him how he would like to be knocked down and told him to pick on someone his own size. My knee's bleeding, it's sore.' Her words tumbled out in a rush.

'Ask your dad to clean up your knee. He's in the garden. I need to get this washing out on the line.' She could tell from her mother's hunched shoulders that there was no point expecting any more attention. Washing heavy towels and wringing them out through the mangle was guaranteed to put her mother in a bad mood. She was not long back from a lengthy spell in a convalescent home, recovering from a nervous breakdown left over from an unrecognised and untreated postnatal depression. Her youngest child was frequently not on her radar, or the two older siblings for that matter. Normally Fran's dad did the wringing on washing day on a Saturday, but he was planting cabbages in his vegetable patch, taking advantage of the dry weather.

Fran had been sitting on the pavement clutching her bloodied knee, her bike a tangled heap beside her. Billy Robson looked like he might be moving in for another kick at her bike when a whirling streak of long, jodhpurs-clad legs on a lanky body, topped with a head of bobbing blond curls, took him down. What this avenging angel actually said as she sat astride him, forcing his head to the ground with one hand was, 'How do you like it you little shite? Away home to your mammy and stay away from this wee girl. She's half your size. Come near her again and…' she left her threat hanging.

Billy Robson slunk away without another word when Fran's rescuer got off him. She came straight over to Fran. 'Let's have a look at your knee. It's not too bad.' She picked up Fran's bike and handed it to her. 'I'm Iona, we live at No. 45. We just moved in.'

'I'm Fran,' she had answered shyly, overawed that this strange, older girl had helped her. 'I live at No. 21.'

'I have to get to the stables; I need to muck out the horses before I get a ride. But if that boy bothers you again, you let me know.' She smiled at Fran and squeezed her shoulder. 'See you.' Iona jumped on her own bike which she had flung down on the road and rode off at top speed, her blonde curls flying out behind her.

Horses? Stables? Fran was agog, she had never known anyone who lived such an exotic life. All the children in her street ever did was play hopscotch, or the luckier ones rode up and down the street on their bikes. It was also the first time Fran had heard a swear word being used in her defence. It was shockingly thrilling.

Iona became Fran's secret heroine, admired from afar as she cycled madly back and forth from the stables or walked to the secondary school. She must have been about eleven, Fran guessed. She always acknowledged Fran with a cheery wave any time she saw her. She tried to be outside her gate when she knew Iona would be cycling or walking past and her heart would beat a little faster. Billy Robson did not try to bully her again. Sometimes Iona would stop and have a chat with Fran, always asking her if she was all right. As the next few years passed, Iona started confiding in Fran about how much she enjoyed riding and that she had a crush on someone at the stables, and occasionally she spoke about her mum and dad fighting. Her parents both drank and their fiery Irish tempers would flare up. Especially on a Friday when her mum got paid and came home with a few bottles of Guinness. Although she had no real advice to offer, Fran realised that Iona was grateful to have her to talk to and they would often meet up in the park on a Friday so that Iona could get out from under her hot-tempered parents' Guinness-fuelled arguments. Fran was just content that Iona was treating her sometimes like a best friend.

Fran's older sisters had left the secondary school by the time it was her turn to go, so she was walking anxiously to school alone on that first day when Iona caught up with her.

'Hello Fran. First day at big school eh? You can walk in with me if you like. I'll show you around.' Fran was delighted, Iona, her friend and protector had taken her under her wing.

What a relief she felt as she mingled with the big kids at the secondary school. At last she could blend in. She had grown so quickly between the age of nine and eleven and was the biggest child in her primary class, even taller than her primary school teacher. Although on reflection, he was rather vertically challenged anyway and bristled scarily with Napoleonic energy. Fran had been a prime target for teasing and name-calling, especially from the little boys who lived at the rougher end of their housing estate. Many of them looked pale and undernourished with scabby knees and dirty nails. At least her street had trees. But she had been too visible, in the wrong way. She never got away with any small misbehaviours at primary school.

'A big girl like you should know better,' Mr Thompson her teacher would growl.

She learned to be compliant and well behaved so as not to draw any attention to herself. It did not always work.

'Fran, come and sit beside Colin McBride at the front here and help him with his reading.' Fran would have to squeeze in beside anxious wee Colin at his too-small desk and try not to gag at the smell of his unwashed body and urine-drenched trousers. Thus, Mr Thompson reinforced in Fran's psyche that she would always take the role of rescuer because 'she was a big girl and should know better'.

Colin McBride's smell lingered in her nostrils for ages afterwards. She hated it. She never did teach him how to read and did not see him again after she moved up to the secondary school. Her first lost cause. She had done well in her eleven-plus test and was put into the A stream at school and her expectations for academic success became a possibility.

Both her sisters had left school at fifteen, worked at boring office jobs and had equally boring boyfriends. They had left home and were sharing a house with two other girls. All they wanted to achieve was to get married and have children and stop working. Fran had always been aware that she wanted much more for her life. Although she was not sure how to go about achieving 'the much more' or indeed what it might be. Possibly living somewhere with a fitted carpet would be a good start. She was embarrassed by the threadbare rug in the middle of their living room, exposing acres of dark brown stained floorboard, around the edges. Iona's hallway and living room were carpeted wall to wall with a grey and green patterned Axminster. Luxury. And the walls boasted interesting wallpaper, repeating pattern of orange fir cones in the hallway and a big floral design in black and pink in the living room. Fran was particularly envious of the dark maroon moquette three-piece suite which Iona said her mum had paid for out of her tips for serving petrol on the garage forecourt. The walls in Fran's house were still in post-war bare plaster, which her dad had sponge-stippled all over with a green and pink abstract design. Fran so longed for wallpaper. Their living room was furnished with a sagging bed settee which her mum and dad had to sleep on when Grandma came to stay and was given their bedroom. Two mismatched armchairs in faded and fraying fabric, a sideboard and dining table with six chairs placed under the window, took up the rest of the space. She was acutely aware that their house was shabby compared to Iona's house and some of the other neighbours' houses that she had been in and wished fervently that her house could look nicer inside. It had made her determined from an early age when her social awareness kicked in, that she wanted a better future for herself.

Iona caught up with Fran one Friday afternoon on their way back from school. It was the last day of the summer term. 'Fran, my mum wants to move back to Killarney, she's lost her job at the garage. They installed self-service pumps and she has been made redundant. I don't want to leave, especially you. I'll miss the stables so much too. I love going there.' Her voice quivered as she added, 'I feel so angry with her, but now that Dad's gone, she wants to be closer to her family.'

Fran was appalled. 'But Iona can't your mum get another job somewhere else? Do you really have to leave?' Her throat constricted at the horrible prospect of losing her best friend.

Iona just shook her head 'I don't have a choice Fran, Mum has already given up the house and enrolled me in a school in Killarney. We are leaving in a few days. I'm so sorry to leave you, but as soon as I get to sixteen I'll come back. I promise.

Goodbye Fran' Iona squeezed Fran's arm hard with one hand and rushed off, her pale blue eyes brimming with unshed tears.

Fran did not see Iona again before they left the street. Iona was fifteen.

Fran was bereft. The sharp pain of loss she experienced for the first time in her life could not be shared with anyone who might have understood. Her sisters thought that Iona was too old and too precocious for Fran and she could not tell her mother or father that Iona's leaving was making her feel so unhappy.

Despite their age difference, Iona had befriended her and had been happy to confide in Fran about her turbulent home life. Iona's dad had died suddenly from a ruptured spleen; he had been a heavy drinker. As life-changing as that had been for Iona and her mum, Fran never dreamt that her friend would leave. Although her parents were both fiery characters and Fran was a bit intimidated by them, Iona had adored her dad. She had been named after their honeymoon destination, Iona, as she had been born exactly nine months later.

Fran never forgot the summer that cemented her friendship with Iona. Iona's dad drove a black cab and one summer, two years after they had moved into the road, he and John Dunwoody, another black-cab driver who lived next door to Fran, took all the kids they could fit into their taxis to the beach. They drove for ninety minutes west of Glasgow to the seaside town of Saltcoats, where Fran, Iona and the other children from their road (not the Robsons!) enjoyed an amazing day at the beach, paddling (too cold to swim), building sandcastles and sharing the sand-crunchy sandwiches their mothers had packed for them. It was the first time she had been at the seaside and Iona had spent the whole day with her.

Fran was not allowed to go to the funeral service in the Catholic church, but stood beside Iona later at the graveside. Iona had cried softly and squeezed Fran's hand hard when the priest intoned the Rite of Committal prayer. Fran experienced a deep connection with Iona as she grieved over the loss of her beloved father.

The long weeks of summer dragged on the year that Iona left. The children spilled out onto the street for the day straight after breakfast and usually drifted down to the local park in a group, playing rounders, or spending hours on the swings, trying to avoid the attention of the creepy park keeper. Fran often went along with them, but without Iona, she felt lonely most of the time. Iona's friendship had given her life shape, opened possibilities for a different future. But she was still too young to change anything or identify what she *did* want. Confused and unhappy, she withdrew into her imagination, her soul's journey suspended.

At school, she focussed on her work and the years slid by, unmarked by any major changes in her home life. Except for the eventual appearance of a fitted carpet and a three-piece suite, after her mother went out to work. Fran felt a little better.

Continuum

'Fran, it's me, I'm back. I've moved in with Liam.' Iona's voice was husky, excited.

'When? Where?' was all Fran could manage. She couldn't believe that Iona had come back to Glasgow from Ireland. It had been five years since she left with her widowed mother to live in Killarney and the girls had only exchanged Christmas cards occasionally. Fran had not expected to see Iona again despite her promise to return. She had not forgotten how intense her friendship with Iona had been and had never stopped missing her. She spent a lot of her spare time hanging out with a small group of school friends from her year, but always felt a bit detached from them, still painfully self-conscious and unable to participate in the easy banter with the boys that her girl-friends seemed to be so good at.

'Listen Fran,' Iona continued rapidly. 'I'm working at the Veterinary Hospital as a groom. Liam's stables are just down the road. He's been coming over to Killarney to see me-and- I -I'm in love with him...'

Iona had mentioned Liam in one of her Christmas cards, but Fran had no idea that their friendship was so serious. She knew that Iona had had a crush on him before she left Glasgow for Killarney, but he was old, at least thirty! He was divorced and he owned the stables. Could this be real? She was stunned, thrilled and confused all at once. Her friend was back, but deeply involved in a relationship that Fran had no concept of. Would Iona still be interested in rekindling their friendship? All Fran had to offer in the way of news from the past five years was that she was still a schoolgirl with plans to sit her Highers the following year and them perhaps go to university or college. She was determined not to follow in her sisters' footsteps. They had both recently married with three months of one another, falling out over Fran's hair length. Her older sister had married first and insisted on Fran, the bridesmaid, cutting her hair short. Her middle sister was enraged as she had wanted Fran's hair to be long for her wedding, three months later. Bridesmaid again. There was so much stress and disharmony around both events and Fran strongly disliked her brothers-in-law anyway, that she decided that she would never get married. And she hated her short hair. Hardly earth shattering events to share.

'Can you come over later? There's a bus stop right outside the stables.' Iona continued. 'The cottage is at the entrance. It would be great to see you again and I want you to meet Liam.'

'Yes, I can come.' Fran's voice shook a little, she was delighted to be seeing Iona again but nervous about having to meet the mysterious Liam. She had never gone to the stables with Iona when she was younger and had never seen Liam. What would he be like? What on earth would she talk about? All she knew of horses could be said in about two sentences. Would they think she was boring and naive? Trying not to overthink what she should wear to meet Iona again and her much older horsey boyfriend, Fran shrugged into her slim-fit black trousers with stirrups under her feet that pulled them straight, making her legs look longer and slimmer and a turtleneck thin, blue-striped sweater that suited her colouring. She slipped her feet into her new flat black shoes and hoped they would not rub up a blister on her heels. Her dark hair was growing back after the severe bridesmaid cut and waved softly around her face. She just wished her puppy fat had disappeared completely. It still made her feel self-conscious.

'Och, you're just big-boned like your Grandma,' her mother said unhelpfully when Fran complained. However, she quite liked her wide-spaced grey eyes when she peered obsessively at herself in the mirror. She would have to do, the bus up to the cottage only ran every hour. She grabbed her black suede jacket and shoulder bag and rushed to the bus stop. She was sixteen.

Fran's heart beat a nervous staccato as she lifted the horse brass door knocker. The door opened immediately. Iona had blossomed into a stunningly beautiful young woman. Tall, slim and very toned from the hard physical work she did at the stables. Her hair was long, fair and curly and her pale blue eyes widened with pleasure when she saw Fran. They were almost the same height, Iona just a fraction taller than Fran.

'Bejesus you've grown up Fran! C'mon in, Liam is still at the stables. He'll be here soon.' Iona's years in Ireland had left their mark on her accent. She pulled Fran into a fierce hug and Fran's nerves melted away.

Fran was so relieved that Iona was alone. It gave them a chance to catch up on the last five years and almost immediately, Fran felt the old ease and familiarity that she had always experienced in Iona's company.

'To be sure, I wanted to come back when I turned sixteen like I said. But then Mum got ill and it turned out to be stomach cancer. I couldn't leave then. My auntie, Mum's sister, married an Ulster man and they left Killarney for New Zealand. It wasn't safe for them to stay because of the troubles. The nuns at the nursing home took care of Mum when she got too ill for me to look after her at home and I got a live-in job in a hotel. God, I hated that place! But it was near Mum's nursing home and I was able to see her nearly every day until she died.'

'Oh, I'm so sorry Iona that must have been hellish for you.' Fran couldn't imagine what it must have felt like for Iona to have lost both her parents and to be all alone in the world.

'Liam was with me at the funeral. He comes over to Ireland a lot, his family are from Tralee and he would come and visit me and Mum every time. After Mum got ill, he would often stay with us for a day or two and take Mum and me to the coast. She loved looking at the sea.' Iona's voice dropped to a quiet whisper.

'When did Liam become your boyfriend?' Fran asked shyly, not sure if that was what to call him.

'Do you mean when did I first sleep with him?' Iona laughed as Fran blushed. 'Actually, not properly until after Mum died and then it all got a bit intense and we couldn't bear to be apart. He asked me to come back to Glasgow and move in with him – and here I am!' Iona flung out her arms and twirled around the kitchen. 'I can cycle to work from here, but I've got a car too. I can ride whenever I want and I get to sleep with Liam every night. Perfect!'

Fran listened enthralled to this dramatic, tragic story with a happy ending. Iona, the orphan, carried back to this love nest by her older boyfriend and they were besotted with one another. It was like a fairy tale!

The kitchen door flew open with a crash. Fran jumped.

'Hello Darlin', how's my girl? Liam (had to be) strode over to Iona, pulled her into his embrace and kissed her long and hard on the lips.

'Eejit!' Iona pulled away from Liam's arms but her eyes shone with adoration as she said, 'Liam, this is Fran'.

He turned to Fran and took a step towards her. 'Well, you're goin' to be breaking a few hearts for sure girl.' His voice, low and lilting with a soft Irish cadence, calmed her anxiety. She could imagine him soothing the wild, untamed creatures to do his bidding with gentle words and hands. As he stepped closer to her she could smell the horsey odour from his clothes; jodhpurs, a green checked shirt open at the neck and a khaki-coloured sleeveless jerkin. He was squarely built, just slightly smaller than Iona and Fran, with unruly, dark curly hair and black, gypsy eyes. His maleness and the warm, musky smell of his body was quite overpowering for Fran's senses and in an instant, she knew why Iona was so attracted to him. She did not understand what animal magnetism was, but felt its power pouring out of him. He held her by her shoulders, leaned in and kissed both her cheeks. She could feel her face flame in embarrassment. She had never been so close to a man before or ever even been kissed. Especially by such a powerfully attractive man. She was overwhelmed and gazed in confusion at her feet, wondering if Iona would be annoyed about her boyfriend kissing her.

'Oh, away with you Liam! You're making the girl blush so you are. Just ignore him Fran, he's a terrible flirt so he is.' Iona placed one arm around Fran's shoulder and pushed Liam away with her other hand.

Relieved that Iona was not annoyed, Fran relaxed would not have minded hearing more of Liam's opinions about her. This was her first compliment and she was glowing inside.

'Iona talks a lot about you Fran. You two must have a special friendship. Don't let anything get in the way of that whatever happens. Life can be hard sometimes.' Liam suddenly sounded serious as he pulled Iona close into his side again. 'C'mon you two lovely girls, let's have a drink to celebrate you getting together again.' He added, at once light-hearted again. 'Would you be after trying a wee drop of Guinness, Fran?'

'Oh, I've never tasted it before, I'm not sure.' Fran said, shy once more. The thick black drink that Liam poured for himself with its creamy frothy head, smelt very strong to her.

'Here, have a taste.' Liam held the glass up to her lips, she took a tiny sip and nearly gagged.

'Oh sorry, that's horrible Liam.' He laughed loudly as she pulled a face and he turned to Iona.

'Looks like I can't convert you and Fran to Ireland's favourite drink. Never mind, all the more for me. Do you want to join Iona in a whiskey instead? That's her tipple.'

'No thanks, do you have any sherry?' Trying to sound sophisticated. That was the only alcohol that Fran had ever tasted and only at Hogmanay to bring in the New Year. Liam produced a sweet sherry for her and they sat around the big wooden kitchen table eating a hearty Irish stew that Iona had cooked. Fran picked out the vegetables and tried discretely to push the chunks of meat around her plate. She hated meat but didn't want to offend Iona. Neither of them seemed to be bothered or even notice that she left most of the meal, but Iona produced a plate of crackers and cheddar cheese and placed it near Fran as she and Liam refilled their glasses. Fran managed to stretch out her sherry and the evening flew by. When finally, she left Iona and Liam standing entwined at the door of their cottage, Fran was beaming with happiness. She felt accepted into their inner sanctum of horse talk and their irreverent, bohemian take on life. They did not challenge or judge her for her unworldliness, but simply absorbed her into their space. The well of loneliness in Fran's soul began to fill up again.

She was trying to write an essay about Emily Dickinson for English class when Iona called her. 'Hello Fran, I heard from one of the girls who works in the laboratories that they are advertising for a research technician for the Large Animal Surgery at the Veterinary Hospital. I thought you might be interested.'

'I've got my Highers soon Iona, I-I was planning on going to university if I got through all my subjects.' Fran's English teacher had high hopes for her going on to study English language and literature at Glasgow University.

'OK Fran, not to worry, it was just a thought. By the way, I'm going over to Ireland for a few days with Liam, there's a filly he's interested in buying, so I'll catch up with you when we get back.'

She couldn't stop thinking about the conversation with Iona. The prospect of leaving school early was exciting. She had never thought before about working in a laboratory, but she loved the science subjects at school. She also loved animals and would have liked to become a vet, but had dismissed the idea as she struggled to understand mathematics. Maybe being a research laboratory technician was the next best thing she reasoned with herself. All her friends from her class were going into boring office jobs when they left school, but at least they would have a pay packet and have money to spend. Fran was quite daunted by the prospect of university with no money available to her. Her parents would struggle to support her if she was not going to be working full-time and still living at home. Also, she wanted her life to be immediately more exciting like Iona and Liam's. She was desperate and impatient to break out of the mould of her predictable family life. She made the phone call.

Awakening

'Mum, Dad. I'm leaving school. I got a job in the Veterinary Hospital as a research assistant. The pay is quite good. £5 7/6 a week.' It had not occurred to Fran to discuss her plans with her parents beforehand.

'I thought you were going to sit your Highers, Fran?' her dad said mildly, looking up from his newspaper, the *Scottish Daily Express*.

'That's quite good money for a first job Fran. When are you starting?' her mum enquired with sudden interest. Fran knew that her dad's pay packet was only a few pounds more. She had seen the brown pay packet by mistake once when she had gone into their bedroom looking for a handkerchief. She had a streaming cold and wanted one of her dad's big white handkerchiefs with the brown and blue borders which were kept in the chest of drawers. Her parents were out at the bowling green, the only activity they shared away from the house. His pay packet was lying on the top of the folded handkerchiefs. £9 3/6.

Fran had been shocked. She had no idea that her dad was so poorly paid. He had been working as a progress clerk for the Glasgow based optical lens manufacturer, Barr and Stroud, for years. No wonder her mum was eager for Fran to start work. Clearly a regular pay packet was valued above any airy-fairy notions of going to university.

Iona was pleased. 'That's great Fran! Are you sure you really want to leave school and not go on to university?'

'Yes! Positive! I can't wait to start working. I'll be able to see you every day as well.'

'I'll tell Liam. He'll be pleased too. I'm always moaning about not having any girlfriends at work. The other girls, the kennel maids, think I'm weird.'

Fran laughed. 'Well I don't think you're weird, just mad! I'll see you next Monday. My first day.' She was excited and nervous. Had she made the right decision? It would be great seeing Iona at work, but what about Liam? She had trouble getting the memory of his intense, dark-eyed gaze and the feel of his scratchy, stubbly kiss on her cheeks, out of her head. He had unsettled her, made her long for something she could not put a name to. Hopefully she would not have to see him too often, he belonged to Iona.

She could not sleep the night before she was due to start her first job at the Glasgow Veterinary Hospital. She had already met Professor Wilson who was Head of Large Animal Surgery. He had shown her around the vast operating theatre and outlined the research project she would be working on with him in the laboratory. He was a jovial, twinkly-eyed man and Fran liked him immediately. And he was English! Fran was pleased to be moving into what she perceived as such sophisticated territory. She could not wait to become part of this new environment, so far removed from her stultifying life with her family. She tumbled, like Lewis Carroll's Alice, into a world completely outside her experience and imagination.

'Fran, can you check this chap's pulse please? Might as well make yourself useful.' Professor James Wilson beckoned her over to the operating table where a huge anaesthetised bull lay on its side, its eye disconcertingly open in a glassy-eyed stare. Fran was on her lunch break, but she was fascinated by the operations on the large animals and spent a lot of her spare time observing the surgeries when Iona often darted home to see Liam. She moved quickly over to its head, ready to press its neck for the pulse. Thrilled to have been asked to help. 'No! No girl, the other end.'

What! Surely not! She groaned inwardly, face beetroot red. One of the assisting vet students, grinning wickedly, handed her a huge tub of lubricating cream, to rub into her hand and arm. There were no gloves in sight. She listened in horror as Professor Wilson instructed, 'OK Fran, hold the tail up and push into the rectum, keeping your palm upwards until you find the arterial pulse.' She felt the perspiration pooling under her arms and moistening her hairline, but she was determined to appear unfazed and professional.

She cleared her throat and stepped up to the bull's huge flanks, lifted the resisting tail and inserted her hand into the squishy tunnel. Trying not to let her face contort into sour lemon mode, she gamely pushed her arm in further until it was swallowed up to her elbow. Her fingers felt what she assumed was a pulse and she carefully counted the beats.

'Forty-five,' she announced triumphantly.

'Good enough. Thanks, Fran.' Professor Wilson's eyes were twinkling behind his mask. 'You can pull out now, nice and slowly.'

The bull's rectal muscles clamped onto her arm as she tried to withdraw. She seriously thought she might be trapped until the bull woke up and shook her out.

It was a set-up of course, and a month later, her picture, pulling her arm out of the bull's bottom appeared in the students' rag magazine with a vulgar caption. Fran had dyed her bob-length dark brown hair black and cut a severe straight fringe in an attempt to look more grown up. They had nicknamed her Cleopatra and the bull was called Anthony. Iona and Liam teased her mercilessly about it when she told them.

'Oh my God Iona, what's wrong?' Fran had been sent to the stable block to ask Iona to bring down a lame gelding to the large animal surgery. Iona was shaking uncontrollably, a river of tears coursing down her cheeks. Her pale blue eyes, wide open and staring unfocussed at Fran.

'It's Liam, he- he's been taken to hospital. The filly – she threw him- his neck- broken.' The floodgates of her anguish opened. Fran rushed over to her.

'Oh Jesus, no! How? Where?' She realised she was gripping Iona's arms hard and shaking her as if trying to force a denial from the traumatised girl.

'Dawsholm Park. He was on a hack with his brother and the new Irish filly – first time out – she got spooked at something – threw him – he landed on his head – no hat.' Iona's voice cracked. 'Oh Fran, he might be paralysed. I've got to get to the hospital.' Iona looked around wildly and started making for the stable door.

'Wait Iona, I'm coming with you. Jim!' Fran shouted to one of the stock men. 'Tell Professor Wilson I've gone to the hospital with Iona. Her boyfriend has had an accident. Take the gelding to the surgery would you please? Come on Iona, did you bring your car in today?'

Iona nodded wordlessly and they made their way to Iona's ramshackle Triumph Herald in the car park. Miraculously, Iona managed to keep control of her car, although white-faced and shaking. Fran kept her arm across Iona's shoulders in a futile attempt to keep her calm, although she too was in turmoil. What if Liam was paralysed? The thought of his strong torso and limbs immobilised forever was too much to bear thinking about.

A nurse collected them from the A&E check-in desk and led them to the relatives' room.

'The doctor will come and talk to you.'

'Where's Liam? Can't I see him now?' Iona was gripping Fran's hand. Fran's heart was beating hard and fast, rising panic matching Iona's.

'Sorry dear, but you are not his next of kin. His brother is with him now.' The nurse left quickly.

'This is ridiculous!' Iona raged. 'Frank is only visiting us – he lives in Tralee. I should be with Liam.'

Time stood still. The door opened and Frank, Liam's brother stood framed in the entrance to the room. He was a swarthy, rougher, older version of Liam. He looked at Iona for a moment, silent.

'Frank! Say something! How's Liam?' Iona stepped towards him.

'I'm sorry girl. He's gone – a few minutes ago. They tried to revive him – but…'

Fran would never forget the unearthly shriek that Iona made as she flew at Frank, fists flailing hopelessly against his chest.

'No! No! He can't be! He promised never to leave me!' Iona sank to the ground, consumed by shock and grief.

Frank pulled her back to her feet. 'Come on,' he said, his own voice breaking, 'You need to say goodbye.'

Fran was left alone in the relatives' room, bereft, shocked. How could that powerhouse of energy and charisma that had been Liam be extinguished so cruelly? Snuffed out like a candle. She couldn't believe what had happened. Iona and Liam, the future they had planned, all the passion and intensity of their loving, all gone in an instant. She suddenly remembered that Liam had always refused to wear a riding hat and thought about his serious words about life being hard sometimes when she had first met him. Did he have a premonition about his own life ending so suddenly? Somewhere deep inside, she knew that Liam would rather be dead than live the rest of his life paralysed and dependent. But Iona was facing a bleak future, alone again, left only with the loving spirit of her beloved to comfort her. Fran was afraid for Iona. Would she survive this terrible loss? She was not sure how she would be able to support her friend through the fathomless sorrow of the dark days that lay ahead.

It was several weeks after the funeral before Iona resurfaced. She spent days lying in the big double bed she had shared with Liam, staring unseeingly at the wall, her eyes swollen and empty from the hours of hopeless crying. Fran spent as much time at the cottage as she could, trying to comfort her friend and tempt her to eat. All Iona wanted to do was to drink the whiskey that Liam kept in the bedroom. Sometimes she would ramble on for hours about Liam, the passion they had shared and the future they had planned. Reading the heart rending poems she had written about him. The only outlet for her pain. Fran kept vigil with her, listening, crying sometimes too. Hiding her own loss. Doing her best.

'I've made you toast and milky coffee, Iona, will you sit up and have it please?' Fran pleaded. She had spent the night lying on top of the sour-smelling sheets beside Iona who had drunk herself senseless on whiskey. Iona had refused to change the sheets since Liam had died, lying with her face buried in his pillow, trying to absorb his essence.

Iona lurched up unsteadily and sat on the edge of the bed drinking the weak coffee. 'Frank's selling the stables with the cottage, I've got to leave here soon. Liam didn't have a will and Frank is his next of kin. He said I can take something of Liam's to remember him by.' She stared at Fran with empty eyes. 'As if I could ever forget him. All the mementos in the world would never help me to get over losing him. I just want him back Fran.'

Fran nodded helplessly, she did not have any words of comfort other than to murmur as she had so often in the last horrendous weeks, 'I know, Iona, I know.'

However, the coffee and toast seemed to revive her a little. 'I'm not coming back to work at the Veterinary Hospital Fran. I can't bear it. It's too close to the stables and anyway, I don't want to work with horses any more. How could I, knowing how Liam died? God, these sheets are minging.' She suddenly staggered to her feet and pulled the dirty sheets off the bed. 'Do you mind running a bath for me Fran, I stink.'

For the first time since Liam's funeral, Fran felt a surge of optimism for her bereaved friend. Maybe this was the first step towards Iona's recovery? In truth, it was a heavy emotional burden for a teenager, trying to console and support Iona through this nightmare. Fran experienced a rush of relief that she might not have to continue feeling so responsible for her friend's survival.

But she did feel panicky. 'Where will you go?' Crossing her fingers in hope that Iona wouldn't go back to Ireland.

'Frank and Liam's cousin, Siobhan, lives in Byres Road. She came over from Ireland last year. Transferred by her bank to a branch in Glasgow. She has a spare room in her flat. I'm moving in with her.'

'Do you know her already?' Fran asked doubtfully, trying to imagine her free-spirited friend sharing a flat with a banker.

'Aye. She's all right. A bit of a bam-pot actually. Reminds me of Liam sometimes.' Iona smiled sadly. 'I'll need to get a job somewhere.'

Fran was silent, suddenly fearful that Iona would move on again and that she would lose their friendship.

Iona seemed to have read her mind. 'Don't worry Fran, we won't lose touch. I don't know how I would have managed to survive these last weeks without you.'

Fran's heart swelled to hear those words. She always felt less insecure around Iona. More grown up. Iona had packed so much into her young life already. She had scaled the heights of passionate love with Liam and plunged to the abyss with grief and loss, all before reaching her twenty-first year. Fran felt so naive, so out of her depth with this level of sorrow, but somehow, she had found a way to give Iona the support she needed. She had a purpose after all.

Iona only took from the cottage a small horse brass depicting a woman holding the reins of a rearing stallion that Liam had kept in the pocket of his riding jacket. He had called it his lucky charm.

A few weeks after she finally left the cottage, Iona called Fran. 'Can you come and meet me Fran? I've started working at the *Express* offices in Albion Street. I am having a drink with some of the journalists after work tonight. We'll be in the Press Bar just next to the office. They're a good laugh.'

'OK Iona, but I don't know what to talk about with journalists.' Fran was anxious.

'You'll be fine. Graham Gordon will be there, he's the science writer. You will have something in common with him. Mind you, he likes his booze, so don't know how much sense you will get out of him. Anyway, you'll have me to talk to.'

She was just pleased that finally, Iona seemed to be moving on a bit and was starting to socialise again, and equally pleased that she still wanted to include Fran in her new circle of friends. She wondered how Iona was adjusting to working in an office job after a life of mucking out stables and dealing with horses. But after meeting a few of the hard-drinking journalists, she decided that Iona was probably still in her comfort zone, they were an earthy, hedonistic bunch and Iona could keep up with their quick-witted repartee – and their whiskey consumption.

Graham Gordon, the science writer, seemed very interested in Fran's background. Fran was studying anatomy, physiology and biology at day-release college for her Institute of Medical Laboratory Technology certificate. 'How would you like to help me with my column Fran? I never have time to read through all the science journals.' He peered at Fran through bloodshot eyes, already half-sozzled from the beer and whiskey chasers he was downing. 'I'll pay you of course. Just write out any interesting bits of new research that you think the public would want to hear about and I'll include them in my column.' His hand trembled as he raised his glass to his mouth. Fran looked at him in amazement, wondering if this was a genuine offer. He had only just met her! How did he know if she was capable of stringing scientific facts together? But there was something vulnerable about him that her innate rescuer responded to. He looked shabby and worn out, disillusioned with whatever disappointments life had dealt him. She wanted to help him.

'OK Graham, I'll have a go, but I've never done anything like this before.'

'You'll manage, you sound like a bright lassie, here take this pile of journals with you and get something back to me by next week. I'm away home now.' Graham rose unsteadily to his feet and weaved his way out of the pub, leaving Fran a little overwhelmed and excited about this unexpected turn of events. She hoped she could do this extra work for Graham. He had said he would pay her. That would be amazing to get some extra money in her pocket. It gave her self-confidence a boost and she found that she could join in the lively chat with Iona and the other journalists. She loved their quick wits, and handled being teased by them reasonably well. She was much more at ease with them than she was with the vets. She couldn't keep up with their drinking though. A lemonade shandy was enough for her, before she started feeling woolly-headed. Iona was drinking a lot, too much. Fran hoped that as her sorrow for Liam's loss eased with time, she would cut back on her alcohol intake.

Fran spent a lot of time peering at herself from all angles in the hall mirror. Oh, how she hated her shape! She felt so fat and ugly. The frisson of pleasure from Liam's compliment had worn off – she wanted to be slender like Iona, she was so popular with the men who all vied for her attention. Without telling anyone, Fran went to see the family GP and was pleased when he prescribed slimming pills for her. It hadn't been difficult to persuade him that she needed to lose weight. He hadn't disagreed with her.

'I will give you a three-month supply, but you must come off them after that. They can become addictive you know,' he said cheerfully, ripping the prescription off his pad and handing it to her.

Fran could not believe the adrenalin rush she felt when she started taking the pills. She found herself talking too fast and her appetite virtually disappeared. The weight fell from her bones, her cheekbones hollowed, showing up her grey eyes. After two months, she was finally happy with her new, slimmer shape. She squirrelled away the leftover pills in case she needed them again. How extraordinary that her parents, particularly her mother, had not noticed the change in her appearance. Obviously still invisible. Iona had noticed. 'Jesus Fran, have you stopped eating? You're fading away.'

She didn't want to admit that she had taken slimming pills, it felt like cheating. 'No, I've started jogging at lunchtime, it must be that.' She had started running in the grounds of the Veterinary Hospital with a couple of other laboratory technicians from another department and her weight stayed off. Eventually, she threw away the remaining pills. She was attracting a bit more attention from the journalists and some of the vet students were flirting with her now. She was pleased, feeling a little more confident.

The next part of herself she had wanted to lose was her virginity. The endless talks with Iona, made her long to experience the passion Iona had shared with Liam. But who with?

'Listen hen, you could squeeze all of the virgins in Glasgow into a telephone box.' When she confessed to Graham Gordon that she had never had a serious boyfriend. This pearl of wisdom from him was her final catalyst.

Metamorphosis

Clive Robson-Forbes was a final year vet student who came from a family of landed gentry somewhere in East Sussex. He was tall and blond and usually wore yellow cords and a cravat, a bit of poseur, with a loud braying laugh. Not really her type, but she was seriously impressed by his upper-class persona. Secretly she wished that he would at least notice her. Although, *her* lover would be a dark, brooding Byronic type who would sweep her off her feet, writing deathless prose and declaring his undying passion for her. All that exposure to English literature she supposed.

Fran had never forgotten the derisive comment her English teacher, Mr McPherson, had uttered when she told him she was leaving school to work at the Veterinary Hospital. '*Et tu*, Frances?' He had expected Fran to go to university. Not many of his pupils ever did. But really? Comparing her to Brutus, Caesar's friend turned murderer, was going a bit far. However, she had never forgotten his words or how immediately, she was rubbed out of his expectations. She felt bad about letting him down, but, thought, with hindsight, that he could have tried a bit harder to persuade her to stay on at school.

'There's a vet student party on tonight in Byres Road, Fran. Do you fancy going?' Iona phoned Fran at home. 'It's just down the road from my place. I bumped into one of the final year guys and he told me about it. Asked if I would bring you along too.'

31

'OK Iona. If you're sure. I've not been to one of their parties before. Who asked you to bring me?' Fran felt a mixture of nervousness and excitement. Maybe it was Clive, or C.R.F. as she silently called him. He might be there. Her pulse quickened at the thought. Many of the vet students lived in flats in Byres Road in the west end of Glasgow, conveniently near the Veterinary Hospital.

'Em, I think his name is Brian, you know, the Welsh guy with the squint.'

Fran was deflated, she knew Brian, he was always trying to flirt with her when she was helping in the operating theatre. Nice chap, but the squint was just too disconcerting. She certainly did not fancy him. Still, she wanted to go, just in case…

Fran went to Iona's flat in Byres Road first and they had a drink together. A lager and lime for Fran (Dutch courage) and Iona had her usual whiskey and lemonade. They walked the few blocks down the road to where the party was well under way on the first floor of the four-storey sandstone building. Fran was wearing a soft red dress nipped in at the waist that had belonged to her oldest sister, which Fran had been too big to wear until the slimming pills and the jogging honed her curves. The neckline was low and Fran kept tugging at it to try and hide her still-generous cleavage. However, she felt quite pleased with her appearance. Iona wore a white silk shirt and tight black trousers, she looked stunning. As usual, the students hovered around Iona, moth-like in her incandescence. Suddenly, Fran felt clumsy and overdressed, all her confidence evaporated. Brian, he with the squint, shambled over to her, offering her a glass of punch.

'You look lovely Fran, nice dress.' Brian looked at her with admiration, but Fran had trouble meeting his deviating eyes.

'Thanks Brian. Is this your flat?' Brian nodded. 'Who are you sharing with?'

'Oh, just two third-years. I'll bring them over to meet you.' Brian wandered off to find his flatmates in the crowd.

Fran felt disappointed, so C.R.F did not live there after all. Would he come she wondered? She had not mentioned to Iona that she quite fancied him. Iona would have found him unbearably pretentious. She sipped at her drink and started heading towards Iona who was surrounded by admirers at the far end of the large living room. Before she reached the group, Clive Robson-Forbes suddenly loomed over her, breathing acidic fumes from the vile tasting punch they were all drinking. Cider and lemonade with wilted slices of orange floating in it. It had quite a kick though. Fran's head was swimming. His heavily-lidded eyes scrutinised her and her cleavage, speculatively.

'Nice dress. Let's get out of here and go to my place for a decent drink.'

Who could resist that as a pick-up line, delivered with such self-assured hubris? She knew exactly what the subtext was, but she was determined to join the ranks of the sexually initiated. It might as well be with him. He must have been aware that she liked him, as she always blushed any time he caught her looking at him when they crossed paths at the Vet School. She glanced towards Iona, but her back was turned so she did not notice Fran leaving with C.R.F. She was quite glad of that really. His flat was just across the passageway from where the party was now revving up in cider-fuelled mania.

So. No romantic walk along the quiet roads, holding hands, talking, getting to know each other then. No. Just a drunken stagger across a dank, dark green tiled hallway into a slightly musty-smelling flat with no curtains at any of the windows. He led Fran through to a bedroom but did not put the light on, probably because the overhead bulb had gone, but still managed to pour them both a shot of whiskey. Fran hated whiskey. They sat on the edge of his bed drinking. Suddenly, without preamble, he pushed her back on the bed and kissed her. His tongue snaked around inside her mouth, probing and demanding. Fran felt like gagging, but she was committed now. There was no turning back.

'Take your clothes off, Pam.' He was scrabbling at his own clothes.

'It's Fran. My name's Fran.' Could he not even remember her name? What was she doing? A sudden upsurge of fear. Would it hurt? But she obeyed his invitation, glad of the darkness and anxious about the next bit. She just wanted it to be over. And over it soon was. After a cursory squeeze at her breasts and a quick fumble between her legs to identify the target, he rolled on top of her. Roughly, he pushed her legs apart and thrust into her, pumping her body like a pneumatic drill. Almost immediately, he shuddered, uttered an expletive and rolled off her, sat up and lit a cigarette. Didn't offer Fran one.

'This was my first time,' she whispered. Not sure how she was supposed to feel, but having to fight off the unexpected tears prickling her eyes.

'Shit! Why didn't you say? Are you not on the pill then?'

'No.'

'When was you last period?' He sounded panicky.

'It's just finished.'

'You should be all right then.' Relieved. He was pulling on his trousers. Yes, the yellow cords. Did he ever wash them? She felt embarrassed talking about periods with her first lover. Even though he fell far short of her Byronic fantasy.

'Let's get back to the party.' He was already walking towards the door as she frantically pulled her clothes on.

'Um. No. I want to go home now.' What she really wanted was to have him hold her, tell her she was beautiful and beg to see her again.

'OK Can you see yourself out?'

She left, feeling foolish and discarded – and dirty. The sticky, wet stuff in her knickers felt horrible. She was desperate to get home and wash. She did not want to tell Iona what had happened, but knew that Iona would have wondered where she got to.

'Are you all right Fran? Welsh Brian said he saw you leaving with that big drip Clive.' Iona was on the phone to her early the next morning.

'Oh Iona, it was awful. I did it with him. It was all so quick and he just left me afterwards. I was too embarrassed to come back into the party.'

'What a shit he is, to be sure. Fran, I'm sorry to tell you, but he's getting married this weekend. Brian told me.'

'Oh great! Trust me to lose my virginity to a bridegroom. I was obviously his last sexual conquest before he tied the knot. He didn't mention his pending nuptials at my deflowering ceremony!' Fran tried to be flippant, but she was crushed, feeling ashamed and worthless.

He completely ignored her for weeks when he got back from his honeymoon. Fran was miserable and humiliated for a while, but had to admit that the soulless coupling with him had done nothing for her. She just wanted to forget the whole sordid experience. Iona cheered her up as they always referred to him as Mr W.B., wham bam, after that.

'Mr W.B. has finished me off with vet students Iona. I won't be going near any of them again in a hurry, that's for sure.' In truth, Fran felt like avoiding relationships with men altogether.

'Yes, I get that Fran. One day you'll meet someone decent and fall in love. That's when sex works best for women. Just give it some time. Why don't you come into town tonight? I'm having a drink with a few of the journalists after work. We'll be in the Press Bar as usual. Graham Gordon asked me to find out if you were coming. Something about his science column?' Iona had called Fran's extension in her laboratory. This was Friday night and all the journalists who were not out on assignments would be congregating in the Press Bar in Albion St, right next door to the newspaper offices.

'Sure, why not? I'll meet you there later. Graham only wants me to go through a pile of science journals for him, to see if there is any material suitable for his column. I think he is always too drunk and can't be bothered to do the research himself.'

'I heard on the grapevine that the editor has given him a final warning. He hasn't been submitting his work on time for the print deadline. He drinks like a fish. Always pissed. Been getting worse recently. See you later, Fran.'

Fran had already written a piece for Graham. The last time they had met up to discuss suitable topics for his column, he had slurred, 'Can you write it up for me Fran, there's a good girl. Let's have another drink.' Her exact words were printed in his column and for a while after that, she would ghost-write his column quite regularly. It gave her quite a buzz to see her words in print and another buzz when Graham paid her a five pound note for her work. A fiver! That was almost as much as her weekly wage. She so enjoyed writing the articles. Another seed was planted.

Graham didn't stay long in the Press Bar after Fran had discreetly handed him the piece for his column. 'Thanks doll, you're a champion.' He slipped the note into her hand and stumbled away. He preferred to drink at home. Fran insisted on buying Iona her drinks that night. She felt quite proud of herself. It was a heady feeling to have a bit of extra money to spend.

'Come over here you two lassies. I'll buy youse both a drink.' The strong Glaswegian voice of Harrison (Fran never did learn his other name) roared at them across the bar. The first time Fran met him, he was sitting on a high barstool. It was only when he slipped off the stool that she realised he was tiny, just tipping five feet. 'You two big lassies are the best lookin' women in Glasgow, ye ken that? '

Just as well he approved of them thought Fran, he was the newspaper's political, satirical cartoonist. He kept Iona and Fran vastly entertained and anyone else who cared to listen, with his wicked, acerbic wit, particularly aimed at Tory politicians. She didn't fully understand his excoriating observations as she hadn't the first clue about politics at seventeen.

'Let's get out of here, girls.' Harrison always insisted on having Iona and Fran escort him to his taxi. The girls towered above him in their vertiginous heels. They must have made a comical spectacle. He gave Fran and Iona a cartoon that he had drawn of them all. The little chap flanked by the two Amazonian women, like matching bookends, clutching his elbows in a vice-like grip to stop him falling over. He could drink his own weight in whiskey. The other journalists couldn't understand the affection the two girls had for Harrison, the pint-sized Lothario. He made them laugh. That's all.

After easing him into his taxi, Iona would often take Fran to the nearest, new, innovative, Reo Stakis restaurant, where, following Iona's lead, she would opt for a chicken-in-a basket meal. The height of sophistication, she always thought. Fran's experience of restaurant etiquette was limited. The fish and chip shop near where she lived didn't count. Iona was Fran's anchor, helping her to be herself and not to take life too seriously. Often, the two of them would end up laughing insanely at the absurdities of Glasgow night life happening around them in the mean city streets.

'Look, that bloke over there gawping at us, is B.C.' Iona dug Fran in the ribs, her voice raised indiscreetly. Whiskey always did that to her.

'Before Christ? He doesn't look that old!'

'No. No. B.C., bunchy cock, look at the front of his trousers.'

The two girls dissolved in hysterics. That became their secret code for leering men.

How they remained unscathed was a mystery.

Moving On

Now that she was slimmer and writing Graham Gordon's columns for him and earning a bit of extra money, Fran felt a bit more confident about herself. Except when Clive Robson-Forbes appeared with his group of final year buddies. Despite her and Iona having a laugh about their name for him Mr Wham Bam, seeing him around still made her uncomfortable. He had taken to calling out to her.

'Had your hand up any more bulls' bottoms lately?' was his pathetic attempt at getting a cheap laugh at her expense. She wished he would just ignore her as he had done since returning from his honeymoon.

'Your mouth produces more hot wind than a bull's arse,' she retorted with some spirit. How she despised him now, supercilious moron! But the truth was, she realised the disastrous encounter with him had sapped her self-confidence, leaving her even more inhibited and unsure about her appeal, sexual or otherwise, to any man.

'I bet Mr W.B. has told the others about his last stand conquest with gullible me, the virgin. They gossip like old women.' She poured out her wounded feelings to Iona. 'I feel sorry for his new wife. I bet he won't stay faithful to her.'

'Don't bother with him Fran. He'll be gone soon, after his finals. I hope he won't try working with horses. I remember they flattened their ears and tried to kick him any time he went near them. Good judges of character horses are.' Iona always managed to make her laugh.

'Fran, isn't it?' She was just getting into the lift to go up to the third floor where her laboratory was, when behind her, in walked the tall figure of Ian Green. He was one of the senior lecturers. She had often seen him around the place, but they had not spoken before. He was quite attractive in a slightly old-fashioned tweedy way. Fran felt herself blushing. He was a bachelor in his mid-forties, but exuded a strong heterosexuality, despite the thick glasses which magnified his eyes to owl-like proportions.

'You're James's lab technician, aren't you?'

'Yes. I am working on Professor Wilson's research project.' Fran replied primly. She objected to being referred to as 'James's lab technician'. Made her sound like a pet possession.

He grinned disarmingly at her. 'I've seen you helping out in the large animal surgery.'

Oh no. Not the bull saga again! 'Yes, I do help out quite a lot now.'

'Have you worked with anaesthetics?' Before she could reply, the lift door opened and he stepped out, blocking her way. 'I need some help this afternoon,' he continued. 'I am operating on a valuable breeding tup with urolithiasis and all the final year students are doing exams. I wouldn't trust any of the third years to help.'

She was flattered and astonished that he had sought her out to ask for her help. Urolithiasis was a serious condition for a breeding ram. The urethra would be blocked with calculi, a build-up of mineral deposits causing pain and urine retention. Fatal if left untreated. The experience she had gained in the operating theatre was strictly unofficial, but she loved it and Professor Wilson had encouraged her involvement.

'Oh, I would love to help, but I would need to clear it with Professor Wilson first.'

'Don't worry. I will talk to him now. Can you meet me in theatre in thirty minutes?'

'Absolutely.' That was her buzzword. Flustered and anxious now, she hurried into her laboratory. Quickly, she tidied up her bench space, writing up the results of an earlier experiment and scribbled a note for Professor Wilson. She was praying that Ian Green had got permission for her to assist him. Professor Wilson had been expecting a meeting with her this afternoon to discuss the research results.

By the time she arrived at the operating theatre, Ian Green was already there, injecting the wild-eyed ram with a sedative so that it could be heaved onto the operating table. The stockman who had brought the ram down to the theatre, helped them lift the flopping, fleecy body onto the table. Once the ram was positioned and secured on its back, Ian intubated it and Fran had the job of monitoring the mixture of anaesthetic and oxygen, keeping the animal asleep while Ian operated. She also handed him the surgical instruments, scalpel and clamps that he needed to expose the urethra. The procedure did not take long once the urethra channel was opened. He manually removed the calculi blocking the exit and irrigated it well with saline, closed the incision with neat sutures, and finally, dusted the wound with antibiotic powder.

'Good job, Fran. James has taught you well. Have you ever thought about studying veterinary medicine?'

Was this turning into the veterinary version of *Pygmalion*?

She spluttered her reply. 'Not a chance. I left school before my Highers, and anyway, I'm useless at maths.'

'Pity. I think you would have made an excellent vet. Never mind, I dare say you have plenty other skills at your fingertips.' He looked directly at Fran, his eyes magnified and shiny behind the thick lenses of his glasses.

Lord! Was he flirting with her? Had he overheard Mr W.B. talking about her? Did she have a reputation or something? The stockman cleared his throat noisily, glowering at her. He did not approve of her working in the operating theatre with the vets. He had made a pass at Iona before Liam's accident and had been rejected. Fran too, was guilty by association. *Hell hath no fury like a stock-man scorned.* She was sure that it was him who had started the gay rumour about her and Iona. Iona had just laughed off the rumours when Fran told her what was being said about them. Fran however, had been mortified. After the humiliation of the horrible episode with Mr W.B, it was almost too much for Fran, still unbearably unsure of herself, to be the subject of such gossip.

She and Ian helped the malevolent stockman to load the sedated ram onto a trailer attached to a small tractor. With a last baleful glare at Fran, he drove off quickly, to return the ram to its postoperative recovery pen. The bed of deep straw was to protect the animal when it woke up from the anaesthetic and staggered to its feet. Speed was of the essence at this stage, as animals often started waking up while they were still on the trailer. This was not too much of a problem with sheep, but trying to stop a horse from rearing its head up on the flatbed trailer was a different story. It would take a team of people, Fran and Iona included, to position the horse on the deep straw in the recovery stable and jump out of the way quickly before it got to its feet. She loved all this drama with the animals. It was so much more interesting than the repetitive laboratory research experiments she was doing.

'Well, I think we should celebrate our success this afternoon. Neither of us managed to kill the ram, which is worth a drink at least, wouldn't you say?' He ran his hands through his thick, springy dark curls, already lightly peppered with grey. Yes, he *was* flirting with her.

Oh well, nothing ventured, she thought. He was quite an interesting and charismatic character and she was flattered that he approved of her skills in the operating theatre. So more in the spirit of wanting to share a bit of gossip with Iona, she replied. 'I agree, a live ram deserves at least one drink.'

'Jolly good. I'll check up on the ram at half past five. You can come and meet me at the recovery pens if you like. Make sure our patient is recovering.' He had quickly removed his operating scrubs and was vigorously washing his hands.

'Of course, I'll meet you there,' she replied self-consciously, experiencing a sudden panic. What was she letting herself in for? He was as old as Methuselah.

Without another word, he strode out of the operating theatre, leaving Fran to tidy up the detritus from the operation and to take the instruments to the steriliser.

The ram was already on its feet greedily chomping its way through the feed, barely stopping to raise its head from the trough as Ian checked it over.

'Looks like he is making a good recovery, Nurse Fran, so let's go and raise a glass to his good health.'

By the time they walked to his Jeep, the car park was almost empty. It occurred to her later, that this was probably a deliberate strategy to avoid being seen leaving together. He drove them to a country pub on the outskirts of the city. She liked that about living in Glasgow. A fifteen-minute drive out of town and the countryside swallowed you into its unique tranquillity. It was one of those rare early summer evenings when it was warm enough to sit outside, but also early enough in the season not to be eaten alive by midges. She wished she had not worn her scruffy brown cords and scuffed boots to work that day, but there was no dress code at the Veterinary Hospital. Large animal veterinary medicine and stockings, tight skirts and high heels were not a good combination. Fran squirmed as she remembered turning up one day, not long after she started working, wearing ridiculous high heels. Professor Wilson had asked her to go to the holding pens and ask the stockman to bring up a bull to the operating theatre. One of her heels got stuck in the cobblestones in the yard and broke right off. She had been horrified, but Iona had come to her rescue with a pair of dirty trainers, which she had to wear for the rest of that day. After that, she always dressed casually, and much more comfortably for work.

At least her white linen shirt, worn loose over her trousers, was clean and she had washed her hair the night before. He ushered her into a comfortable, cushioned wicker chair. One of two, around a wooden circular table. The pub was set well back from the road. The courtyard at the back where they were sitting, faced towards the distant, purple and green-hued Campsie Hills. It was still early in the evening and they had the outdoor space to themselves.

'Red or white wine?' Hooray, not whiskey this time.

'Red please. 'She had never had either before. Only a sweet sherry at Hogmanay at home, or more recently a lemonade shandy or lager and lime at pubs or parties. Oh yes. That vile cider punch. Thinking about that made her remember the humiliating episode with Mr W.B. She gazed intently at the grooves on the rough wooden table, hoping that Ian would not notice the sudden flush flooding her cheeks.

'Right-oh.' Ian disappeared into the depths of the pub, stooping to avoid bumping his head on the low door. He reappeared after a few moments, holding a menu and a bottle of Merlot in one hand and in his other hand, two wine glasses criss-crossed at the stems.

'If we are going to share this bottle, we should eat. I can recommend the steak, it's excellent.'

Fran was hungry. Her source of second income, Graham Gordon, had been off sick for weeks, she missed the extra money he gave her for researching and writing his science column. It was near the end of the month and she was short of funds for buying food, so she had not been able to afford lunch that day, making do with an apple from home. But, a whole bottle of wine between two? She was way out of her depth.

'I don't eat red meat.' She blurted out rather brusquely. Her social skills were still in their infancy, particularly out of her comfort zone with this much older, sophisticated man.

'How about chicken then?' Ian enquired, smiling, ignoring her gauche manners. He poured out two glasses of wine and passed one over to Fran, brushing her hand lightly as he did so. They agreed on the chicken and clinked glasses.

'*Slainte*!' they said simultaneously and she drank hers rather quickly.

By the time the food arrived, she was giggling helplessly as Ian regaled her with funny stories from his own vet student days. Her eyes sparkled as brightly as the wine glasses. She had always liked people who made her laugh and she soon relaxed in his company, aided by two more glasses of the excellent Merlot and the scrumptious chicken dish. She quite forgot that he was ancient.

The courtyard filled up with the Friday night people. It was still pleasantly warm, even as the sun was slipping below the horizon and the sky morphed into purple velvet, streaked with silver. The noisy chatter made it difficult to have a conversation, but she didn't care. She was enjoying herself now and was aware that one seriously good-looking young lad was trying to get her attention over Ian's shoulder. Ian stood up abruptly.

'Come on. I had better get you home. It's getting a bit too crowded here.'

She would quite liked to have stayed longer, but didn't argue. She and the young lad exchanged a regretful glance as she followed Ian around the side of the pub to where his Jeep was parked. Despite downing two-thirds of the bottle of Merlot, Ian happily drove like a maniac along the narrow country lanes, arriving miraculously safely at her house.

'Thanks for the meal. I had a nice time.' Fran suddenly felt shy and quickly opened the passenger door to get out. Ian leapt out and came round to her side to help her down. She was a little wobbly on her feet. Ian put his arm around her to steady her. She needed to go in urgently, having completely forgotten to visit the toilet at the pub. She lifted her head to say goodnight and he swiftly planted a kiss on her mouth. She had noticed earlier, after the second glass of Merlot, that his mouth was full and sensuous and had idly wondered what it would feel like to kiss him. It felt wonderful. Her first proper kiss. His mouth was soft and warm and she felt herself responding to him.

'I knew it!' He pulled his head back.

'What?' She looked up at him, startled and confused. Did she have bad breath or something worse?

'You're not gay!' With a cheery wave, he left her swaying and speechless at her garden gate. As he jumped back into his Jeep and revved away, he wound down his window. 'We must have dinner again.' He roared in his plummy English accent. A few curtains twitched.

The relationship was kept strictly under wraps. He clearly didn't want his colleagues to know that he was seeing a seventeen-year-old laboratory technician. Especially, Professor Wilson's research assistant. He was head of the Veterinary Hospital and Ian's boss. Fran didn't want any of *her* peers to find out either. Ian was just so inappropriate, but he made her feel special. A new experience. In truth, she was flattered that he was showing an interest in her. She had not had a boyfriend of her own age before and Ian was very complimentary about her looks which helped her to feel better about herself. Although sometimes when they were out together in public, she would feel a bit awkward to be seen with him. Always hoping that they would not bump into anyone she knew.

They always made elaborate arrangements to meet after work to avoid being seen together and had the occasional stolen kiss in the side room of the operating theatre where the steriliser was kept. It was all so dangerously illicit and exciting and she was enjoying the drama and the intrigue of it all. At least once a week, she would catch a bus outside work and get off two stops later, where Ian would pick her up. They would go to a quiet little country pubs for a meal and a shared bottle of wine. She was becoming quite a connoisseur of decent red and white wines. He always ordered one of the most expensive ones from the wine list. Mercifully, he did not seem to be in any rush to consummate their relationship. Always the gentleman, merely kissing her when he dropped her back home after one of their secret dates. Fran felt quite safe with him and enjoyed the kissing. She had told him about her experience with Mr W.B. and that she was not very experienced sexually. She heard later that Mr W.B. had to re-sit one of his final practical exams. Surely nothing to do with his examiner, Ian Green?

Then the inevitable happened.

'Are you free next Saturday Fran? We could spend the day at my cottage. I'll do lunch for us.'

She agreed reluctantly. Why couldn't they just carry on as they were? She worried about spending a whole day in his company. What would they talk about? His interests were light years away from hers. He picked her up in the morning and they drove north, away from the city, for about thirty minutes. He pulled off the main road and drove along a private lane for a hundred yards, stopping at a wooden barred gate. Fran jumped out to swing it open for him. His driveway was laid with pebble stones and ran the whole length of his cottage. She couldn't see any other visible dwellings beyond the boundary of hawthorn hedges. It certainly was in a remote spot. The cottage was very old and long, built from the heavy grey stone, commonly used in Scotland and the roof tiles were of dark grey slate. Quite a few of them were chipped and looked as if they might slide off at any minute It was early July, the sun shone gently from a rare, cloudless sky. Fat, aerodynamically-improbable bumble bees droned and squeezed in and out of an untidy tumble of lupins and antirrhinums, or snap-dragons as Fran's dad called them. A rampant wisteria had tangled its way across the whole of the front of the cottage, almost completely covering one of the windows. Not a gardener then, she thought. Her dad kept their garden neat and tidy and she felt slightly repelled at this sign of casual neglect. There was no garden at the back, just a narrow strip of flagstones. Beyond the boundary fence, stretched acres of sheep-dotted fields, with the low-lying Campsie hills providing a protective back-drop. Apart from the occasional distant bleat of a sheep, the silence was thick and heavy, as only it can be in the country.

She was quite enchanted. 'Oh, this is beautiful, Ian! You must love living here.'

'I do. I do, but it gets a bit lonely sometimes in the winter. I've been snowed in twice since I moved in here. A bit of company would be nice then.' He placed a long arm around her waist.

Breathe in Fran, she told herself, in case he feels the small muffin top that was developing above her trousers. All those bottles of wine and puddings shared with him were leaving their mark.

'Come and see my work room.' Typical man, wanted to show her his hobby room before showing her where the bathroom was. He led her into a barn attached to the side of the cottage. Every bench was cluttered with angle grinders, lathes, chisels and wood-carving tools. Long curls of hard Perspex and wood shavings littered the floor and the benches. Ian clearly was not a tidy soul. The shelves held some crudely carved woodland animals and stacks of Perspex circular coasters with snowdrop-style designs cut in them. His early work she assumed. A pleasant, heavy smell of linseed oil hung in the atmosphere. In pride of place on a table in the middle of the barn, gleaming in the light from the overhead bulb, lay a set of exquisitely carved bagpipes. The wood was dark and shiny and the carving both on the chanter and the drones; a column of the Scottish thistles interwoven with a delicate spider's web. A tiny spider was etched into base of each pipe. Carving artistry for sure.

'I carved these pipes myself,' he announced proudly, holding them out lovingly to show her. 'The bagpipe maker in Glasgow said they had the best tone he had ever heard.' He continued fondly, as he gave them to Fran to admire.

'Oh, they're great. Well done. Fantastic carving. Can you play them?' she enquired dutifully. What else to say?

'I practise in the field behind the cottage, but I am not very good yet.'

Visions of the sheep running wildly to the far corners of the fields popped unbidden into her mind and she felt the first bubble of hysteria pushing against her diaphragm. She managed to suppress it. She couldn't wait to share this nugget with Iona, she would love it! Finally, he showed her around his cottage. Inevitably, the indoor space too, was untidy, with piles of books and veterinary journals on every surface. The natural light had been cut down by the heavy curtain of wisteria growing outside, across the window. All the furniture was dark and heavy, but the enormous crinkled brown leather sofa and matching armchairs, were scattered with exotically patterned cushions and the worn Persian rugs on the wooden floor, leant the room a homely and inviting air. Almost every spare inch of available wall space was covered in an eclectic mix of hunting prints, dark and brooding Scottish landscapes, portraits (his ancestors?) and a few more contemporary oil paintings of horses and dogs. A huge open fireplace dominated one wall, flanked by a log-filled gleaming brass scuttle and a set of brass tongs on one side. A well-used toasting fork was propped up against the blackened fire surrounds on the other. The room smelled faintly of wood smoke, beeswax and with a slight aroma of wet dog. If he had a housekeeper, she would have had a nightmare trying to dust and polish around his clutter. They ate a simple lunch of cold, poached salmon and salad, washed down with a couple of glasses of another smooth and mellow white wine. Fran had never drunk alcohol in the middle of the day before and just felt like falling asleep. No chance. Ian whistled for his brown and white collie Meg. She bounded in from outside, slithering obsequiously across the floor to sit, leaning heavily against his legs, looking up at him with adoring eyes.

'Come on, I'll show you around my land.' He grabbed her hand and off they went, striding across his fields. Meg zig-zagged deliriously around them trying to round them up, but obediently ignored the sheep, who regarded them warily. Possibly getting ready to flee in case the bagpipes appeared.

They walked for a long time and Ian kept up a steady stream of stories about his leasing arrangements with a local farmer, who in return for the grazing rights to Ian's fields, kept him supplied with eggs, homemade bread and beer. Also, his freezer was stuffed with an Armageddon-proof supply of lamb shanks and chops. Riveting. By the time they returned, the sun was dropping behind the hills. Ian lit a huge log fire. It can still be chilly in the evenings in Scotland, even in the summer months. They ate again, biscuits and cheese and drank a few more glasses of his excellent white wine. Ian settled into his big armchair and Meg and Fran shared the rug in front of the fire.

The beautiful arias from Puccini's *La Bohème* filled the room. She had told Ian about her love of classical music and how she had grown up listening to her father's collection of operatic arias. There was no television brought into the house to distract them until Fran was sixteen, so all they had for entertainment at home was the gramophone and the radio. When the rampant music of the Beatles, Rolling Stones and Elvis burst into her awareness, earlier in the sixties, she felt herself both repelled and compelled by their raw energy and sexuality. She had so wanted to share the unbridled hysteria of her teenage friends when they got together at weekends to listen and jig around to the pop music, but some part of her stayed detached. An observer, wondering how she should be.

As Puccini's final heart-breaking aria between the tragic lovers, Mimi and Rodolfo, 'Sono Andante' came to an end, Fran was almost in tears. She blinked them away rapidly and leant back against Ian's legs. He stroked her hair, no longer the raven-black fringed pageboy cut, but grown back, long and wavy, a glistening, dark chestnut brown. His fingers kneaded the tense muscles in the back of her neck. Her stomach fluttered nervously, waiting in the wings.

He groaned. 'Oh Fran, you are so lovely, so innocent.' He slipped his arms under hers and pulled her up onto his lap. She tensed. 'Just relax darling girl, there is nothing to worry about.' His warm mouth sought out hers and soon she felt herself yielding to his caressing, knowing fingers.

There were a few firsts for her that night. After the first-time, mind-blowing sensations his fingers had coaxed from her body, leaving her feeling like a rag doll, he then lifted her up and carried her through to his bedroom. She couldn't believe this was happening! *Ah me, the stuff that dreams are made on.* He helped her undress and made her stand naked, in front of him. His eyes took in the contours of her curvy young body with an approving, practised eye.

'You have the most beautiful shape, Fran.' He murmured huskily in his plummy English accent. His compliment was quite reassuring for the painfully inhibited girl, but she could have done with a few more specifics than that.

She answered politely, 'thank you,' and scuttled quickly under the covers. He carefully removed his own clothes, laying each item neatly on the back of a chair. First the checked shirt, followed by the vest (oh no, a vest). The corduroy brown trousers and large white Y-fronts soon joined the rest. Lastly, he removed his glasses and laid them on his bedside locker. He stood up straight, watching her peek at him from under the sanctuary of the bed covers. Clearly, he did not have any inhibitions about *his* body. He had quite a big tummy that shone whitely in the dim light of the hallway, although his chest, arms and legs looked strong and toned. Very little body hair she noticed. She had never seen a man's penis up close before. The episode with Mr W.B. had been over so quickly, she had not had a chance to look at his one. She shot a quick glance at Ian's business end and decided that it looked like what she had expected. Thankfully not too enormous. Ian did look a bit odd without his glasses. His eyes seemed naked and unfocussed. It was only as he climbed into bed beside her that she realised he had left his socks on. Oh my God.

His body was warm and the soft tummy felt quite cosy against her back. It was comforting to have his arms wrapped around her and she nestled back into him, expecting his magic fingers to arouse that ecstatic sensation in her body once again. After a few moments, when nothing much happened, she heard snuffling noises at the back of her head and realised Ian was asleep. She felt vaguely disappointed, but soon the warmth and Ian's rhythmic breathing lulled her to sleep too. It was still dark when she awoke to feel his hands stroking her body in long slow movements. She rolled onto her back as he reached into her 'special place,' as he had called it a few hours earlier. (She never knew she had one before then.)

'Darling,' he moaned, pulling her on top of him. She had to stretch her legs quite wide to get across the big tummy, but as he slowly and carefully entered her, she could understand now why people wanted to do it. It could become quite addictive.

She kept on seeing Ian, because he asked her. She was always worried that people would find out about them, particularly her dad. He would have been horrified that his teenage daughter was involved with such an old man. Fortunately, Ian never once suggested meeting her parents. He always dropped her off at the bottom of her road. She had a sneaking suspicion that Professor Wilson, might have guessed something was going on between her and Ian. He was quite protective towards her and she sensed an edginess between him and Ian when they were operating together. She had even stopped telling Iona about her ongoing fling with Ian. They had laughed so much together about his foibles in the early stages, that Fran felt that she should have moved on by now. She would have liked to stop, but it was so difficult when they worked in the same place. She could not avoid him.

Life at home was getting more difficult too. Fran's father was recovering from bowel cancer and needed a lot of support from her, the youngest and only one of his three daughters still living at home. Her mother simply couldn't cope with his care needs.

'I'm sorry you are having to look after all of this for me Fran, but you know what your mum is like. She's not good with any sort of illness. When I'm gone. will you promise to look after her?'

'Oh Dad, please don't say that. You are going to get better. But Mum will be all right. I will always look out for her whatever happens.' She squeezed his hand. She felt closer to him now than she had ever done. She kept him company in the evenings when her mother was out at whist drives or spending the evening sharing a drink and blethering with her widowed friend, Peggy. He told stories from his childhood that Fran had never heard before. He had been a taciturn man and all they had ever shared when she was younger, was listening to his beloved classical music records together. He had also allowed her to trot after him around the garden, helping him tend to his flowers and vegetables. He told her that only he and one brother survived to adulthood. Five siblings died from tuberculosis. Their home had been a two-roomed tenement building on the east side of Glasgow. They had to share a communal toilet on the landing with another large family.

'How did you stand that, Dad? It must have been hell.' She found it hard to visualise such crowded living conditions. Fancy having to share a toilet for a start! The kids were washed in a big copper hip bath in the kitchen-cum-living room and once a week, they all trooped down to the public baths for a 'proper' wash.

'I didn't know anything different. You just accept what you are born into.' (Not me, thought Fran) 'But we have done all right. We were lucky to get this house. The war changed everything. I had been training with an optician when war broke out. I was making prescription lenses.'

'Really?' She was fascinated. 'What happened? Could you not have gone back afterwards?' She knew her dad had not been sent to fight when he enlisted, because of his varicose veins, but instead, had been put to work on the canal barges. The Forth and Clyde canal was a valuable conduit for moving munitions around – all under cover of heavy tarpaulins to avoid detection.

'It was heavy work,' he said tiredly. She thought that was probably an understatement, her dad was not a particularly robust man.

'When you were born at the end of the war Fran and because we had three children, we were given this Corporation house. I had to find work close by. The optician was on the other side of Glasgow.'

'Did you never want to find another job, Dad?' She asked him carefully, not wanting him to guess that she knew about his pathetically low wage.

He looked at her for a long moment before answering. 'Aye, well, your mother wouldn't have wanted to move away. There was a chance of a better job in London but…' His voice trailed away. She squeezed his hand again, understanding now, that his need to provide for his family and to keep her mother happy had stamped flat any ambition he might have had.

He died suddenly, without warning. The cancer had metastasised all over his body, the coroner told them. He had just turned sixty. Fran was glad that she had heard his story and had cared for him in his last weeks before he passed away. Her mother took to her bed and Fran was left to make all the funeral arrangements.

Then the ties that bind tightened further. With her dad gone, she knew that her mother would transfer her dependency. She had to find a way to escape from Glasgow before she got completely enmeshed in a life as surrogate minder to her mother. And there was Ian, her middle-aged Svengali, reversing their roles and becoming more possessive and needy. She had promised her dad that she would look after her mother, but she was still only nineteen. She wanted her life back! After all, her mum was only forty-nine, not much older than Ian. Surely she could find a way to create a life for herself? Without Fran. She had to get away.

'Over here Fran.' Iona waved at her through the smoky, crowded press bar filled with the usual Friday night crush of drinking journalists, most of them chain smoking. The atmosphere was convivial and very noisy. 'I've kept a seat for you.' Iona patted the empty chair beside her.

She slid in next to Iona, joining the animated company of Harrison and Graham Gordon. Both men were reasonably sober for once. It was early in the evening.

'Hello hen, what are you drinking?' Graham called the passing barman over and ordered them all a drink. Iona was already on her second whiskey. Fran asked for a lemonade shandy and Harrison asked for his usual double malt whiskey. 'Bring me ma carry-oot son.' Graham winked at the young barman. He would be leaving soon for his solitary binge at home, so Fran quickly told them her news.

'I've been offered a job in Grayson's Research Laboratories in Middlesex. I'm leaving next week.' She tripped over her words. Saying it out loud made it feel very real.

'Jesus Fran. You're deserting us to live amongst the Sassenachs. Shame on you!' Harrison roared, knocking his whiskey back in a oner. 'Who's gonna prop me up now, eh? You got another big lassie to take her place Iona?'

'Sorry Harrison, you're on your own. I've handed in my notice too.' She turned quickly to Fran. 'I was going to tell you tonight Fran, but it looks like we both had a big surprise for one another.' Iona shrugged, lifted her glass and drained it.

Harrison snorted and stomped over to the bar. Fran heard him order another double as he heaved himself onto his high bar stool, his back turned to the girls. For once, sense of humour failure.

'Where on earth are you going Iona?' She had not seen so much of Iona for a while as she had been distracted with her father's illness, sitting her final exams at college and trying to fit in time with Ian.

'I met Max Cohen a few months ago. Our editor asked me to arrange an interview with him for the paper. We hit it off and I've been going out with him ever since.'

'Max Cohen! He owns half of Glasgow Iona!' Fran was astonished. 'And he's ancient!'

'I know, but I don't care. I like him a lot. He's very into art and literature. He has an amazing collection of first edition books and original paintings, even a copperplate etching of Picasso's.' Iona's eyes brimmed. 'I'll never get over losing Liam, Fran. But Max is the first man I have wanted to be with since Liam died. He is very charismatic. He wants me to stop working at the *Express* so I can go to college. Maybe get a degree. I want to write poetry and I want to finish my education. I gave up too soon.'

'Are you going to get another job?' Fran's head was spinning with this unexpected development.

'No. I'm moving in with Max. He has a house in Lenzie and he wants me to be a sort of P.A. for him. He's only forty-five, not really that old!'

Fran felt guiltily relieved to hear that. She had been dreading telling Iona that she was leaving Glasgow. Like a deserter.

Clearly Iona had made her choice too. Max Cohen was wealthy; he would keep Iona comfortable. Keep her safe.

'Are you sure that's what you want Iona?' She had seen photographs of Max Cohen, property magnate, in the newspaper. She had not been drawn to his rather rigid, unsmiling features, although he did have a large, sensuous mouth. He must have some other endearing qualities going for him. Iona would not be with him just for his money. She was too free-spirited for that.

'What else is there?' Iona looked at Fran, her blue eyes brimming. She blinked rapidly and quickly lit a cigarette.

'I'll come back as often as I can. I must keep an eye on Mum. I hope she will cope without me. She's quite hopeless at times.' Fran was at a loss, not knowing how to respond to Iona's sorrowful comment.

'I'll keep in touch with her for you Fran.' Abruptly, Iona pushed back her chair and stood up. 'I'm going now; Max is waiting for me. Take care.' Never one for hyperbole, she squeezed Fran's shoulder and left. The cigarette, abandoned and burning in the ashtray.

Fran shivered, a visceral tightening gripped her in a nameless anxiety. A sudden shadow dimming the beckoning future.

Graham's 'carry-out', a bottle of scotch in a brown paper bag was deposited in front of him. He stood up immediately, pushing the bottle into an inside pocket of his baggy tweed jacket. 'Cheerio then Fran. Thanks for everything. You should have gone into journalism. Peering down microscopes isn't your style. Never mind, good luck anyway doll.' He walked unsteadily out into the night.

She tried to swallow, her throat was constricting. She had not realised that it would be so difficult to leave her friends. Particularly Iona. Plucking up her courage, she went over to the bar and tapped Harrison on the shoulder. She did not want to leave without saying farewell to him. He swung around, their eyes were on a level. He glared fiercely at her. She panicked and wished she had just left quietly instead. Then unexpectedly, his arms went around her, holding her in a crushing bear hug. 'Don't you ever vote for the Tories.' he growled in her ear. Fran grinned at him. She was absolved.

'I won't Harrison, honestly.'

Ian too, had wrapped his arms around her when she told him she was leaving. 'I don't suppose I can persuade you to stay?' he had murmured wistfully into her hair. 'At least promise to contact me any time you come back up to Glasgow?' He gave her a solid silver bracelet as a parting gift. He was probably quite relieved she told herself. He was looking for a promotion as Head of Large Animal Surgery and was the heir apparent to the soon-to-retire Professor Wilson. Such a young girlfriend might have been a bit of a deal breaker with the Selection Stuffed Shirt Board.

When she phoned his home number the first time she went back to Glasgow, a woman answered. 'Edith Green. Who's speaking please?' She sounded exactly like Fran's mother, same querulous tone. Fran hung up quietly. She found out from Iona that Ian had married Professor Wilson's secretary, Edith McPherson, a widow in her late forties. She was pleased that he had not wasted any time settling down, but even more pleased that it had not been with her. He got his promotion.

Her mother clammed up when Fran told her she was leaving, her mouth narrowing into a thin line. She refused to ask Fran any questions about her new job, or even where she would be staying. A few days before Fran left, her mother went off on a holiday with her friend Peggy. They went to Southern Ireland and probably drank their way around most of the pubs she guessed. Fran took a taxi alone to Glasgow Airport. As the Trident jet lifted off the runway, diminishing all she had ever known into tiny, unrecognisable images, the last thing she saw was the shimmer of sunlight on the river Clyde before the aircraft climbed above the clouds, headed due south.

Leaving

Fran was getting stiff sitting in the uncomfortable chair beside Rob's bed in the I.C.U. He seemed to be breathing quietly, so she stood up, stretched and went off to find something to drink. When she came back, clutching a cup of coffee in a takeaway cup from the newly opened cafeteria in the main entrance, the curtains were pulled around his bed and she could hear the quiet but urgent murmur of voices behind them. Her heart rate accelerated. What was going on? After what seemed an eternity, but was probably only a moment or two, the curtains parted and a white-coated female doctor stepped out.

'Mrs Patterson.' She gestured for Fran to follow her to an empty side room adjacent to Rob's bed. 'I don't want to alarm you, but your husband's heart stopped beating for a few seconds, however, we have managed to resuscitate him.'

Fran was stunned. 'Is he going to be all right? I only went to get a coffee.' she added pointlessly, as if deserting her vigil at his bedside had somehow caused the emergency.

'He's still not too great,' the lady doctor patted Fran's shoulder kindly, 'but if we can keep him stable until the antibiotics start working, he will probably pull through. You can sit with him again if you want to. I see you have a coffee. If you want tea later to keep you going, we have a vending machine just outside the entrance to the I.C.U.'

Fran was still shaking from the unexpected shock of Rob nearly dying again. Twice in one day was pushing the boundaries. She sat down at his bedside again as the nurse quietly wheeled away the defibrillator unit.

'I can't take my eyes off you for a minute without you getting into trouble,' she whispered, at his unconscious frame. How ironic it was to expect him to respond in any way to her attempt at humour. She held his hand, offering silent comfort, trying to connect. But even fully awake, he just didn't 'get' her. He never had really. Not even at the beginning...

Norman Anderson, her new boss in the West London branch of Grayson's Research Laboratories, was tall and painfully thin, with a huge Adam's apple that bobbed up and down, when he spoke. It seemed to have a life of its own. Fran couldn't concentrate on what he was saying as he explained the project she would be working on with him. She was dismayed to learn that she would be sharing her laboratory space with him. His desk was opposite her bench and he spent most of the day pouring over his notes. He was a vet but totally academic. She couldn't imagine him getting his hands bloody inside a sheep's stomach, or swearing, or taking the testicles from a castrated ram home for tea like her old boss, Professor Wilson, the now-retired head of the Large Animal Surgery at the Veterinary Hospital in Glasgow.

'Lovely rolled in oatmeal and fried with garlic and onion.' Professor Wilson would declare gleefully, tossing the newly removed testicles into a stainless-steel dish. Fran had the job of rinsing them and wrapping them up for him to take home to his equally batty wife, Betty. How Fran missed the earthy vibe at the Veterinary Hospital. She had to keep reminding herself of her other reasons for leaving Glasgow. She simply had to get away from her mother and Ian Green. They would have enmeshed her into a life she did not want. For the first time, she was happy to be young, single and unencumbered with responsibilities.

'Fran, I want you to come with me today to help set up a

leptospirosis vaccine trial with sheep. Have you handled sheep outdoors before?' Norman asked hesitantly. He did not look as if he were relishing the prospect himself.

'Definitely!' she responded enthusiastically. At last they were getting out of the stuffy laboratory where she spent hours peering down a microscope at wriggling leptospiral bacilli which were kept alive in hapless hamsters. Graham Gordon, her old scientific journalist buddy from Glasgow had been right, she wasn't cut out for spending long hours in a laboratory. Maybe she should consider a change of career she mused.

She giggled inwardly as Norman struggled to attach a bag to the ewe's rump while she supported the animal against her legs. This was more like it! Poor Norman, he was way out of his comfort zone doing field work. She so enjoyed the outings to the farm every week during the trial, when the sheep were released from the indignity of carrying the heavy bags full of droppings. They would trot off like spring lambs, skipping and kicking out their hind legs. Norman would unbend a little on these outings and seemed to enjoy Fran's obvious delight at the ewes' behaviour. Her pleasure and sense of freedom soon evaporated when she was back at the lab with kilos of sheep droppings to analyse.

'Fran, I've got bronchitis, I feel awful.' Her mother sounded dreadful, her voice rasping until she was overcome with a paroxysm of coughing. 'Can you come home? I can't get out of bed and Peggy is away in Dunfermline at her daughter's.' It was Friday lunchtime when Fran took the call on the phone in her lab.

'All right Mum, don't worry, I'll try and get a stand-by ticket. I should be home by tonight. Just stay in bed.' Fran sighed heavily as she put down the phone. She had been planning to go to a Proms concert this coming weekend with her two flatmates from New Zealand. She also had a first date with Matt. He was a lively young Londoner who played the saxophone in a jazz club most weekends. She had just met him in a pub nearby her shared flat in South Kensington. She had been instantly attracted to him, he was funny and intelligent and best of all, in his early twenties. At last, a possible relationship with someone nearer her own age. She had been looking forward to meeting up with him again. I hope he still wants to see me when I get back. I wish Mum hadn't needed me this weekend. Fran had a frustrated internal monologue but there was no one else to look after her mother. Both her sisters had emigrated with their families; one to New Zealand and one to Australia. Fran's hair length issue at their respective weddings, still getting in the way of a reconciliation between them. It just reinforced Fran's determination not to get married, or if she ever did, to keep it simple. No white wedding for her.

Norman swung his chair round to face Fran. He had obviously overheard her end of the conversation with her mother. 'Look Fran, just leave early if you need to catch a flight back to Glasgow. I can wait for a few days for your results from this latest batch. Take as long as you need.'

Fran felt a rush of warm gratitude towards her normally slightly anal boss. 'Oh, thank you Norman, that would be really helpful. I might need to take a day or two off next week as well, but I will get back as soon as I can. I will phone you on Monday with an update.' What a kind soul he was she thought, reconsidering her opinion of him as she rushed off back to her flat to pack a few things before heading for Heathrow Airport.

She managed to get a cheap stand-by ticket for an early evening flight and was back in her old home before dark. She felt quite oppressed to be back home looking after her mother once again. Will Mum ever manage to cope on her own? I can't keep dashing back from London every time she gets ill, she thought with some frustration. The doctor came to the house and prescribed antibiotics for her.

'Keep her warm and in bed. Plenty of fluids and bland food for the next few days. If she does not start improving in forty-eight hours, call the surgery. This is a serious chest infection and could develop into pneumonia. Encourage you mother to stop smoking, that would help.'

She followed the doctor's instructions and kept her mother lubricated with hot whiskey toddies and endless cups of tea, until, after a couple of days, she seemed to be improving a bit, still in bed, but sleeping a lot. She phoned Iona.

'I'll come over to your house if you don't want to go out and leave your mum.'

'Oh great, thanks Iona, I'll make something for us to eat. Max won't mind you coming out to visit me, will he?'

There was a small silence. 'No, he-he's away on business now, won't be back until tomorrow morning. I'll be over soon. Can I stay the night with you?'

'Of course, Iona, there's two beds in my old room.' Fran was puzzled, Iona sounded subdued, not with her usual cheery tone.

Half an hour later, Iona pulled up outside Fran's house. She was driving a shiny black Mini, it looked brand new. When she came in Fran looked at her in shock. Iona was stick thin, dark circles sullied the skin under her pale blue eyes, her blond curls were long and tangled, giving her face a small, ethereal look. She was still hauntingly beautiful despite her Twiggy-like thin face and body. She gave Fran a quick hug. 'I brought some whiskey in case you don't have any in the house. I know you don't drink it normally. Can I pour one for myself?'

'What's wrong Iona, you look rough. Have you been unwell? Is living with Max working out all right?' Fran asked. She had not met Max yet but didn't like the look of him from the photographs she had seen. She also knew that he had a reputation for being ruthless in his business dealings in the property market. Iona had hinted at that once or twice the few times they had phoned one another.

'It's all right if I am willing to sit beside him when he plays poker. He says I bring him luck.' Iona stared into her whiskey glass, swilling the amber liquid around in hypnotic circles.

'How often does he play poker?' Fran asked, unable to imagine Iona sitting passively at Max's side, probably drinking too much out of boredom.

'Twice a week, he has his mates over and they sit up all night. It drives me mad, but the rest of the time I can do what I like. He is very generous to me Fran.' Iona said a little defensively. 'I have plenty of time to write and I am going to art classes now. I have started sketching horses and dogs belonging to Max's friends and I am learning how to paint in oils. One of Max's friends keeps horses. I get to ride whenever I want. I didn't think I would want to go near a horse again, you know, after Liam-but it has been all right actually. It's a great feeling to be galloping on a horse again. I had almost forgotten how exhilarating it is.' She quickly emptied her glass of whiskey and poured another one.

'Are you eating enough Iona, you've lost a ton of weight.'

'Oh, don't try and mother me Fran, I'm fine. I like being thin. Max has a horror of fat women.' Iona sounded irritated.

Her mum started coughing again in her bedroom where she still lay and slept most of the day. 'I'll just see to Mum.' Fran hurried out the room, glad of the chance to drop the touchy subject of Iona's alarming weight loss. She was knocking back the whiskey as well. Worrying.

After a few more whiskeys, Iona's mood lifted and she was soon laughing and making her usual ironic observations about some of Max's rather eclectic circle of friends and 'business associates'. Fran shared some of her funny stories about her Kiwi flatmates and her unlikely veterinary boss, Norman. Exaggerating a bit to make Iona laugh. Around midnight, the friends collapsed into the two beds in Fran's bedroom. Fran's face was aching with the laughter they had shared. It was just like old times.

She was wakened by the quiet sounds of Iona getting dressed in the early morning darkness of the bedroom. 'Do you have to leave so early?' Fran was struggling to keep her eyes open. 'Do you want some breakfast? A cup of tea or something?'

'No. Sorry Fran, but I need to get back before Max. He doesn't like it if I'm not there when he comes home. Bit of a temper on him, so best to keep him sweet. I'll see you. Thanks for letting me stay last night. I'll come back and see your mum when I can.' Iona disappeared quickly. Fran heard her car engine start up and then she was gone. Fran could just make out the time on her bedside clock. It was 5 am.

The Ties That Bind.

'Fran the company will fund you to upgrade your I.M.L.T. qualifications to degree level if you want. It might be worth thinking about. If this department expands, you could head up the technicians' research team, but only if you have a university degree. Biochemistry and Biology would be the most appropriate one to opt for.' Norman stood beside Fran's desk, his long white fingers tapping nervously on the surface.

This felt like a royal command to Fran. She was the only one in the Biology Department without a degree. Biology, was fine, her speciality. But Biochemistry! Far too left-brained for her. She was hopeless at maths. She signed up for the course. How could she not? Especially after Norman had been so understanding about giving her time off to look after her mother. She felt she owed it to him and allowed her innate desire to please, override her instinct to avoid such a difficult challenge. Afterwards, she wanted to kick herself for getting trapped into this. She had just locked herself into two further years of attending college and study.

Her salvation turned out to be Matt. 'I can help you unravel the mysteries of Biochemistry Fran. I did a year of it at university before switching to electrical engineering. Not just a pretty face you know.' He laughed as she flung her arms around him.

'Oh Matt, thank you. That would be marvellous. I was having nightmares about it.' Matt had no idea just how many brownie points Fran gave him for that generous offer and he was true to his word, helping her to understand the language and concepts of her dreaded subject. She hoped fervently their relationship would last the course. He was such a comfortable person to be with and she was having a lot of fun in his company.

Two months later her mother called her at Grayson's. She couldn't cope any longer with living by herself in Glasgow. She wanted to move South. Fran was horrified. 'What about Peggy, Mum? She will miss you. You see her every day, don't you?'

'Not any more. Peggy has moved to a smaller house and it's quite a long walk to her place. It's down near the park.' The park was only a fifteen-minute flat walk from their house in Glasgow. But her mother was not to be persuaded to stay put. Before Fran could say anything, her mother continued quickly; 'I can't sleep in the house by myself and I can't manage to look after the garden.' Her voice became whiny. 'Anyway, I'm going to have to leave my job, they're giving me too much extra work. I can't cope with it. The stress is making me ill and there is nobody here to look after me now.'

That was it. Fran felt the walls closing in. She sighed deeply, defeated. 'OK Mum, don't worry, I will try and find us somewhere to live nearer Grayson's. But, you must make your own arrangements about closing down the house and packing up to leave.'

'Oh dear. Will I? I don't think I can manage that. I will ask Peggy to help me, unless – can you come back?'

'No Mum. I'm sorry, but I have exams soon and I can't miss any of my classes.' She was just about keeping on top of her studies with Matt's help. The last thing she needed right now was the upheaval of leaving her flat in South Kensington, her jolly flatmates from New Zealand and trying to find a suitable place for her mother and herself to live. She wondered how Matt would take the news, he was a real city lover. She could not shake off the sense of being trapped by this pending development.

In the end. it was Peggy and her daughter and son-in-law who did all the packing, cleaning and arranging transport for the furniture her mother wanted to bring with her. She was still utterly helpless.

Fran managed to find an unfurnished, two-bedroomed flat above a row of shops in the suburbs, only two Tube stations away from her work and only two changes needed to get to her college in Paddington. She moved in by herself after signing the lease, to clean the place up and redecorate it. Every room showed signs of bad neglect by the previous tenant. Matt came over and helped her when he could.

'Hey babe. Shall we stop painting for a bit? That mattress looks kind of inviting.' Matt had come up behind Fran, slipping his arms around her waist and kissing her neck. Fran leant back into his solid body. He was wearing a pair of scruffy, paint-spattered shorts, but his upper body was naked. He had been hinting for a while now that he wanted a bit more than just kissing. Fran hadn't had a full physical relationship since leaving Glasgow. Ian's paranoia about keeping their affair a secret had left her with an enduring notion that a sexual relationship was a little bit 'wrong'. But this was her last day of freedom before her mother arrived. She had a sinking feeling that event would challenge her friendship with Matt. She liked Matt, he was kind and funny. The only thing that put her off a bit was the smell of his sweat. He ate a lot of curry and his body odour was decidedly curry-ish. Fran was camping in the flat while she waited for the furniture from her old house in Glasgow to arrive with her mother. The mattress on the floor, a kettle and a couple of cups and plates and some cutlery, were all the items the flat boasted at that moment.

She turned in his arms as he pressed her close into his body. She could feel the hardness of him through her shorts. 'Oh Matt, I don't know if I'm ready for this yet,' she protested weakly. But the insistent pressure of him against her lower body, made her legs tremble.

'Let's find out then, shall we?' Matt lowered her carefully onto the mattress keeping up the contact with his mouth and tongue on her mouth, neck and ears. She shivered with anticipation as he helped her to wriggle out of her shorts and T-shirt. Perhaps it was a final act of desperation before the constraints of having her mother move back in with her, but she yielded fully to him. They made love in an explosion of passion that had them both gasping and laughing. A little later, they came together again, gently, kindly. Matt stroked the damp hair off her face. 'I guess you were ready for this then?' He smiled and Fran sighed, suddenly feeling bereft for what she sensed would come.

'Can you get me more cigarettes dear? I've almost run out.' Fran gritted her teeth as her mother called after her just as she was going out the door. They had run out of milk and the corner shop was about to close. Why couldn't her mother have gone earlier? She had been at the flat all day doing God knows what. The living room was still piled high with packing boxes that could have been emptied by now. Fran had to dash to get to the corner shop to buy milk before they closed. Buying her mother's cigarettes was leaving her short. At least her mum would soon be able to contribute to the running costs of the flat when she started her new job, but she still expected to be looked after. Fran felt oppressed again and another emotion crept in that she recognised as resentment. But, she had made that promise to her dad to look after her mum, and it seemed that was her destiny – for now. Running away from Glasgow had not worked.

Now that she was no longer living conveniently in London, Matt and she were only meeting up in town after her college day on a Thursday and sometimes on a Saturday. Matt played his saxophone every Thursday and most Saturdays with a jazz quartet in a small club in Dene Street. His day job was with London Underground sorting out complicated logistics in an office somewhere. Fran had not fully grasped exactly what he did.

They had not had an opportunity to revisit their passionate lovemaking at the flat. Matt was always working and she was studying for exams. He would take her to his club every

Thursday, after they shared a curry at Matt's favourite Indian restaurant, conveniently, two doors down from the club.

'Sorry gorgeous, but can you wait here for me while I play this set?' The first time that happened, she felt a bit conspicuous sitting alone at the bar, but Matt kept an eye on her and would rush over to whirl her onto the tiny, crowded space that served as a dance floor, as soon as his set was finished.

'Ooh, you're all sweaty,' she protested. Matt just laughed and pulled her in closer. His other lovely qualities cancelled out the curry smell from his body – almost. They had nowhere to go to be alone and Fran could sense that Matt was getting frustrated. Against her better judgement, she invited him over to her flat one Saturday when he wasn't playing.

'Mum, this is Matt.' Fran introduced her mother who as usual, was sitting comfortably on the sofa, her packet of cigarettes and an overflowing ashtray on the small occasional table at her side.

'Hello dear. Would you like a cigarette? No? Oh well. Fran, do you mind making me a cup of tea? So, what do you do for a living Matt? Fran says you play the trumpet in a band.'

Fran could hear Matt trying to explain that he played the saxophone in a jazz quartet, and his day job was in 'logistics' for London Underground. Fran banged around in the kitchen making tea. God, why can't she go to bed? It was late. Couldn't her mother see that Matt and she wanted to be alone? He would have to leave soon to catch the late train back to town. She just could not bring herself to ask her mother to leave the room. Her heart sank. This was not going to work; she just knew it. Why did she have to feel so responsible for her mother? She just had no awareness of Fran's need for privacy. Fran was angry and frustrated with herself for not having the courage to set the boundaries. Matt came over once more, but he couldn't out sit her mother who wanted to be the centre of attention, dominating the conversation and turning the air thick with her cigarette smoke. Fran guessed that he was probably fed-up with her for not making her mother give them space. He stopped calling her. She tried to remember that the smell of his curry-flavoured sweat had put her off a little, but she missed him. At least she had a slightly better understanding of Biochemistry thanks to Matt.

It still took two attempts at the Biochemistry, but finally Fran passed her exams and got her degree. She had not been able to socialise with anyone for ages after she and Matt stopped dating. Her head had been buried in her books forever it seemed.

'Come on Mum, let's go to the pub to celebrate me finally getting my degree.' The truth was, she reminded herself ruefully, that she did not have any friends living locally to celebrate with. All the people she mixed with at work lived in London. 'John, that Scottish man I told you about might be there tonight.' John had started chatting to Fran in the corner shop when he heard her accent.

'Where are you from then?' was how he initiated the conversation the previous day. 'Not too many Edinburgh folks in these parts,' he added.

Fran laughed. 'I'm from Glasgow actually. How about you?'

'Aye well, me too lass, but not from the same end as you. You sound posh. I'm John by the way.'

Fran laughed again, immediately warming to this open and friendly middle-aged man with the achingly familiar accent of her home town. They chatted on a bit and she discovered that he was a widower. His wife had died almost a year earlier. He also told her that he was a regular the local pub, The Plough. 'I can't stand being alone in the house at night,' he had said sadly.

'Tell you what', said Fran the rescuer. 'Why don't I introduce you to my mum, my dad died recently too and Mum has moved south and is living with me now. I'll bring her over to the pub sometime.'

'That would be grand.' John beamed. 'Is she as good-looking as you?'

'Almost.' Fran grinned. 'Maybe we'll see you tomorrow night in The Plough?'

Her mum got quite skittish when Fran told her about meeting up with John at the pub and spent a lot of time that evening, trying on different frocks, finally settling on a green paisley-patterned shirt waister dress which showed off her neat figure. She was still a very attractive woman, Fran supposed, suddenly seeing her mum in a new light.

'I can see where Fran got her good looks from.' John clasped Fran's mum's hand and smiled widely.

'Och, you're a blether.' Fran's mum's face had flushed quite pink and she nervously lit a cigarette.

'Sit down girls and I'll get you a drink.' John took their orders and went over to the bar. Soon John and her mum were deep in animated conversation, swapping stories about their lost partners and their shared histories in Glasgow. Fran listened contentedly, hoping that something would spark between these two. She so needed her mum to get a life of her own.

Intervention

Fran noticed him as soon as he walked into the pub. She experienced an immediate sense of deja-vu when he looked straight at her. Flushed, she had lowered her gaze. Later when she went up to the bar to buy them all another round, he appeared very quickly at her elbow. She could feel the heat from his arm through her jacket.

'What are you and your friends drinking.?' His voice was deep and pleasant. She turned and looked straight into his deep-set, dark brown eyes. His hair was black and wavy and his skin had an olive hue. He smiled. Lovely white teeth, Fran noticed.

'Why do you ask?' As if she didn't know. 'I am buying drinks for my mother and a friend. I'm celebrating, I don't normally come into this pub.' Oh God, she was babbling.

The brown eyes stared unwaveringly at her. 'Well, let me help you, your mother and her friend celebrate… whatever it is you are celebrating. Put your money away, I'll get this round. My name's Rob. What's yours?'

'Fran.' She liked his confidence. He didn't proffer his hand. 'All right, if you insist,' she managed. 'Thanks very much.'

'I'll bring the drinks over.'

John and Fran's mum, Jen, were mildly surprised at Rob's sudden appearance at their table, bearing a tray with two double whiskeys, a half pint of lager for himself and a vodka and lime for Fran.

Rob did not give Fran time to do the introductions, but quickly shook hands with John and Jen. 'Hello I'm Rob, Fran tells me you are celebrating. So, cheers.' He sat down and clinked glasses with everybody as if they were already best friends.

Rob insisted on buying another round but reappeared with just two more double whiskies. 'Fran and I are off to watch the sun go down. Nice to meet you, Jen, John.' He took Fran's hand and pulled her gently but firmly to her feet. She felt she should have been a bit annoyed at this presumption. He could have asked her first. In truth, she was quite carried away with Rob's decisiveness and self-assurance. He was obviously a man who knew what he wanted. And, he was so good-looking. Fran had taken every opportunity to examine his features in the pub when he was talking to her mum and John. His square jaw was off-set by the high cheekbones and the long straight nose. His forehead jutted out a bit over the deep-set brown eyes, but not enough to create a Neanderthal profile. She smiled inwardly at the silent appraisal she was making. She reckoned he was around the six-foot mark, a couple of inches taller than her in her high heels. But she particularly liked the shape of his body. He was broad-shouldered, and solidly built with strong, square hands. She had a horror of being with skinny men as she felt that they made her look enormous beside them.

'Good to meet you son.' John had stood up to shake Rob's hand. 'Thanks for the drinks and look after Fran.'

She could have died of embarrassment. What was John thinking? Behaving like her dad. Must have been the whiskey addling his brain. Fran's mum pursed her mouth and lit another cigarette.

'Don't worry, I intend to, John. Enjoy the rest of the evening you two.' Rob kept hold of Fran's hand and they walked out of the pub into the mild warmth of the summer evening.

Rob told her a few weeks into their relationship, that he had fallen in love with her at first sight that night in the pub. She too had experienced a strong visceral attraction to Rob, but she wasn't quite sure then what real love should feel like. Was it that flip-flop feeling in her stomach the first time she met him at Heathrow straight after one of his flights? He was still in his uniform and looked so handsome as he strode towards her, beaming his wide smile, just for her. She noticed other women staring at him as he approached her, feeling a huge stab of possessive pride when he pulled her into his embrace.

'Did you miss me, darling?' Rob's voice was deep and sensuous as he nuzzled her neck. He had been on a long-haul trip with a three day lay-over in New York. They had not slept together yet and Fran was not quite ready to take that next step with him.

'Yes, I did.' Had she? 'Did you miss me?'

'Of course I did. There's a squash tournament starting at my club tomorrow. Will you come and watch me play?'

Rob was very competitive and while the tournament was on, nearly all their time together was spent at the squash club. He was either playing in a match or having a 'friendly' practice game with one of his competitors.

'Are you Rob's latest girlfriend?' the bartender asked Fran nosily as she was waiting for him to shower and join her at the bar.

'Have there been a lot of earlier girlfriends then?' Fran enquired sarcastically but uneasily. Rob had not mentioned any ex-girlfriends from the club.

'Well, there's two of them over there.' The barman ducked his chin in the direction of the far corner of the bar as he continued rinsing and drying beer glasses. 'He's always got someone in tow.' Fran glanced quickly at the two girls chatting animatedly together. Both dark-haired, slim and attractive. They looked towards Fran for a moment and continued their discussion. Fran felt uncomfortable and quite exposed. They were probably wondering what Rob saw in her. She couldn't believe it when he came into the bar and went over to the girls to say hello before joining her.

'Fran, come and meet my friends, perhaps you can arrange to have a game of squash with them. I've coached them they are quite good players.'

'You're joking, aren't you? Fran was aghast. 'I heard you have dated both of them!' Her voice rose in a shrill whisper.

Rob looked at her in total surprise. 'Don't be silly, they don't mean anything to me now. We are just friends.'

Fran wondered how the two girls felt about Rob. Had they dumped him? Had he dumped them? She was feeling very insecure about Rob now. Maybe he would discard her too when another pretty girl came along.

'Actually, I don't really want to go and sit with them Rob. It's just too weird to talk to your ex-girlfriends. I would feel too judged by them.'

Rob shrugged. 'All right, let's go.' He placed an arm around her waist and pulled her in firmly to his side. They left.

After a few more dates, which always ended in long, intense kissing sessions in the cramped confines of his two-seater MG sports car, Rob finally suggested, 'Why don't we go up to your flat tonight?' They had been to the pictures and he was due to leave on a ten-day trip the next day.

Oh no, thought Fran. Here we go, the kiss of death with Mum on the scene. John was in Scotland visiting his sick sister and Rob had not seen them again since the first night in the pub. John and her mum were spending more and more evenings in the flat which she had mixed feelings about, although it had taken some of the pressure off Fran to keep her mother entertained. However, she still expected Fran to make her and John cups of tea when she was at home.

'I suppose you're going out with that Rob again.' Her mother had taken to calling Rob 'that Rob' for no other reason Fran supposed that she was feeling a bit threatened by the amount of time that Fran was staying out and not devoting the same hours as before to shopping and cleaning the flat for them.

Rob chatted politely with her mother while Fran, as usual, made cups of tea for them. It was 11 p.m. and Rob had been sitting beside Fran with his arm firmly around her shoulder and finally pulling her onto his lap. A clear signal that they wanted to be alone. But her mother lit another cigarette and settled herself comfortably for another round of conversation. Oblivious.

Rob stood up and grabbed Fran's hand. 'Right, we're off to bed. Good night Jen.' All she saw was the astonished look on her mother's face as Rob marched her out of the room, straight into her bedroom. He shut her door firmly and stood grinning at her.

'What are you doing?' Fran was appalled. 'She will be offended…'

'She is going to have to get used to it.' Rob wrapped her in his arms and pulled her onto her bed. She knew it was coming to this, but she had been sure that meeting her mother would have put him off as it had with Matt. Worryingly, she still thought about Matt from time to time, wishing Rob had the same sense of humour as him. Or at least, delayed this moment until they found a more suitable and private place to consummate the relationship. Either way, she had not invested too much in this outcome, staying detached, merely accepting it as inevitable.

There were no fireworks for Fran, no breathless giggling and mutual joy in this ageless union of their bodies, just an act of love, carried out with well-practised skill and ease by Rob. Her body responded, but her soul remained still and quiet.

'That was wonderful Fran you are almost perfect. I think I love you.' Rob cradled her in his arms and fell asleep before she could reply.

Almost perfect? She would call him on that one. Was he almost perfect she mused? Not quite. She was disappointed to learn that he was still married, but separated and had a two-year-old son. She had always supposed that she would be sharing such significant experiences with her husband, when and if she acquired one. None of it would be new to Rob. She wished too that he had a sense of humour or at least read books. He would talk at length about flying or his squash tournament with Fran, but little else seemed to be of much interest to him. Still, he was a match for her demanding mother. And he felt solid and smelled lovely. Maybe it was her turn to be looked after. Fran snuggled into him and buried her doubts in the moment.

Her mother never warmed to Rob after that night.

'I'm going up to Glasgow to visit Iona, Rob. She's had a baby girl and I want to see them.' Fran had booked a few days' holiday from Grayson's Laboratories. She had seen Iona a few times in Glasgow and once when Iona had come to London and they had gone to a Johnny Mathis concert together. Iona had finally left Max Cohen. Fran had never liked him; she had always thought that he enjoyed his mixed status as a 'person of culture' with his equally well-heeled Lenzie neighbours, as much as he liked his reputation as 'a hard man' with his business associates. Fran been horrified to see Iona grow increasingly thin and drinking heavily when she lived with him. She described to Fran what happened when she told Max that she was pregnant. He was furious.

He ranted. 'I didn't take you in to watch you turn into a fat milkmaid with a kid hanging off your tits. I have kids, I don't want any more. Get rid of it.' He had reached into his inside jacket pocket, taken out a wad of cash and flung it onto the coffee table. 'Don't come back here until it's gone.' He left, slamming the front door behind him and roared off down the driveway in his Jaguar, leaving Iona shocked, shaking and speechless.

Iona filled her Mini to the brim with her clothes, books and paintings. She was working on a few commissions of animal paintings. She would be needing to sell as many as possible to stay afloat. The cash Max had flung down would keep her going for a while, maybe even until her baby was born, but after that she had no idea how she would survive.

She had gone back to the flat in Byres Road in Glasgow that belonged to Siobhan, Liam's cousin. Seven months later, she gave birth to a dark-haired, brown-eyed perfect baby girl. Iona fell in love again, seeing in the child a reflection of her indelible memory of Liam that she would always carry in her soul. A month after the baby was born, a large sum of money was deposited in her bank account with an unidentifiable reference code. Iona was contacted by their old friend Harrison, the political satirical cartoonist from the *Glasgow Express* newspaper. Iona had told Fran that she still met up with the journalists in the Press Bar from time to time and they knew what had happened with Max. He was not admired by any of them.

'Hello hen, thought you might like to know that you will be getting a tidy sum of money every year for the wean from Max Cohen.'

'How come? Iona was astonished. 'He wanted me to get rid of the baby.'

'Well let's just say, it came to my attention that he was trying to bribe someone in the Council Planning Department. He was trying to push through a planning application to convert a warehouse into luxury flats near the docks. I had a quiet word in his ear about a nice cartoon of him that I could publish in the *Express* unless he felt like giving you a yearly maintenance instead.'

Fran had been delighted to hear that Max had been outwitted by clever wee Harrison and pleased that Iona was getting help to raise her baby.

'Hello Iona. Congratulations. Oh my God, she's gorgeous! She looks more like Liam than Max oddly enough.' Fran cradled the infant, entranced by her perfection. 'Oh by the way, this is Rob.'

Rob had a few days leave and had insisted on driving Fran up to Glasgow. Fran was pleased, she wanted to introduce her handsome boyfriend to Iona and hoped that Iona would approve of him. Hoping too, that Iona would recognise some quality in him that she Fran, had not yet quite grasped. Rob had barely spoken to Fran on the journey up north, only talking when she initiated a conversation. He had kept one hand on her thigh though most of the way, but she thought his 'strong silent act' was a bit odd.

'Pleased to meet you Iona, Fran speaks about you a lot. Sounds like you two girls were tearaways around these parts.' Rob smiled warmly at Iona, leaning in to kiss her on the cheek.

'Well we had our moments to be sure, although I think I was the bad one, leading her astray.' Iona gently took the now grizzling baby from Fran. 'Not much opportunity for any of that these days with this little darlin' to look after.' The baby quietened immediately in Iona's arms, looking over her shoulder with wide-eyed eternal curiosity at Fran and Rob.

'She really is beautiful Iona.' Fran moved over close to Iona searching her friend's features with concern. 'Are you managing all right?' Iona was still very pale and thin.

'I'm all right Fran, don't worry. Leaving Max was the best solution. I'm not drinking as much now and since Max paid me the extra money, thanks to Harrison. I can relax a bit and focus on my poetry and painting and of course, this wee one.' She kissed the infant and laid her back down in her cot.

Rob was standing at the far end of the room examining some of Iona's paintings, completely zoned out of the baby talk. Fran wished he could be a bit more interactive, or say something amusing or interesting.

'What do you think of Rob.' she mouthed looking hopefully for Iona's reaction.

Iona gazed back at her with a fathomless expression. 'He's very good-looking,' she said quietly. 'Is that going to be enough for you?'

Fran was eager to show Rob some of the beautiful Scottish countryside and they drove further north through the eerily atmospheric Glen Coe and stopped on the shores of Loch Leven. The rare winter sun was sparkling the water and Ben Nevis rose majestically in the background, the cap of snow at its summit limed in silver. Rob leapt up onto a bank of rocks and turf, silhouetted against the mountain, beaming his amazing smile down at Fran. As she gazed up at him, seduced by the beauty of their surroundings, Iona's words faded from her mind and she decided she was in love.

Pat Abercromby

Uncertainty

Fran was always glad to see Rob when he returned from his long-haul trips, but was perfectly content without him when he was away. It was hard to analyse why and she chose to ignore the anomaly. Maybe she was just someone who was all right with her own company she decided. Her mother and her boyfriend John, were always together in the flat, behaving like an old married couple, turning the air hazy with their perpetual smoking. They rarely went over to the pub now. Clearly John was a home-loving bird. There was no privacy and the walls were too thin. The thought and sounds of her mother and John in bed together was too much for Fran. It was just too weird, especially when Rob and she were in her bedroom with her mother and John only yards away through a thin wall. Rob had a small bedroom in a shared house in Ealing and they would spend the night together there quite often. Still short on privacy, but better than the flat.

But Fran was restless, *was* this enough for her? Iona's words frequently echoed through her mind. She felt hemmed-in again. Her mother was heavily dependent on her for financial support and Rob seemed to be content with his living arrangements. Not surprising she thought wryly, as he spent most of his time being spoiled in luxury overseas hotels. She had accompanied him on a short, three-day trip to Los Angeles and had watched with amused interest from her back seat on the flight deck as the glamorous cabin crew girls fussed and pandered to the constant requests of Rob and the two other flight deck crew for cups of tea and coffee every half hour. The three-day layover was spent lounging around the hotel swimming pool, eating delightful food, drinking cocktails and having lots of sex. Apart from the lots of sex bit, she hoped, she knew that this was Rob's normal lifestyle when he was flying. No wonder he was not in any hurry to settle down at home.

It just was not enough for her after all. But what could she do? Her only work experience was in medical laboratory research. She could hardly claim to be a journalist on the strength of helping Graham Gordon to write his science column in the *Scottish Daily Express*. Once again, she started to look for a way out. She saw the advert in the *Telegraph*. A pharmaceutical company near Frankfurt had indicated that they were looking for another qualified, English-speaking researcher to head up a new research project in California. But initially, the successful candidate would work in the laboratory in Frankfurt until the visa process was completed. She applied. She was excited about the prospect of living in the U.S.A. and checked the mail anxiously every day. Nothing. She had given up thinking about it, assuming, disappointed, that all immediate possibility of escaping to America was not going to happen. Then, just when she had almost forgotten about it, she was invited for an interview in a hotel near Heathrow airport. Two weeks after the interview, a bulky envelope arrived, postmarked Germany. It contained a letter of appointment, a contract and an open one-way airline ticket to Frankfurt. The start date was January 1st, 1970. New year. New life.

She called Iona to tell her she was leaving soon for Germany.

'What about Rob? Will he keep?' she enquired doubtfully. Fran could hear Iona's toddler, Keira babbling in the background.

'To be honest Iona. I haven't given that much thought. I just need to get away. My mother is driving me insane and anyway, Rob's not ready to commit to any long-term relationship. He is still just separated and his ex won't divorce him.'

'Well if it's meant to be… How long before you go to the States? Once you get there you probably won't want to come back.' Iona's voice sounded a bit slurred. Was she drinking again?

'Whatever happens, I'll come back as often as I can, I promise. How are you and Keira getting on now?' Fran felt anxious about Iona, maybe trying to cope on her own with a toddler in a flat was proving too much for her. If she was back on the whiskey, that was bad news.

'We are fine, Fran. Keira goes to nursery five morning a week. Max's money pays for that and my pet portraits are selling quite well these days.' She hesitated. 'And a volume of my poetry has been published.'

'That's marvellous Iona, how did that happen?' Iona was a dark horse, never one to show off about her achievements. Fran was always the one checking up on her.

'It was Harrison who encouraged me. He comes over here occasionally and he read some of my poems. I thought they were rubbish, but he did a series of lovely pen and ink drawings to illustrate a few of them and the next thing I knew; he had found a publisher for them. They are mostly about Liam and Keira, the only people in my life who have inspired me.'

Fran experienced a little jolt of sadness when Iona said that. Iona's friendship meant so much to her, but it seemed that Iona did not feel the same.

'I'll buy a copy Iona, what's it called?'

'Don't be daft, I'll send you a copy. It's called *The Chained Heart*.'

When Iona's book of illustrated poetry arrived, there were two inscriptions inside. One from Harrison.

To my other prop half. Will ye no come back again?

Iona had written. *To Fran, my dear friend. Without your support, love and inspiration, I would not have come back from the abyss of my soul's despair.*

Schmerz der Liebe
(The Pain of Love)

'Rob, I have been offered a job in a pharmaceutical company in Germany, near Frankfurt. I'm sorry, I didn't really want to tell you before.' She did not mention the pending transfer to the U.S.A. They were sitting in her bedroom after another evening spent at the squash club in Ealing. She had waited to tell him in case it put him off his tournament match. She also thought that this news might make him break up with her. She was very attracted to Rob's dark Mediterranean features, his decisiveness and most of all, his ability to handle her mother. At almost thirty, a few years older than her, he was a paradox to Fran. At times when he was with her, he seemed protective and very caring, but at other times he was so focussed and single minded about his squash and his flying career that he was almost cavalier in his attitude to her. Always assuming that she would be available to watch him play and never enquiring about her life when he was away. Expecting her to drop everything and be there for him when he was around. But, she had reasoned, years of her youth had been spent taking care of her parents; nursing her father until he died and then having to support her mother in her helpless widowhood. It was nice to feel wanted and for a change, to feel looked after, at least sometimes. She had compromised and accepted the limitations of her relationship with Rob. It was all she had known, but now she realised, it was not enough for her.

'I guess you've known for a while then?' He looked at her quizzically. Didn't appear to be too bothered. 'Oh well, that will be good experience for you. I'll come and visit you.' End of discussion. Rob pulled Fran into his arms and made love to her with fierce intensity, as if to seal the deal.

On the day of her departure Rob phoned. 'Sorry Darling. I've got a squash match booked this afternoon. It's the first round of the tournament so I can't come to Heathrow to see you off. But I'll come and visit you as soon as I can.'

Fran's mother did not come to the airport either to see her off. John was coming over to stay over for the weekend to keep her company and she had to cook a meal for him. She was quite stressed as Fran normally did the cooking for her.

As she boarded her flight for what she hoped was a new life, a new adventure, she did feel a flutter of misgiving. She wished that she wasn't going to continue working in the Pharmaceutical Industry. Three years closeted with Norman Anderson analysing sheep's droppings had not set her alight with enthusiasm for medical research. Poor Norman had been quite emotional when she left. The only one really. She hoped the type of research she would be doing in this new company would be more stimulating.

Germany that January of 1970 was bitterly cold. It was a Saturday, December 30th 1969 and Fran wasn't starting her new job until the Monday, January 1st 1970. She had to spend two days on her own in a Frühstückspension, one of many small Bed and Breakfast establishments in this suburb of Frankfurt. Homesickness clamped her chest in its vicious grip. It was a physical pain, her heart hurt, squeezed into too small a space and she experienced a pervasive sense of dread. As only bed and breakfast was on offer, Fran had to wander the streets trying to find somewhere to eat. Her command of German was basic schoolgirl level, which just added to her sense of isolation. It was difficult to maintain a meaningful conversation with anyone. The streets with the blank, shuttered windows of the stark grey buildings in this Frankfurt suburb were completely deserted on the Sunday. And it was New Year's Eve and nobody to celebrate with. It was awful, she felt so lonely she wanted to die. Her misery had no outlet. She just wanted to flee back to the familiarity of home and even to Rob's silent embraces.

'*Guten Tag, Fraulein Frances. Ich bin Herr Dr Wolfgang Braun. Wie geht es Ihnen?*' Fran's new boss introduced himself, giving Fran a stiff little bow and shaking her hand.

Fran was so pleased to be speaking to someone after her ghastly, lonely, first weekend in Germany. '*Guten Tag, Herr Dr Braun. Freut mich sehr.*' She quickly ran out of anything more meaningful to say, feeling self-conscious. Happily, Herr Braun continued talking to her in excellent English and introduced her to Polly and Ted, two other English research technicians on the team. Polly was small and vivacious with an unruly mop of red hair. She had been working for the company for five years and came originally from Newcastle. She was thirty, but always lied about her age, Fran discovered. Ted was married with a wife and small child in Milton Keynes. He was there purely for the money, which was much better than the wages offered for the same work in the U.K. Fran immediately bonded with her two English colleagues. Polly was chatty and sociable and Ted had a quick, clever, sense of humour. Fran and he had a lot of fun sparking off one-liners, outdoing one another with absurd takes on German culture. If only Rob had some sense of the ridiculous to match hers, she would have missed him more. Polly and Fran were marking time until their promised transfer to the U.S.A. to head up a new research facility in California. Just as well Fran thought, she was sickened by the animal experiments that were going on. The stringent controls protecting laboratory animals in the U.K. did not seem to apply here. She knew she would not be able to stomach working in that environment for long.

'*Malzeit!*' The call to down tools and go for lunch rang out at exactly twelve noon.

'Come on Fran. We'll show you the way to the canteen.' Ted and Polly were already deserting their work benches.

'I'm starving.' admitted Fran. 'Starting work at 7.30 am is a bit of a shock to the system. I didn't have time for breakfast!'

'You'll get used to it. The food is good here. Make sure you fill up. It's practically free.' Polly illustrated this truth that day and every other day by piling her plate high with a mountain of food; kartöffel, saurkraut, schinken, schnitzels or würst. Whatever was on offer Polly ate, yet remained waif-like. Fran couldn't understand how she got away with staying so slender.

'May I join you?' Fran was disconcerted at first when their boss, Herr Braun wanted to sit with them at their table. However, Polly and Ted seemed quite relaxed about it and chatted on animatedly. Fran reckoned that Herr Braun was quite pleased that he was the only head of department to have three English researchers on his team. He laughed politely along with them, but Fran wasn't sure if he fully followed all the nuances of their humour.

Rob sent letters to Fran every week, short notes declaring his love. *I will come and visit you when the squash tournament is over and when I get back from my next trip*, he wrote in his small, spidery handwriting. She always wrote back, telling him she missed him, which she did some of the time. Especially at night in her bare little room on the top floor of the Madchenheim where all the non-local female employees were housed. She was still very homesick and would have been pleased to see him.

'Come on Fran, we're missing the fun,' Polly yelled up the stairs. Her room was directly below Fran's in the Madchenheim. They were going to a Fasching party, one of the endless celebrations taking place during the carnival season before Lent began on Ash Wednesday, the eleventh of February.

'Coming.' Fran called, grabbing the new red leather shoulder bag she had bought with her first paycheque. She ran down the concrete stairs to join Polly on the street, pulling her ridiculously short, red tartan mini-skirt down a bit further over her freezing bottom, which was clad in red knickers to match her skirt, even though she was wearing black opaque tights. The knee-high boots kept her lower legs warm, but the acres of exposed thigh to where the equally short coat ended, felt arctic. Polly was wearing a full-length, white quilted coat with a fur-lined hood which was pulled up, covering her red curls. She looked like a cosy, miniature polar bear. Much more sensibly clad against the cold than Fran. Experience of German winters triumphing over fashion.

It was early evening, very dark, very cold, but already the revellers were out on the streets, many dressed in garish costumes and singing loudly, hugging and kissing everyone they met. A brass band of rosy-cheeked musicians was belting out oom pa pa tunes in the middle of the market square, attracting an audience of dancing and clapping youngsters. Vendors at street corners were selling steaming cups of *glühwein* and pretzels glistening with embedded salt crystals. Fran loved the taste of the hot wine infused with nutmeg and cloves, contrasting with the saltiness of the huge pretzels, almost as big as tennis racquets. There were other vendors at every corner selling Bratwurst, German hot dogs, in soft rolls with spicy mustard.

'You should try one of these Fran, they're fabulous'. Polly wolfed down a huge hot-dog with gusto. Fran was astonished. Polly had just finished a schnitzel with French fries in the Madchenheim about an hour earlier. Where did she put it all? She had the appetite of a full-back rugby player. Fran would have been the size of a house with half as much food as Polly got through.

The air was filled with smoke, steam and wonderful, mixed aromas from the stands. People stood around the glowing braziers warming their freezing hands. Fran was agog. The Germans she had met in the first few days after her arrival were so formal. Lots of hand-shaking, bowing and stiff greetings. But on the first day of Fasching, everyone morphed overnight into her new best friend, including her boss, Herr Braun; all behaving suddenly like overexcited schoolchildren, loud, boisterous and extremely jolly.

'We're going to a party in Kaiser Strasse to meet up with Chuck and some guys from his unit. It's his friend's Geburstag.' Despite having lived in Germany for five years, Polly spoke excruciatingly bad German. But she had amassed a large circle of friends, both locals and men from the US Rhein-Main Air Base on the outskirts of the town. Chuck was her current love interest. Fran had not yet been introduced to any of Polly's friends and was curious to meet them that evening. Especially the Americans, as both Polly and she hoped to be transferred to the U.S.A. within a few months. They hurried through the streets, swallowing a few *glühweins* on the way – just to keep out the cold. Dodging the embraces of the noisy merrymakers as they went.

'What's his name?'

'Who?' Polly was easily distracted.

'Chuck's friend?'

'Oh *ja*. His *freund*,' Polly happily and indiscriminately spoke both languages in the same sentence. 'Erik.'

Erik! Didn't sound very American or very promising to Fran, but Polly was already disappearing through the door of a large and noisy Bierkeller and down into the basement where the party was already in full swing. They discarded their coats on a row of pegs already heavy with garments. Fran, reluctantly, hung hers up, hoping it would still be there when they left.

'Hi babe!' A tall, chunky guy with very short hair and a huge smile, showing white gleaming teeth, Chuck, Fran presumed, descended on Polly. Smothering her in a bear hug, he lifted her off her feet and swung her round. Polly gasped and giggled, obviously thrilled with his enthusiasm.

'Who's this?' He advanced on Fran before Polly had time for introductions. Alarmed that she too might be the next one to be airlifted, Fran quickly stuck out her arm and shook his hand.

'Hi, I'm Fran, Polly's friend.'

'You from England too honey? You don't sound like Polly, but that's a real cute accent.'

'Fran's Scottish.' Polly quickly stepped in. 'Why don't we introduce her to some of the guys?' She tugged Chuck across the room to a group of three obviously military types, standing in a huddle, deep in conversation. Fran had no choice but to follow.

'Guys, this here's Fran from Scotland,' which had to serve as the icebreaker as Chuck was immediately dragged off to dance by an extremely animated Polly.

The three men broke off from their discussion, disconcerted at being left to entertain the stranger. Polly and Chuck, the social glue binding them, had deserted, leaving the four of them to find common ground.

'Sorry to break up your conversation,' Fran said brightly. 'It looked serious.'

The tallest guy cleared his throat. 'Gee no, we were just telling Erik here that we have a surprise birthday present lined up for him.'

Of course, Erik the birthday boy, a safe subject to start a conversation with.

'Happy birthday-um-Erik.' The name just did not trip off her tongue, but she held out her hand anyway, for some reason, expecting a limp shake. He was in shadow, but he stepped forward and took her hand. Is it possible to fall in love with a handshake? Before she had even registered his features, or the sound of his voice, the firm warmth of his hand holding hers sent her pulse rate up several notches. The room was dimly lit, but she could see that his eyes shone, Viking blue. They stood there looking at each other, neither of them releasing the other's hand. She was dimly aware that his two companions had melted away into the darkness of the room.

'Dance with me.' His voice was low and mellow. She remembered thinking that he sounded like J.F. Kennedy. She moved effortlessly into his arms, the top of her head just grazing his cheek. He took her hand in his and placed them both over his heart. The beat reverberated through their locked fingers. His hair was dark blond, cut short, military-style, which accentuated his strong, but slender Nordic features, the nose high-bridged, the chin clear-cut. The music was mercifully slow and they drifted for a few timeless moments, silently communicating through their bodies, which moulded together in a perfect fit. When the music stopped, he led her over to a corner of the room where they sat side by side in a booth with high-backed seats, shielding them from the chattering group sitting behind them. They sat with their thighs touching, fingers laced, neither of them willing to break the physical contact.

'What's happening here, Fran? I feel like a kid on a first date.' He smiled and she noticed the white line of a scar running from his ear and ending at his chin. He saw her eyes flickering over his face. He held her gaze. 'Collateral damage,' he said quietly.

'Vietnam?' she asked gently, awash with compassion and what could have been fear, for this beautiful man.

He lifted her fingers and kissed them. 'Yeah, but let's not talk about that tonight.'

'Where are you from, Erik?'

'Massachusetts, but I haven't been back there in a while.' He sounded wistful.

Fran remembered how homesick she had felt when she first came to Germany a few weeks ago, and squeezed his fingers in sympathy, wondering if he too had experienced that pain of separation when he first left his homeland. Apart from going to the bar a couple of times to get them a drink, he did not leave her side all evening. It seemed so important to find out all they could about one another. He was in the U.S. Special Forces and surprisingly, for a career soldier, Fran was delighted to learn that he was well read. They laughingly discovered that they had similar tastes in books. Hemingway, William Faulkner and F. Scott Fitzgerald were their mutual American admired writers and like her, he had read Kingsley Amis, P.G. Wodehouse, Daphne Du Maurier and was even familiar with the lives of some of the Bloomsbury set and had read biographies of Virginia Woolf and Lytton Strachey.

'I bet I know who your favourite composer is.' Fran teased.

'Mozart,' they said in unison.

'This is almost too weird Fran. I feel as if I have known you all of my life.'

'I know, I feel the same.' she agreed, feeling a stab of guilt as thoughts of Rob slipped into her mind. 'Maybe we were together in a past life.' She threw that into the mix to test his reaction.

'Past life or this life Fran, we were meant to meet.' Erik held her hand and they sat quietly, absorbed in the wonder of their connection.

Polly and Chuck came over and sat with them for a while and soon they were all laughing together as they exchanged observations of living in Germany. Although both men admitted that living on base was just like being in a Little America as they had all the home-grown range of foods and goods available in the PX store. After a while it must have been obvious to Polly and Chuck that Fran and Erik wanted to be alone again.

Polly whispered in Fran's ear. 'Go for it girl, he's gorgeous!'

'Let's have another dance, honey. Leave these two love birds in peace. Behave yourself Buddy!' Chuck punched Erik lightly on his upper arm, grabbed Polly and whirled her off to dance.

The band playing live music were having their break. The background music changed to a continuous stream of sixties' pop songs when popular music had turned from anodyne beige crooning to colourful, meaningful songs, appealing to the young generation. The mellow tones of Karen Carpenter's rendition of 'For All We Know' slowed the jiving couples into tight twosomes, swaying as one in the dim light.

'Shall we?' Erik stood and held out his hand for Fran. She moved into his arms again. A powerful wave of recognition flooded through her. It was as if she knew every part of his being. He gently steered her into a dark corner of the small dance floor and bent his head to her. For the rest of her life, Fran would never forget that first kiss she shared with Erik.

It was so tender and yet also full of desperate longing. She felt unbelievably connected with him. All thoughts of Rob and home evaporated from her conscious mind. They walked back through the now deserted streets to her hostel. It was still freezing outside, but she did not feel it. He came up the stairs with her to her room on the top floor. They could not bear to say goodbye. He came in and they lay entwined on her narrow single bed until the dawn. For both, it was a homecoming, lost souls, now rediscovered. She saw him as often as his military duties permitted, frequently doubling up in a foursome with Chuck and Polly. But, they always returned alone to the solitude of her small room. It was their sanctuary.

A few weeks later, 'California Dreaming.' by the Mamas and Papas was playing on Fran's radio as they lay together in the afterglow of their lovemaking.

'I will think of you every time I hear that song Fran. Maybe we will find one another in California – if I get back from Vietnam in one piece.'

'Oh Erik, don't say that.' Fran shivered suddenly.' Of course, we will meet again in California, but you're here now so…' She pulled him closer.

Rob phoned her at work the next day. He was coming on the ferry to Ostend and wanted Fran to meet him there the following weekend. 'Darling I really miss you. I can't wait to see you again.'

'I-I miss you too Rob.' Hearing his familiar, warm brown voice again made her want to see him. She was so used to listening to Erik's soft East Coast drawl that she had forgotten how much Rob's voice had attracted her to him.

She and Erik had been planning to go to a pop concert in Frankfurt that same weekend with Polly and Chuck, followed by a Rhine cruise on the Sunday. She had been looking forward to it, but now Rob was travelling to Ostend to see her for the first time since she left England two months before. She could hardly tell him not to come. Erik knew about Rob, she had his photograph on a shelf in her room. He also had a childhood sweetheart waiting for him in Massachusetts. They had stopped talking about it, trying to ignore the shadows of their other lives.

'I'm going to tell Rob about us Erik. I can't keep deceiving him. It feels dishonest.'

Erik held her shoulders and looked into her eyes. 'Fran honey, you must do what feels right for you. You know how I feel about you. If you still want me, I'll be here when you get back.'

Fran buried her head into his chest. 'I'll always want you Erik.'

The following day, Chuck was waiting with Polly when Fran came out of the building at five o'clock. Odd. What was he doing here she wondered? They normally all met in town at their favourite Bierkeller. He walked straight over to Fran and placed his huge arm around her shoulders.

'Fran, I am sorry, but Erik was shipped out earlier this afternoon. He's gone back to Vietnam, Special Forces mission. He said to say goodbye and sorry he couldn't tell you himself. He will get in touch with you as soon as he can.'

Fran was stunned. 'Did he have a choice? Did he have to go?' she asked, her eyes brimming with tears. She was in total shock. It had always been a possibility of course, the silent menace of a rapid departure hovering in the background as the brutal Vietnam war raged unabated.

'No way', Chuck snorted derisively. 'When these Special Forces bastards tell you to jump you ask how high. It's what Erik signed up for.'

'Come into town with us for a drink,' said Polly squeezing Fran's arm. 'It will cheer you up.'

'Thanks for that Pol, but I won't tonight.' When she stumbled into her room, her heart broke and she wept for her own loss and for Erik too. She felt as if she had lost a limb. She could not believe that she might not see him again. But there was no way to contact him now that his unit had moved off the base. They had such a special connection, surely that could not just evaporate? Not knowing what might happen to him haunted her. What if he was killed or injured in Vietnam? What if he went back to his sweetheart in Massachusetts? How would she ever find out unless he sought her out when she was in California?

A few days later, Chuck's unit was flown out too. Polly did not mourn for long.

Fran met Rob in Ostend as planned. She did not tell him about Erik but she did tell him that she was waiting for a transfer to California with the company. Rob was unperturbed.

'Wherever you are, darling, I will always want to be with you.' He kissed her quite tenderly for a moment before tumbling her onto the bed, making love to her in his unaltered, intense and uncommunicative way. He never did do pillow talk. Fran returned to Frankfurt feeling miserable and confused about her feelings for Rob. She still missed Erik intensely, but Rob exuded such a self-assured certainty that their relationship was forever and that Fran was the only one for him, wherever she might choose to live and work. It was hard not to be swept along with it, especially now that Erik was lost to her, even although she knew that Rob would never share the same magical closeness with her. She hoped fervently that going to California to work would give her some clarity.

'Fran, come and meet Billy.' Polly sounded mysterious as she called up to Fran in her top floor room. It was a Saturday morning and Fran had no plans for the weekend. Billy? Was this Polly's latest boyfriend? She had already dated a couple of U.S. soldiers since Chuck had left. Fran laughed with delight and surprise when she saw Billy in Polly's room. He was a beautiful red setter puppy with a coat the exact colour of Polly's titian curls. Billy lolloped over to Fran and crawled into her lap, licking as much of her face and hands with his sloppy tongue as he could reach.

'What a sweetie! I didn't know you were planning to get a dog, Polly.' Fran stroked the ecstatic, wriggling pup.

'I wasn't planning it, Heinrich from the laboratory bought him but his *Freundin* is allergic. Came out in hives, he said, so Billy had to go. I couldn't resist when I saw him.'

'What will you do when we go to California to set up the new research facility?' Fran asked. 'You might not be able to take him with you.'

'If I can't take him with me, I won't be going. I couldn't bear to part with him now. I certainly won't be going back to Newcastle with him. There's no way I would put Billy in quarantine for six months.' Polly was vehement.

'So, does that mean you are prepared to stay here for the rest of Billy's life?' Fran asked, aghast at the thought of Polly being trapped in Germany with only her dog for company. It also made Fran feel quite depressed, as Ted was thinking of leaving too. He was missing his wife and daughter in Milton Keynes too much. Turned out the extra money was not worth losing out on his family life. Now that Erik had gone and Ted was leaving soon too, she felt that the people who had made her life in Germany bearable were now out of her reach. It wouldn't be as much fun in California without Polly, but she was determined to go anyway, with or without her. She secretly hoped that Erik might come back from Vietnam and come and look for her there or that she might be able to make her mind up about Rob. He made it clear that he had no intention of letting her slip out of his life.

Polly thought for a moment before she replied. 'I'm not going to worry about it for now Fran. We haven't heard anything yet about the transfer and I think I will be able to take Billy with me, if where we will be living allows pets.'

'We should be hearing soon.' said Fran continuing to gently pet Billy who had fallen asleep on her lap. 'I don't think I can cope with being here much longer. I'm running out of excuses to avoid carrying out Herr Braun's experiments on the laboratory mice.'

But, the weeks dragged by with no word about their transfer, then Polly came over to Fran one day waving a blue memo slip. 'Fran, Herr Braun wants us to go to a meeting in his office at 2 p.m. Not sure what it's about.' She dropped the memo on Fran's desk and dashed off at her usual manic pace. She was rushing home at lunchtime to walk Billy. Now a massive, soppy red setter and the love of her life. She still managed to fit in a huge plate of food at *Mahlzeit*, but often took home a doggy bag for Billy. She piled her plate even higher than before.

Fran spent an anxious lunch hour with Ted, trying to guess what Herr Braun wanted a meeting for. Maybe he was going to challenge her about the lack of animal testing in their department? Ted was beyond caring; he was planning on leaving soon and had not been summoned to this meeting anyway. Polly arrived back, breathless, with five minutes to spare before their appointment.

'*Kommen Sie bitte herein Fraulein Fran und Fraulein Polly.*' Herr Braun sounded unusually formal. Fran and Polly exchanged a worried glance. The previous week he had invited Fran, Polly and Ted on a wine-tasting Rhine cruise to celebrate the girls' pending transfer to the research facility in Benecia, California. Ted had not yet told his boss that he was thinking of resigning. They had had a blast. Herr Braun (call me Wolfgang), had been in great form, leaping on and off the cruise boat as it stopped at several of the famous Rheingau Vineyards. The superb Riesling tasting sessions at each stop, rendered call-me-Wolfgang more and more riotous. By the time they dropped anchor at the private dock of the renowned Schloss Johannisberg vineyard, he was behaving quite outrageously, slapping Ted affectionately on his back and squeezing Fran and Polly's shoulders in a most un-boss like fashion. Fran and Polly weren't remotely bothered by this. He was just like a big, excited schoolboy. Just like he had behaved during Fasching earlier in the year. Anyway, they too were a bit tipsy and giggly after several glasses of wine. Nevertheless, Fran was particularly impressed by the taste of the Schloss Johannisberger Riesling. It was outstanding. Her exposure to Ian Green's teaching on good wines before she left Scotland, had given her a discerning palate. Combined with the taste of the famous white asparagus grown in the region, there was little to beat the flavourful experience of both.

'I am sorry to tell you that your transfer to California has been delayed for several months. There is some problem with licensing that our lawyers are trying to sort out. I know you will be disappointed but…' Herr Braun shrugged his shoulders, not meeting the girls' dismayed gaze.

'*Scheisse!*' Polly muttered, almost under her breath. Herr Braun pretended not to hear. Polly had investigated taking Billy with her when they went, and had already had him vaccinated against rabies in preparation for their departure.

'However, we are starting a new project here, testing a drug for cardiac arrhythmia, so I want the two of you and Ted, to work out a testing protocol between you. We will be using laboratory cats and monkeys to test the drug.' Herr Braun continued, outlining the objectives for the project, but Fran had stopped listening. She had seen some of the experiments being carried out on the cats and monkeys. They were barbaric. There was no way she could be a part of it. So far most of their tests had taken place in the laboratory (except for the experiments using mice that Fran had so far managed to avoid) and as the transfer to California had up until now, been imminent, she had closed her mind to what was going on with the animals.

She would have to get away; she knew that immediately. But how? She could not wait for months for the transfer to the States, now that the animal experiments were looming. She would have to find another way. Even the faint chance of meeting up again with Erik in California was not enough to make her be prepared to take part in these heinous experiments. The despair she was experiencing was making her feel physically sick.

'Darling, come back. I miss you. I love you.' Rob was murmuring into her hair in a hotel room in Brussels. This was only the second time she had seen him as he had quite a heavy flying schedule and had to fit in the squash matches when he was home. His squash tournament was over (runner-up, much to his annoyance) and he had just returned from a long overseas trip. His regular letters had dropped off a bit, but they were still in touch and Fran had agreed to meet him again halfway, in Brussels. She had burst into tears almost as soon as they checked into their room. Rob, without preamble had pulled her into his arms, preparing to kiss her on the lips, but her tears stopped him.

'What's wrong, Fran? I thought you would be glad to see me.' He took his arms away and stood watching her silently, looking doubtful. Unable to offer any comfort.

'The transfer to California has been delayed for months and now they want me to do unspeakable experiments on cats and monkeys!' Her voiced hitched in despair, 'I-I can't bear it Rob. But I don't know what to do. I'm going to have to leave, but I've nowhere to live.' She wept. Inconsolable. She had sealed her fate. Rob would be her passport to freedom.

'Look, we can rent a place together. But in the meantime, you can share my room with me in Ealing.' Rob had continued when Fran sat on the bed, head in her hands, tears trickling between her fingers. Rob sat beside her for a moment, then pulled her gently onto the bed, enclosing her body in his embrace. The physical, not words, always his solution to any crisis. Fran succumbed and allowed her mind to contemplate the unplanned future with Rob, there was no other option it seemed. Anyway, Rob wanted her, truly loved her he had said. They stayed in their hotel room for hours. It was pouring with rain. Brussels in the rain was a desolate place. Fran did not have the energy to think about anything other than getting away from the looming nightmare of her work at the pharmaceutical company.

'I can't go back and live with my mother again,' said Fran emphatically, 'so if you are really sure that you don't mind sharing your room with me Rob, I am definitely going to hand in my resignation'. They were checking out of their hotel to go their separate ways.

'Of course I don't mind Fran. We can manage until you find another job. You are a clever girl, you can be anything you want to be. Just come home.' That was quite a lengthy speech from him.

This was just what she needed to hear. Rob clearly wanted her to be part of his life. He loved her. She would learn to love him as much in return. Given time.

Ted too, planned to leave the company at the end of the month, in two weeks' time. Now that her decision was made, she was could not wait to get away and wanted to travel back with him. Although she had no job to go back to, she knew without a doubt, that whatever she did, it would not be in pharmaceutical research. That era of her life was over. Graham Gordon, her old journalist mentor from her early days in Glasgow had been right, she was not meant for laboratory work. It had just taken her six years to realise it.

'Oh Fran. I'm going to miss you and Ted. But I don't blame you for leaving. I'm not sure I can stand to carry out the experiments either.' Polly hugged her friend with rib-crushing strength, but Fran had the sense that Polly was tougher than she was making out. She knew that Polly was already involved in the experiments. She just did not talk about it to Fran. Also, she was now going out with the senior technician in the animal research department. He was in his mid-thirties and he and Polly spent every available minute together. Fran was amused to see that he piled his *Mahlzeit* plate as high as Polly's. They were a good match. Fran wondered if Polly would still be prepared to leave her new love interest and go to California. She doubted it.

Herr Braun was clearly disappointed that he was losing two of his imported English technicians and became increasingly formal and distant as the time approached for them to depart. Another '*Et tu Brute?*' moment for Fran. Ted was oblivious. He couldn't wait to get back to his family. In a mad moment, he had bought a sleek, left-hand drive, dark blue, Ford Mustang. It was hardly a family car. Fran imagined his wife's face when he turned up in it. They drove back together, crossing the Channel at Bruges. They laughed endlessly during their long drive back home, euphoric to be leaving Germany behind. Ted had an outrageous sense of humour. And the hours flew by in his company. Her jaw and diaphragm ached from all the merriment. Such a kinder ache than heartache.

The Return

'Let's get married on the 29th February. Then we only need to remember an anniversary every four years.' Rob smiled at Fran over his glass of wine.

'Married? Who needs to get married?' she had said, surprised. This was the first time in three years they had been together, that the word marriage had ever been mentioned.

'Well, there's nothing to stop us now my divorce is finalised.' Rob as ever, a man of few words, had offered this as a logical next step. He just assumed that she would not hesitate. Taken it for granted in his mind that marriage between them was inevitable. He could have asked me properly, she had thought, annoyed.

Fran had moved in with Rob straight away after her flight from Germany with Ted. He shared a large Victorian house in Ealing with three aircraft ground engineers. His housemates were a jolly crowd and treated Fran like one of them. She wouldn't have minded staying on for a while as they were good company when Rob was away on a trip. There were usually one or two girlfriends emerging from someone's bedroom most nights of the week, and always at the weekend, so she was never short of female company either. The biggest drawback for her, was the bathroom. Only one, in a five-bedroomed house. The combined irritations of the permanently raised toilet seat, pubic hairs in the bath, toothpaste smears on the mirror and always, a miasma of male odours, sweat or recent evacuations and others, less definable, made her dread going in there. She often had to hold her breath. The toilet in the downstairs cloakroom never flushed properly. In a house, full of engineers, Fran thought that was ridiculous. 'Well, we're not PLUMBERS,' Rob said indignantly when she had asked him to fix it. Sharing the cramped space in Rob's small, single bedroom was also challenging for her. Last in, smallest bedroom. Normal shared house politics. Rob had moved in with them when he separated from his wife and had been in no rush to move out into a place of his own. It was easier for her when Rob was away on a trip.

Fran got a job interview.

'So Fran, what would you be bringing to the table? I see you have been working in medical research for a few years.' William Strong, who owned the recruiting company in London, peered over his glasses at her. He was overweight, and a film of sweat beaded his brow and upper lip. The offices, on the upper floor of an old office building in Frederick Street in Camden, were stuffy and too warm. William Strong obviously didn't believe in letting in any fresh air.

Fran looked straight at him, displaying an outer confidence she didn't have.

'Well, I understand the needs of the pharmaceutical industry from the inside and how important a strong sales and marketing team is to a company.' She had met a few of the medical representatives from her first job in Greysons when she first came down to work in London. She knew the type. 'Also,' she continued, her grey eyes holding his in a steady gaze, 'I can write, so I can produce adverts and press release articles for the client if required'. She produced a small file of cuttings from her slim, leather briefcase (a present from Rob). She had saved all of Graham Gordon's science columns from the *Scottish Daily Express* that she had penned. Although she had no by-line, Graham had written to her after he retired to Lerwick in Shetland, to thank her for writing his columns for him. '*You might need this one day*

Fran, if you ever decide to take up journalism,' he had scrawled in a rare moment of altruistic sobriety.

William Strong raised an eyebrow and leaned forward behind his desk, until the bulk of his stomach stopped him. 'Hmm, quite impressive.' He read Graham's letter and quickly scanned through the newspaper cuttings. 'His obituary was in the *Times* last month, he had a good reputation. Got a gong from H.R.M. for his contribution to the media. Wrote several books about Shetland and the Outer Hebrides.'

Fran paled. She hadn't known that Graham had died, or that he was erudite enough and sober long enough to write books. She guessed his liver had given out on him eventually. She wondered if Iona knew. They had visited him together just once after he moved to Shetland, a long, overnight ferry ride from Aberdeen. He had seemed quite contented with his isolated life and had taken up with a sturdily built, taciturn local woman who looked after him. The poor woman was probably pleased to see the back of Fran and Iona, who had spent several hours reminiscing with Graham about their hedonistic times in Glasgow. Fran had been very fond of Graham and was glad that he had received recognition for his writing career and grateful to him for acknowledging her contribution. It looked like that might have swung the interview in her favour.

'Tell you what. I'll give you a month's trial and if you can get at least two pharmaceutical companies on board as clients, I will give you a contract. We don't have any of them on our books at present.' He droned on for a few more minutes about the terms of her employment, but Fran was not paying attention. She was experiencing a mixture of jubilation and fear. She knew nothing about recruiting campaigns, or how to go about getting clients, but she had a job! She would find a way. Now that she would be earning a commission, (less than she had hoped for) she could move out of Rob's cramped single room. Oh, to get away from that shared, smelly bathroom!

Fran had some money left over from her time in Germany but not enough for a deposit on a rental flat on her own. Rob did not hesitate to help look for a rental place for them to share, now that she had a wage. He was paying a huge chunk of his salary to his ex-wife and child, so they needed their joint incomes to afford anything in Ealing. It made sense for them to move in together. They got on well enough. Sex with him was satisfactory although he was all action and didn't believe in pillow talk. Her thoughts often drifted back to her time with Erik. They had been so close, so in tune with one another, although they had been together for such a short time. But he was gone. In the past. She had to move on.

'Well done, Fran.' William Strong was beaming at her, pulling his lower lip over his top lip to remove the film of perspiration that always seemed to gather there. Why couldn't he just open his bloody window? Fran was sweating too. His office was as hot as a furnace. 'You've done it. Signed your first client in under four weeks. We'll need to see about getting you to sign a contract now.'

Fran did not remind him that he had wanted her to sign up two clients before offering her a contract. Her first client was Insula Laboratories, an up and coming pharmaceutical company with a new drug for controlling type 1 diabetes. They were ready to launch their product and she had been invited to pitch for their recruiting campaign to introduce the drug to GPs and Endocrinology consultants throughout the U.K. Fran was certain that she would not be the only recruiting consultant chasing this campaign, so she had made sure that she read all the available background information and research on the drug. She also wrote a five-hundred-word press release that could be submitted to the popular newspapers. She had dressed carefully in her best charcoal grey business suit. The knee-length straight skirt and tailored jacket suited her tall frame, and the pale mint green silk vest top, showing underneath the jacket, softened the severity of her attire. Her dark hair was mid-length, so she felt fine about wearing it loose and wavy. She kept her make-up discreet, just eyeliner and mascara to enhance her grey eyes and a touch of soft pink gloss on her generous mouth. Black high heels, black shoulder bag and her new leather briefcase finished off the look. Rob, with his typical physical response to her appearance, had wanted a 'quickie' before she went out the door.

'Come over here, darling. You look really sexy in that outfit.'

'Sorry, no time. Got to go.' With a quick kiss on Rob's cheek, Fran dashed out the door before he had time to delay her further. Shame he had not wished her good luck. This was such a big deal for her.

'What part of Scotland are you from Fran?' John Monroe, the Marketing Director of Insula Laboratories had greeted her warmly at their head office in Letchworth, Hertfordshire.

'Glasgow actually. And you?'

'Edinburgh.'

Fran took a leap of faith. 'Oh well, nobody's perfect.' Shit, she shouldn't have said that!

For a second he looked at her in amazement, then roared with laughter. 'Ah, what a cheek. We'll get on just fine. So, why should I give your agency our business?'

Within three months, Fran had signed up two more clients and was running their recruiting campaigns for them too. She was the point of contact for the client paid advertising responses, interviewing and shortlisting suitable candidates for the positions of medical representatives. Turned out that she was very good at this work. She surprised herself. She had a natural ability to put people at their ease and get them talking freely about themselves – without them feeling that they were being interviewed. This helped her select the best candidates for the client. The ones who were naturally good conversationalists, who had natural charisma and the social skills and confidence to communicate effectively with the medical profession.

'Why don't you start up your own business and run it from home? I'll do your V.A.T. returns for you.' Rob suggested after she had been working at the agency in London for a year.

'I can't do that from this flat, I need an office space.' Fran spread her arms to indicate the limitations of their cramped one bedroomed flat in Ealing.

'Let's buy a house then and convert a room into an office. We can apply for a mortgage now that we are both earning.'

Fran got carried away with that idea. It was a bit galling that she was the one recruiting consultant bringing in more business for the agency than any of the others. She was on commission and earning quite a lot, but the agency took the lion's share of the fees the clients were paying. She was travelling all over the country and thoroughly enjoying her freedom and growing confidence in herself and her interviewing skills. She had met a lot of bright, stimulating marketing people at the high end of the pharmaceutical industry. One or two men had wanted to take her out on a date, but she had always refused. Reluctant to mix business with her personal life, but also out of loyalty to Rob.

She realised that when she first met him, she had been dazzled by his good looks, the uniform and his glamorous job as an airline pilot. His strong masculine energy and particularly his decisiveness in dealing with her mother had bowled her over. Flattered too, that he seemed to be so keen to be with her. He was away a lot on his overseas flying trips and their reunions were always physically intense for a day or two, with Fran forever hoping for a greater depth of understanding between them. Although he never initiated a meaningful conversation with her, he was kind and very practical she had to admit. She always felt quite pleased to be seen with him when they went out together, he was in superb physical shape, a testament to his dedication for exercise.

After years of looking after her mother and trying to cope with all the DIY tasks in their flat, it was such a relief to be with a man who took care of everything with such ease. Rob wanted to be close to Heathrow and Fran needed to be able to commute either by car or public transport all over the country on her recruiting campaigns. They bought their first house in Bagshot in Surrey, conveniently close to the airport and the motorways. Rob's wife had refused to divorce him, so marriage was the last thing on Fran's mind. She had never given much thought to being anyone's wife. They certainly had not talked about it before now.

'Well? Shall we opt for the 29th of February?' Rob asked again, ignoring Fran's immediate surprised response.

'Is this your idea of a proposal?' she challenged him again. 'Why do we need to get married? Are you worried about the neighbours?' One of their new neighbours, a young couple who had moved in a month earlier, had asked Rob and Fran to come along to their Round Table social event. The invitation had been addressed to Mr & Mrs R. Patterson. Rob, surprisingly, had wanted to go, so Fran had accepted for them, without letting on that they weren't married.

'Well everybody thinks we are married, so we might as well be.' Rob continued moodily. 'Anyway, your mum was asking me the last time we visited her when I was going to make an 'honest woman' of you. Her friend, Peggy from Glasgow is coming down to visit her in the spring and your mum says she is a bit old-fashioned and might not approve of us living together.'

'So, that's the only reason you think we should get married, because my mum's friend might not approve of us *living in sin*?' Fran said in exasperation. Why could Rob never manage to say the right thing to her? He was completely lacking in empathy when it came to anything to do with emotions. 'Anyway, I bet we couldn't get married on the 29th February even if we wanted to. There's probably some rule against it.'

'Well, can you find out.' said Rob backing out of the room. 'I need to pack for my trip. By the way, I've joined the Round Table.'

Whatever floats your boat, thought Fran who hated any organised groups, especially ones with a hierarchy. She was not a club sort of person. Rob was dedicated and attended all the meetings when he was at home. Fran grudgingly thought that the boys' club atmosphere appealed to his nomadic soul. He did not have many male friends outside aviation. One thing was for sure, if she did agree to marry Rob, she would keep it as low-key as possible. It was obvious that all their neighbours assumed they were married, and if she was honest, it might be a bit easier. Fran acknowledged to herself that she *was* quite conventional at heart, not a wild bohemian like her pal Iona who couldn't care less what people thought of *her* unconventional lifestyle. She could not think of a good enough reason not to get married to Rob. Maybe it would be all right. She did not phone Iona to tell her the news.

Rob left early the next morning for the airport. 'See if you can arrange a date at the end of February. I have a lot going on in March with the Round Table and the squash tournament kicks off on March 3rd.'

So, no honeymoon then. She felt a stab of disappointment that he had not thought to suggest a holiday for them. She let it go. Fran asked the couple across the road to be their witnesses at the registry office ceremony on February 28th. She had been right, the 29th was not possible. She wore a short, dark-green suede skirt with a pale-green silk blouse and a matching dark-green suede waistcoat. Rob wore his only civilian suit, an oatmeal coloured three-piece affair. She wished he had worn his uniform instead. He looked so handsome in his uniform. His suit was ill-fitting and he seemed diminished by it somehow. They went to a show with their neighbours who had witnessed their marriage, came home and went to bed. The honeymoon.

A few days later, Rob left for a long-haul flight to Australia with layovers in Singapore. Fran flew up to Glasgow to stay with Iona overnight before she was due in Edinburgh to interview some candidates for one of her client companies.

'Auntie Fwan, please will you read me a story?' Keira tugged Fran across the room towards the enormous three-seater sofa where an untidy stack of books and coloured pencils spilling out of an old biscuit tin, took up half the space on the cushions.

Fran had just stepped into the flat in Byres Road where Iona and her daughter Keira, still lived. Iona had taken over the lease from Liam's cousin Siobhan who had married and moved on. Before Fran could put her bag down, the child was hugging her tightly around her waist and begging for a story, gazing up through her beautiful liquid brown eyes and the tumbling, dark unruly curls that framed her face. Irresistible, like distilled sunshine.

'Keira! Let Fran through the door first.' Iona sounded exasperated.

'Oh, don't worry Iona.' Fran dropped her bag and picked up the skinny little girl who clung round her neck. 'Tell you what Keira, I promise I'll read you a story in a wee while, I just need to talk to Mummy for a minute. But will you draw a picture for me?' She carried the child over to the sofa and picked up the coloured pencil tin and some drawing paper. Keira seemed satisfied with that and slid out of Fran's arms to the floor.

'I'll draw you a picture of under the sea.' and she settled down to start her sea scene, slashing waves of blue onto the paper with fierce concentration.

'Bejesus, you're a natural Fran. I can't get her to do anything like that for me. She's quite a handful these days.' Iona gave Fran a quick hug in greeting. 'Do you fancy a landing drink?' Iona laughingly used the aviators' terminology. 'It's not too early.'

It was just after 5 p.m. 'Sure, why not. I brought a couple of bottles of wine and a bottle of whiskey with me.' Fran watched as Iona poured them both a drink. A large whiskey for herself diluted with lemonade, and a glass of red wine for Fran. Iona was still quite thin and was wearing a pair of loose track suit bottoms and a baggy white T-shirt, both covered in splotches of paint. Fran noted that there were dark circles under her light, crystalline blue eyes which shone feverishly in contrast to her pale complexion.

'So, what's going on Iona. You sounded a bit strange over the phone. Is something wrong? Fran was used to the undertones in Iona's voice and sensed that all was not well.

Iona lowered her voice so that Keira would not hear her. 'It's Max, he knows where I live and pushed a note through the letterbox. He said that he saw me with Keira and that he wants to meet her. To be part of her life.' Iona took a large gulp of her drink and started pacing up and down the kitchen. 'I'm terrified that he will try and take her away from me Fran. I couldn't bear that'. Her voice cracked. 'But he is so powerful, he might try and take me to court to get her. I am just going to ignore it as long as possible.'

'But Iona, he told you to have a termination and that he didn't want any more children. What's changed and how did he find out where you were?'

'Finding me wouldn't be difficult for Max, Fran. As you said yourself once, he owns half of Glasgow, his henchmen are everywhere.' Iona drained her glass and poured another drink for herself. 'He only has two grown-up sons, no daughters. He must have seen Keira and decided he wants to claim her.' Iona's eyes glittered. 'I can't let that happen Fran, he would corrupt her.'

'Surely he can't do that. She is almost four now and he has not been in her life. He would be a total stranger to her and anyway his name isn't on her birth certificate, is it?' Fran was silently concerned that Iona's drinking might play a part in Max's bid for custody.

'No, it's not, but – there's something else. It could be a revenge thing. Harrison lives here too now and as you know he virtually blackmailed Max into giving me money for Keira.'

'Harrison lives here!' Fran was astonished. 'Do you mean living with you or just renting a room?' The thought of the vertically challenged cartoonist with her statuesque friend was too much to take in.

'You know what they say. They're all the same size lying down. Don't knock it till you try it.' Iona laughed, her anxiety about Max forgotten for a moment while she teased Fran about Harrison.

'Seriously Iona, what's the story with Harrison?' Fran asked, finding it hard to believe that Iona would sleep with such a wee man. He was also a hard drinker, not the best companion for Iona with her whiskey habit.

Iona laughed again. 'We've been commissioned to produce a second volume of illustrated poetry, so he moved in a few weeks ago, while we are working on it. He does have his own room, but occasionally when the mood takes me… anyway, he's normally too pissed to be bothered. Keira adores him and he draws silly pictures for her. He takes her to Kelvinside park sometimes. Maybe Max has seen her with him too.' Her mood changed abruptly as she mentioned Max again.

'You know Iona; you should fight fire with fire. If the court was to hear about Max's nefarious activities and that he paid you to have an abortion, they would not be likely to give him joint custody. Get some of the investigative journalists to do some digging on Max Cohen's dodgy property deals and threaten to expose him. I bet he would back off then. You know first-hand about his all-night poker games and Harrison knows about his attempt at bribing someone in the Planning Department. He would hate to have his image as Mr Respectable blown apart.' Fran was warming to her theme and would have elaborated further, but Keira came rushing in with her ocean floor drawing to show her Auntie Fwan and the discussion ended abruptly.

Keira snuggled into Fran on the squashy sofa listening with rapt attention to the tales of Rapunzel and Sleeping Beauty while Iona worked on her painting. She had set herself up in the recess of the bay window, her easel sitting on top of a white sheet to protect the carpet from paint drips. She was completing an oil painting of a magnificent grey and cream dappled Appaloosa stallion.

'That's beautiful, Iona. As good as a Stubbs. Is it a commission?' Fran was impressed.

'No, I saw this fellow in a field near Loch Lomond and took his picture. Liam kept an Appaloosa just like this one. He loved him. I might just keep this painting for myself. I mostly paint dogs and cats for commissioned work. A bit boring at times, but it pays the rent.' Iona quickly turned back to her painting, but Fran caught the sadness in her voice, clearly she was still in pain over the sudden death of her beloved Liam from a riding accident, ten years earlier.

'I'm hungry, Mummy,' Keira complained fretfully but didn't move from her place cuddled up with Fran. Fran was hungry too, she had missed breakfast and only had the airline snack on the flight up from London. They both looked expectantly at Iona.

'Harrison is bringing us all fish and chips. He won't be long. I phoned him and told him you were staying overnight Fran. He's keen to see you again.'

'But I'm hungry NOW,' Kiera wailed. 'I don't like fish and chips.'

'Oh, here we go, another tantrum brewing. Fran see if you can find something in the fridge for her would you? I just want to finish painting the horse's face before the light fades.'

Fran scratched around in the fridge for something to tempt Keira. She cut the mould from a block of cheddar cheese, grated it and added grated apple to it. She also found a carrot that still looked quite fresh and chopped that into sticks; and a packet of raisins. She arranged the food on a plate in the shape of a face. The carrot sticks created the basic face shape, the nose and the eyebrows, the cheese and apple mix looked like hair and she used raisins for eyes and a smiley mouth. Keira was delighted and devoured the lot. Fran gave her a glass of milk too and toasted a slice of white bread and managed to scrape the last of the butter to cover the toast. She could not find any jam or honey in the cupboards which only held a tin of baked beans and a half-empty packet of white rice. As they went back into the living room where Iona was just finishing and cleaning her paintbrushes, Harrison came crashing through the door, almost buried under an armful of fish suppers wrapped in white paper.

Keira rushed over to him 'Uncle Harrison, Auntie Fwan gave me a face to eat.'

'Oh aye, hen, well she lives in England now, that explains it.' Harrison quickly put down the fish suppers and swung the child around. 'Now sit down and watch *Blue Peter* or something, I want to talk to your mammy and Fran.' He came over and gave Fran a hug, she had forgotten just how small he was. He smelled strongly of his favourite whiskey tipple.

'Harrison, how are you?' asked Fran, feeling enormous and quickly sitting down on the sofa beside Keira.

'All the better for having you two big lassies in the room together. My two prop halves.'

'Let's eat before the fish suppers go cold.' Iona handed the paper-wrapped meals around to everyone. Fran was pleased to see that Keira, who 'hated fish and chips' wolfed her portion down with deft fingers.

The evening wore on with much laughter and reminiscing about their days when they all first met at the Press Bar. Iona and Harrison drank prodigious amounts of whiskey, although Fran tried to pace herself with the wine. Keira's eyes were drooping as she relaxed against Fran.

'Shall I put her to bed?' Fran could see that Iona was probably beyond noticing that her child needed her bed.

'If you like, I usually just wait till she falls asleep on the sofa. She can be very difficult at bedtime sometimes.' Iona was sitting on the floor at Harrison's feet, they were both getting pissed.

Fran carried the sleepy child to the bathroom where she managed to get her to use the loo and clean her teeth. 'Shall I read you another story Keira?' Fran asked, as she tucked the little girl into her bed.

'No, can you sing me a song please. Mummy sometimes sings me a song but mostly she just cries.'

'Sweetie, sometimes grown-ups have big sad feelings just like children do and crying can help to make the sad feelings better. Your mummy loves you very much Keira and so does Uncle Harrison and me too.' Fran gave the child a kiss and a hug and sang her a song. All she could come up with was 'Summertime'.

Keira's eyes were closed and Fran was heading for the bedroom door when a little voice said, 'I wish I had a daddy to love me too.'

Harrison shared Iona's bed that night and Fran slept in his room. At least Iona had given her a clean sheet and pillowcase for the bed. It all smelt a bit masculine in there. The next day Harrison left early before Fran emerged from his room. Keira was up and dressed, ready for her nursery school.

'Come with us Fran and we can get some breakfast on the way to Keira's school. There's nothing to eat. I need to get some messages from the Co-op this morning.'

They ate breakfast in a small café in Byres Road run by an Italian family who obviously knew Iona well. Keira ate a big bowl of cornflakes with milk and sugar, Fran had tea and toast with marmalade and Iona drank black coffee.

'I'm not hungry' she said quite sharply when Fran offered to share her toast. 'I'll get something later. I've got a headache.'

No bloody wonder Fran thought to herself, you must have drunk half a bottle of Scotch last night. She worried too, about how Iona's drinking might be affecting Keira and now with the added impact of Max Cohen trying to muscle his way into their lives. Keira's plaintive little comment about wanting a daddy to love her, was playing on Fran's mind. Should she tell Iona what the child had said?

They dropped Keira off at her nursery school, bought a few grocery items from the Co-op and went back to the flat. Fran insisted on paying and made sure that there was fresh fruit and vegetables for Keira, hoping that Iona would take the hint. Fran was travelling through to Edinburgh later and wanted to tell Iona that she and Rob had married. She knew Iona would think she was mad. She told her anyway.

Iona did not have much to say about Fran's news. She merely shrugged and rolled her eyes, turning away to boil the kettle for more coffee. Their connection seemed to be broken, but Fran pressed on, trying to voice her concerns about Kiera and Iona's obvious alcohol dependency. What if some of the mothers at the nursery school suspected she was drinking? They might mention it to Keira's teacher. Max Cohen could find out and use that against her. The more she tried to get Iona to talk about everything, the more belligerent and defensive she became.

'Look Fran, I can stop drinking any time I want to. But right now, it helps me cope. I never will get over losing Liam and to be honest, I sometimes wish that I had never had a child. I can barely look after myself, never mind trying to care for a kid as well. But I will never let Max Cohen take her away from me. I will do what you suggested last night and ask the boys from the *Express* to investigate him, but I can tell you I am scared. You don't know what he's like and what he is capable of doing.'

'I know Iona; I just wish I could help in some way.'

'Well you can't, you moved away, and now you've gone and married a handsome, empty shell. You're going to need all your energy to help yourself, you'll see.'

Fran recoiled from Iona's harsh comments and clammed up. This was the first time in their long friendship that Iona had spoken so negatively to her. She suspected the alcohol might have something to do with it, but nevertheless, she recognised the truth of her friend's words on some level. But what she had needed, was to have some support from Iona and maybe even have a bit of a laugh about the vagaries of men in general. That would have made her feel better. As it was, they barely spoke for the rest of the day. Iona started working on her painting, her back turned determinedly away from Fran. Later that day when it was time to leave to catch the train to Edinburgh, Keira hugged her tightly.

'Please come back soon Auntie Fwan. I want you to read more stories to me and I can do another drawing for you.'

'I will sweetheart, I have packed your lovely picture of the sea in my suitcase and I will hang it up on my wall when I get home. But you know, I will always be here for you and Mummy when you need me.' She looked at Iona who gazed back at her, unsmiling, her glass of whiskey reflecting the last rays of the early evening sun.

Hard Times

'You might as well go home now, Mrs Patterson.' The same nurse who had spoken to her earlier had brought Fran a cup of tea as she continued to sit by Rob's bed. 'He is more stable now, so you should try and get some sleep. You look exhausted. We'll phone you if there is any change in his condition. You can come in any time tomorrow. We don't worry about formal visiting hours in the I.C.U.'

Gratefully, Fran took her leave. It had been a long, harrowing day. Rob had started coughing up blood in the morning and by the time the paramedics arrived, he was practically unconscious. She had been sitting in the various family rooms and by his bedside all day, waiting to find out if he was going to pull through from this sudden and virulent attack of pneumonia. All she had had to drink was a bottle of water and two or three cups of tea out the machine, all of which tasted like soup for some reason, and one decent coffee. She was worn out and hungry. The adrenalin rush she had experienced when his heart had stopped earlier, had left her drained. I've had five solid years of dramas like this, on duty night and day, she was thinking as she drove home through the darkened, quiet streets. I've forgotten what is to have an uninterrupted night's sleep. It would have been better if he had just slipped away. He can't possibly be happy the state he's in now. It's unbelievable when I think how active and fit he was before his stroke. I can't wait to get home and have a long soak in the bath, my clothes smell of the hospital. I had better wash my hair too. Oh God, I really need a break. I'm not rushing back to the hospital first thing, unless they call me.

She was back before lunchtime and spent most of the next ten days sitting beside Rob in the intensive care ward as he gradually improved. He had been so close to dying for the second time in the past five years, but, not ready to let go just yet it seemed.

With a heavy heart, she brought him home and the dull rhythm of their life continued as before. Except, that he was weaker and reluctant to leave his room. She could not ever leave him alone in the house for too long in case he had a seizure and fell over, which happened regularly now since the stroke. Once he had fallen in the bathroom, crashing backward through the shower cubicle and got stuck in the small space, convulsing and bruising his flailing arms and legs against the tiled walls. She had managed to clamber over him to administer the midazolam that brought the seizure under control, but in the process twisted her back which took weeks to heal. She had to call out the paramedics to get him back into his bed. He was a dead weight and impossible for her to move him. But at least she had been at home. What if she had been out? She shuddered at the prospect of him having a prolonged fit on the floor, possibly breaking a limb in the process. Imagine the chaos that would create for his care needs! She couldn't bear to contemplate it.

The walls closed even tighter around Fran as insidious fragments of her own life and freedoms slipped away from her year by year. Life, as you thought you knew it, can change in a heartbeat, she reflected, cradling a welcome cup of tea before going into the kitchen to make Rob's lunch. Reduced now to the tedious and thankless task of caring full-time for a husband, totally oblivious as to how *her* life had been impacted. He was incapable of thinking beyond his own needs, always had been. Her lips tightened in frustration. Five years ago, she remembered, she had been sitting at her computer printing out her work schedule for the following week. Happy with the work she was doing, training therapists and offering workplace stress management seminars. Loving the interactions with interesting adults and feeling that she was contributing to society. Enjoying spending time with and the companionship of her grown-up daughters and the one grandson who had been born prior to Rob's stroke. Before she had time to press PRINT, her whole future collapsed at that moment when Rob had dropped, convulsing, to the ground. The memory of that awful day brought tears of self-pity welling up in her eyes, as she thought back to the life she and Rob had known, and lost…

'I hope you're not planning on having a family just yet and leaving us, Fran. You are too valuable to us! We will be doubling our sales force this year and we are relying on you to run the recruiting campaign for us again.' John Monroe, her first client from Insula Laboratories was now a firm friend. She had successfully run all their recruiting campaigns for four years and attended all the company's marketing meetings. John squeezed her shoulder as she admired the most recent family picture on his desk. She counted four little girls' faces, all beaming happily at the camera. John and his wife, Camilla were gazing with adoration at their newest addition cradled in Camilla's arms, their first boy.

'Don't worry about that John. I have no plans to start a family yet and when I do, I will employ a nanny,' she announced airily. She and Rob were enjoying the fruits of their joint incomes, spending freely on eating out when they were both at home at the same time and entertaining their friends and neighbours to dinner on a regular basis. Having a lot of money made them both recklessly improvident. Rob enjoyed splashing out and loved paying in cash for everything they bought. Fran never thought about saving. Their future needs were simply not on her radar. Clearly, not on Rob's either.

Fran could not get John Monroe's comments about starting a family out of her head. She was twenty-nine, that was quite old. Her mum was thirty when Fran was born and she was the third and last child.

'I think I would like to have a baby. I'm going to be thirty next year.' Her sudden announcement to Rob took them both by surprise. The recruiting campaign at Insula Laboratories was well under way and she had reached a point when she would need to employ an assistant consultant to help her run the business. She had turned down one assignment recently as she simply could not have handled the extra work-load on her own. She told Rob after they had enjoyed a meal at the newly opened Pizza Express. They were sharing a bottle of red wine and Rob was mellow and quite relaxed, looking forward to bedtime with her.

Rob was appalled. 'You can't be serious! Your business – you would have to give it up!' He spluttered, looking at Fran crossly. He had just bought first-class airline tickets for their annual trip to Australia to visit his family and Fran's sister and her family and her other sister in New Zealand. Rob's idea of a holiday. He never suggested going anywhere else in the world. His blinkered view was, that as he had flown almost everywhere interesting on the globe, he had no desire to revisit those destinations for a holiday. 'Anyway,' he reasoned with Fran, 'we both want to see our families and they won't be able to leave Australia anytime soon.' There was no point arguing with him. At least they always stopped off in Singapore or Kuala Lumpur for a couple of days to break the long journey.

'I'll keep the business going, I'll just employ a nanny and an assistant to help me with the recruiting campaigns. I can still run most of it from home anyway.' Fran squeezed his hand across the table, now very sure that this was what she wanted. A baby might encourage him to become more of a family man. She hoped she had a boy so that he could kick a football around the garden with him. She shared this fantasy with him, but all he said was, 'I already have a son and I hardly ever get to see him.' Fran had always thought he should put more effort into trying to get access to his son, but he never did and only saw him about twice a year. Rob finally gave up protesting when Fran assured him that she would not be giving up the lucrative cash-flow from her business. She fell pregnant very quickly.

Loss

'Fran, it's Harrison. He was attacked outside the Press Bar. He's unconscious in hospital.' Iona's voice cracked. 'I think Max might have had something to do with it…' She was unable to say more.

'Oh my God, Iona! Surely not?' But Fran's instincts knew that Iona was probably right. Max Cohen had a reputation for ruthlessness. The fact that Harrison had threatened to expose him could have been enough for him to exact his revenge. Plus, Max may also have been jealous of Harrison's relationship with his daughter, Keira.

'I'm coming up, Iona. I will catch the first available flight.' All Fran's hurt feelings around Iona's comments about Rob, faded instantly. They had not been in touch for almost a year, but, her friend needed support. That was enough.

They went to the hospital together. Keira stayed with a friend from school. This feels like a repeat of bad history thought Fran remembering the fateful dash to the hospital years ago when Liam died, before Iona got a chance to see him. Poor wee Harrison, he looked so small and shrunken. His face was bruised purple and black, one eye completely closed, almost unrecognisable. A large bandage was wrapped around most of his head, which had been stamped on by the thug who attacked him. He was unconscious, hooked up to a life support system. A young policeman waited outside his room.

'Harrison, can you hear us, it's me, Iona and Fran's here as well.' Iona held his hand up to her face and Fran walked around the bed and held his other hand.

'It's your two big lassies here to prop you up.' Fran whispered into his ear. She thought there was a faint pressure on her fingers. Maybe he had heard her? They sat with him for a few hours, but there was no obvious response.

Iona went off to find a doctor and when she returned her expression was set, her eyes dull. 'Let's go Fran. I need to get back for Keira.' Fran kissed Harrison's hand and reluctantly followed Iona out of the ward.

Iona did not speak again until they were outside the hospital. 'The doctor said he is brain dead. His family will be making the decision when to turn off his life support.'

Fran's eyes welled up with tears. 'Oh Iona, I'm so sorry. Poor Harrison.'

'I'm the kiss of death to any man I get involved with.' Iona said bitterly. 'First Liam and now Harrison.'

'Don't say that. It's not your fault. But if you think Max is behind this attack on Harrison, you should tell the police.'

Iona stopped in her tracks and gripped Fran's arms, hard. 'No! No! I can't. You don't understand. Keira knows that he is her dad now. She loves him. He bought her a pony.'

'What! How the hell did that happen?' Fran could not believe this. The last time she had seen Iona, she had been adamant about keeping Max out of Keira's life despite the demanding note he had pushed through Iona's door a year earlier.

'He found a way to get to her by donating a large amount to Keira's nursery school so they could buy new playground equipment. Naturally they wanted to know why he was being so generous and he told them he was Keira's father. I picked Keira up from school as usual and the head teacher called me in to her office. Keira came with me of course. Max was sitting in her office looking smug.

'Mr Cohen would like to meet his daughter Miss O'Brian, do you have any objection?'

'Keira immediately said 'Are you my daddy?''

'I could have killed that teacher, she had no right to do that, but she thinks I am scum because I'm not married. Bitch. Well it was too late then. Max crouched down in front of Keira and said, 'Yes, I am your daddy and I want to get to know you and make up for all the time we have missed.'

'Keira flung her arms around his neck and said, 'I've always wanted a daddy like the other children in my class.'

'She was totally sold. The next thing he has bought her a pony and now he picks her up every Saturday morning and takes her to the stables at Lenzie to ride. Of course, she is completely besotted with the pony and thinks Max is the best thing ever.'

'Are you not worried that he might try and get custody of her?' Fran asked, very concerned indeed that Max was now firmly in Keira's life.

'Well he hasn't so far and now that I let her stay overnight at his place sometimes, I'm hoping that will be enough for him. After all, having a kid around all the time would cramp his style. So, you understand why I can't involve the police, Fran, it could really backfire. He is a dangerous bastard and I need to keep him sweet so that Keira will be safe.'

Fran stayed silent, accepting the reality of Iona's strategy with Max. He was after all, Keira's father and had rights, which he would enforce if Iona tried to block his access to his daughter. But she grieved for Harrison and the terrible price he had paid for loving Iona. How could she hold this shocking secret? What if Max *had* ordered the beating? That would be culpable homicide. Someone should be brought to justice for this crime. Somehow, she vowed to herself, she would find a way to expose him, but for now, while he had control of Keira's affection. She would have to bide her time.

Back at the flat, Iona cradled Keira and tried to explain that Uncle Harrison was very badly hurt and would have to stay in hospital for a while. Keira took the news well, hugging Iona and looking into her eyes, liquid brown pools of compassion.

'Poor Mummy, don't worry, Uncle Harrison will get better. I'll tell Daddy, maybe he can help him.'

'Don't bother your daddy, Keira, the doctors will look after Uncle Harrison.' Iona shook her head slightly at Fran as she kissed the dark tumble of curls on her daughter's head. Keira went quietly to bed Fran noticed. She was changing, less wild, less needy. More aware. Growing up. Iona poured herself a glass of whiskey and brought a bottle of wine and a glass over to Fran.

'No thanks, I'll just make myself a cup of tea.' Fran walked into the kitchen, her hand protectively covering the tiny fluttering in her womb. She would tell Iona tomorrow before she left, but not tonight. Not with Harrison lying inert, his wit and warmth, hovering above his destroyed body, needing to depart.

'Thanks for coming up Fran. I wish you could stay longer, but…'

'Me too, but I need to get back, I've got to get ready for a recruiting drive for one of my clients. I'm going to Athlone actually.'

'I wish I could come with you; I haven't been back to Ireland since Liam died.' Iona looked lost. Who could she turn to now with Harrison gone and the threat of Max's pernicious influence hanging over her daughter's future?

'Iona, I'll be here for you as much as I can. But I need to tell you, I'm pregnant.'

Iona was obviously surprised. 'Did you plan it? What does Rob think about it? You told me he likes spending the money.'

'Rob's on board with it, Iona. I won't be giving up my business, I'll hire a nanny to look after the baby when I am away on business trips.'

Iona raised her eyebrows. 'Really, are you sure? Are you getting on all right with Rob since you got married? We haven't had a chance to talk about him.'

'It's fine. He's away a lot. Not sure how it would work if he was a nine-to-five husband. Anyway, I'll be in touch regularly now. We shouldn't let so much time slip away from us again without talking.' Fran reluctantly left, but was glad in a way that the horrendous event with Harrison had mended the rift between her and Iona. Their friendship was too precious to let the pettiness of a damaged ego (or maybe an over-reaction fuelled by alcohol) to get in the way.

Harrison's family took five months to decide that they should turn off his life support. He was not an organ donor. The two friends shared a quiet laugh about that over the phone.

'Just as well,' said Iona, 'all his organs would be pickled in whiskey.'

Fran's pregnancy was too advanced for her to fly up for the funeral. There were at least two hundred people at the crematorium Iona told her.

He had been greatly admired by his peers. Irreplaceable. Unforgettable.

Fran fell in love with her tiny, three-weeks premature daughter. Suddenly, unexpectedly, fiercely protective and unable to bear the thought of handing this mewling, dependent bundle over to a nanny. She struggled on for a while, juggling the baby's needs with the business. Rob was as useful as a chocolate teapot. He was either away on long-haul flights or spending much of his time at home playing squash or running to keep fit.

'Not much I can do for the baby since you are breastfeeding her. When she's older I can take her out for walks. Maybe even teach her to play squash,' he added cheerfully.

She could not find a suitable candidate to be her assistant. The men were reluctant to take on an expenses and commission only job and the girls she interviewed were unwilling to undertake the recruiting campaigns, which meant being on the road for days at a time, interviewing and shortlisting potential candidates. It was a tough call for a woman, living out of a suitcase in faceless hotels. Fran had enjoyed the challenge and always felt gratified when she had identified just the right selection of good candidates for her clients. Her strike rate was very high and she had been highly regarded as a recruiter, particularly for the pharmaceutical industry, which was dominated by men. It gave her a lot of quiet satisfaction knowing that she was recognised as being very good at her job by her clients. After a few more months when she had stopped breast-feeding Jess, she would find a reliable child minder for the baby so that she could get back on the road. It would all work out.

'No, I can't be!' Fran was still breast feeding baby Jess, now six months old. She had started feeling nauseous and was losing a lot of weight.

'I would say you are about five or six weeks along.' Her lovely G.P. who had helped delivered Jess, looked at her sympathetically. 'I take it that this was not planned?'

'Definitely not!' Fran dropped her head into her hands in disbelief. Her baby slept peacefully in her buggy. 'I am trying to keep my business going and have just started interviewing childminders to look after Jess for one or two days a week…' Her voice trailed off. 'I am not going to be able to do that when another baby turns up in eight months' time.' She felt a surge of rage against Rob. He hated using condoms and had insisted that he would be 'careful'. She had thought also, that breastfeeding Jess would have helped to protect her against pregnancy. Why couldn't he just have left her alone anyway? She was far too tired to want to have sex. Bloody men and their libidos. She looked up from her internal rant to find her G.P. watching her carefully.

'What do you want to do, Fran? Shall I arrange a pregnancy care plan for you again?'

'Yes, I suppose so.' she answered, automatically placing her hands over her belly in the age-old gesture of protection. 'There really is no other option, at least not one I could live with.' The walls closed around her once more. Of course, she had wanted to have another baby, but at a time of her choosing. Maybe when Jess was about three. She could have managed to keep her business going with just one child, until she had found a reliable assistant recruiter to help her in the field. Her thoughts raced through her mind on the drive home. There was no other choice for her. By the time she arrived back, she had made her decision.

Rob was incandescent when she told him she was pregnant again, as if it was her fault.

'How are you going to keep your business going with two kids to look after? It is hard enough with just Jess.'

'It takes two to make a baby. You insisted that you were being careful and wouldn't use a condom. It's hardly my fault, is it?' The pointless argument burned out only to flare up again when Fran said she was giving up her business. Rob stomped off in a furious huff, unable to articulate his true feelings. Probably scared stiff thought Fran, but we should be all right with just the one salary for a while. I'll get back to work as soon as I can.

Her first and best client, John Monroe from Insula Laboratories, was sad to see her go, but he fully understood that mothering two babies had to become her priority. He and his wife had just produced another boy, now they were a family with six children.

'Don't have six of the little ankle-biters whatever you do, Fran. It's bedlam in this house these days.' He said this with a laugh, taking any sting out of his words. Fran knew that he adored all of them. 'But seriously, if you ever want to come back into the industry, we would welcome you with open arms. You will be a hard act to follow. Good luck, Fran. Keep in touch.'

Fran glowed. It was so gratifying to hear those words. Not once had her mother, or Rob, said they were proud of her for her achievements. Why did it still matter to her? She wished her dad was still alive. He would have been proud of her and would have told her so. Also, he would have loved his two grandchildren. Rob's family lived in Australia, so they only had irregular contact with them. Fran did not have any other relatives on her side to take an interest in her children, or help her to raise them. Her sisters had emigrated and her mother never volunteered. Rob was away so much. As it was me that wanted to have children, it's down to me to take full responsibility for looking after them she decided, and closed her mind to any possible financial fallout. Neither did she entertain any doubts about getting back into the recruiting business eventually, even if she had taken herself out of the picture and would surely lose her clients.

Rob became moody and irritable and they argued a lot as Fran's pregnancy progressed. Their life seemed to reflect the turbulent mid-seventies political economy. Oil prices spiked, interest rates went up. Unemployment rose as the Labour Government was sinking slowly under the weight of its Social Contract, while Margaret Thatcher waited in the wings to pounce. Fran, never one to take much interest in politics began to feel oppressed, fearful – and guilty – as their own pre-baby lifestyle was impacted by the recession. She gave birth alone, to their second daughter, Catrina, also three weeks premature. Rob was away on a trip. They struggled on for a year but their outgoings soon outstripped Rob's income.

'We just can't afford to stay in the U.K. I am not earning enough to pay all our expenses now. The mortgage has gone up too. I wish you had found a way to keep your business going.' Rob's voice rose in frustration.

Fran walked out of the room as the fretful wail of her teething baby provided her with an escape. She was deeply hurt. Was that all she meant to him? Her value measured by what she could earn?

It took a while, but Rob was finally offered a two-year contract with Vultura Airlines operating out of Frankfurt, and went ahead of Fran. She struggled to manage all the arrangements for renting out their house and packing up for the flight to Frankfurt. Her mother was working full-time and couldn't help. She wished Rob had taken time off and come back for her. Still, she reasoned, he probably couldn't get leave so quickly from this new job. She was quite lonely, missing the stimulation of her business associates, and isolated at home with the two toddlers. Rob had been so moody and irritable since

Catrina had been born. Hopefully they could make a fresh start in Germany. At least the worst of their money worries would be over. She cheered up at the thought of a new beginning.

Iona came down from Glasgow with Keira and stayed for a few days to help her pack up. Keira, was gorgeous and Fran could already see the beauty she would become in a year or two when her body caught up with her long, uncoordinated arms and legs. Fran's two little girls were entranced by Keira and she played with them for hours.

'Fran, could I leave Keira with you for the afternoon? I want to meet Hugh at the Tate, he is covering an exhibition of Scottish and Irish artists for the *Express*.' Hugh Mason was the art and theatre critic for the newspaper and Iona had met him at a small art gallery in Glasgow where she was exhibiting some of her work, including the Appaloosa stallion.

'Are you involved with him then?' Fran asked, recognising the slightly feverish energy around Iona when her interest in a man was ignited.

'Not yet!' she answered with an impish grin as she fled out the door to catch the train up to London.

Fran had questioned Iona about the developing relationship between Keira and her father, Max Cohen. He wanted Keira to attend Pinehill School, one of the highly regarded independent schools for girls in Glasgow.

'Keira's very bright Fran and Max will pay for her education there of course.'

'But won't that give him too much control over her and her future?'

'He already has, so she might as well get some benefit from it. I just hope she will see what a manipulative control freak he really is when she is older.' Iona had sounded defensive and defeated. 'He has set up a trust fund for her, so at least I know she will be covered if anything happens to me.'

Fran was appalled that Max had gained so much ground with Keira. Iona had tried at first to prevent him, but it seemed as if she had given in, her fighting spirit quenched in the force of Max's determination. He had always wanted and prized the possession of beautiful artefacts, books and paintings. It made her think that Keira, a child of unusual and rare beauty, was just another part of his prized collection. Something else (someone in this case) with which to impress his well-heeled neighbours and business associates.

Betrayal

'Good flight?' Rob was in his uniform. Fran's stomach gave a little lurch of pleasure. His handsome features always took her by surprise when she first saw him after they had been apart. He beamed at them happily, apparently delighted to see his family again. She had a thumping headache. The flight over had been horrendous as both children had upset tummies. The last few frantic days before they left had been so stressful. She just wanted to get to their new home and have a bath.

It was so strange being back in Frankfurt, the area where she had lost her heart to Erik, her U.S. special forces soldier. She felt the old familiar stab of loss and emptiness as she remembered him. Had he survived that last mission in Vietnam? Remembering too, that she had lost all contact with Polly who stayed on in Germany after Fran left. She knew that, even if Erik had survived, he would not have known where to look for her as neither she nor Polly had made it to California. Anyway, that was all water under the bridge. She was Rob's wife now and mother of their two adorable girls. She had made her bed, as her mother was fond of saying. (Her mother had still not forgiven Rob for taking Fran away.)

Rob had rented a large, newish house for them on the outskirts of Frankfurt. One half of the estate was still a building site as some of the houses were not completed. The owners all contracted their own builders, so at times their street was swarming with trucks delivering bricks and other building materials. Most of the houses on their side of the road were fully built, all large, three-storey villas with huge basements. Their house had several rooms in the basement including the laundry, except, bizarrely there was no washing machine! Two of them were locked, presumably containing the owners' personal belongings. Fran wondered if a large Bosch washing machine was lurking behind one of them? The owners were overseas for a few years, so Rob had taken out a two-year rental term to cover the length of his contract with Vultura Airlines. Fran was a bit concerned that the huge living room, fully fitted out with wall-to-wall dark wood bookcases, display shelves and a heavy, immovable, three-piece suite with carved wooden arms on both the sofa and armchairs, would stand up to the creative attention from her two lively toddlers.

Their next-door neighbours came over to introduce themselves. Fran had been hoping for a chance to practise her German, but their neighbours spoke perfect English and it seemed pointless trying to conduct a conversation in halting German when she didn't know half the words she wanted to say anyway. Rob had a few days off, but he had secured a casual job as a squash coach at a club in Munich and left Fran to 'settle in' as he put it. As the washing machine had not yet arrived, she had a hellish time trying to deal with the results of the children's vomiting and stomach bug, which she caught twenty-four hours later.

'Can't you stay here and help me out. I don't know how I'm going to manage on my own and I don't feel too well now either.' She had protested weakly as Rob was preparing to leave the house. 'We don't even have a telephone!'

'We need the extra money. Anyway, I'm sure the neighbours will help you out if you ask them. I have coaching sessions lined up with my squash students. I can't let them down.' Rob had muttered when Fran had protested at being left on her own again in a new country to cope as best she could. She remembered the awful homesick experience when she had first arrived in Germany almost a decade ago. Then she had been single with the resilience of youth to see her through the first few dark days. But now, she was a thirty-something mother, fully responsible for the two toddlers. Once again, Rob had expected her to get by on her own without his support. She would have to find a way.

She got quite ill with the gastric bug but managed to feed the children who were still not fully recovered, before collapsing on the sofa, unable to move. She had no way of contacting Rob. Fortunately, her lovely German neighbour had brought soup and seeing how ill Fran and the children still were, called in a doctor. The German doctor had put pessaries into the children's bottoms to stop them vomiting, much to Fran's horror. No way, she thought as she dry-heaved into a bowl, he's not coming near me with his ghastly pessaries. They got through it eventually and had recovered when Rob returned.

'There's a new Flight Engineer called Tom who has just joined the airline. Told me he brought his wife and daughter over. They live at the other end of Frankfurt. Tom wondered if you girls would like to meet up?'

'Yes! Yes! When can we arrange a get-together? I would love to meet them, specially her. What's her name?' Fran was desperate for company and pushed Rob for details and for his and Tom's availability for them to come over for the day. It took a week, but eventually Tom, his wife Bonny and their little girl Tracey, the same age as Catrina, their youngest, arrived for their visit.

Bonny was a hoot. The two women got on famously and Fran's life became much more bearable and less lonely. After a couple of months, the apartment directly opposite Fran and Rob's house came up for rent and Bonny, Tom and Tracey, moved in. It was perfect, the three little girls played happily together, most of the time. Jess was told enough to attend the local kindergarten and was soon prattling away in childish German, copied by Catrina who parroted everything Jess said.

Fran and Bonny formed a close friendship very quickly and Fran began to relax into her role as full-time wife and mother, missing her business less and less as the months passed. Tom and Rob's schedules seemed to synchronise quite often, so the two couples could socialise quite a lot. Although Rob and Tom didn't form the same sort of bond as Fran and Bonny had. Rob was very much the alpha male type and Fran guessed that Tom was a bit too soft for his taste. Tom wasn't into sport, had a slight lisp, and was a bit too namby-pamby for Fran as well. Nevertheless, she was so grateful to have Bonny as a friend. Like Fran, Bonny had a zany sense of humour, so they laughed a lot together. Just what Fran needed to offset the communication gap between her and Rob. In the last few months of the two-year contract, Rob was away in Munich a lot. Sometimes for work, but more often coaching at the squash club.

'Tom was saying that he tried to meet up with Rob in Munich at the squash club. They were supposed to have a meal and a beer together, but Rob wasn't there and hadn't left a message. Tom was pretty pissed off about it.' Bonny sounded a bit pissed off as well.

'Oh sorry, Bonny, Rob's hopeless. He told me that he feels obliged to treat his squash students to a meal occasionally. He must have forgotten that he had an arrangement with Tom. I'll get him to call and apologise when he gets back from Arizona. He is on a two-week instructor's training course there. He left early this morning.' Bonny seemed to be mollified.

'Fine, do you want to go into Frankfurt with the girls later? We could check out the new IKEA, I need to get some bits for the kitchen.' Bonny was on the end of her phone, although they could see one another from their kitchen windows.

Fran groaned, but held up her thumb to Bonny. 'Yes, sure. How about we leave at ten-thirty?' The last thing Fran felt like doing was trailing herself and her two children through the cavernous, endless departments of IKEA. She hated shopping with small children, but at least they would be amused with the huge container of coloured plastic balls to jump in. She would far rather have gone to the park, but after Rob's *faux pas* with Tom, she felt she owed Bonny. At least the extra money he was making coaching would come in very useful if she went shopping. He had left her quite a lot of cash to spend.

His letter, addressed to Fran, arrived after he had been gone about a week. *Darling Suzanna, I miss you so much. I can't wait to make love to you in our special way...* Fran nearly threw up. No other emotion she had ever experienced before, was as raw and mind-altering as this. Her heart raced like a hunted animal and her stomach heaved painfully. Her breath hitched and caught, trapped in her throat as the scorching tears streamed, blocking her nose. She had to wait several hours before she could call him. Arizona's time was behind Germany. She had to stay calm, for the children.

'Who the fuck is Suzanna!?' She screamed down the phone, all control gone as she heard his voice. There was a stunned silence from Rob. All she could hear was the crackling on the line, louder than any confession or denial could ever be.

'I'm sorry! I'm sorry! Please darling, it's you I love, only you! I promise, I was planning on breaking up with her when I got back...' His voice trailed off, probably remembering the sordid contents of his love letter. 'How did you find out?'

'How do you think, you lying bastard? I read what you said to her! Did she get my letter then? What shite did you have to say in mine?' Fran's voice pitched higher and higher as she choked on the rage, flooding with adrenalin, shaking uncontrollably.

'Please darling, please! She means nothing to me...'

'Mummy, what's wrong?' Fran spun around, still clutching the phone. Her two little girls were standing in the doorway, staring at her, frightened, wide-eyed, tears trembling, ready to spill over. She banged the phone back into the cradle without another word to Rob and ran over to them. Crouching down, she gathered their little bodies close into hers.

'Darlings it's all right. Mummy is just cross with Daddy. It will be all right. I promise you.'

'Is Daddy coming home soon?' Came the muffled voice of Jess, her four-year-old. Jess was very attached to her father, although he rarely seemed to notice her.

'Yes, he is, but tell you what. Why don't we go and visit Grandma first for a little holiday? It will give her a lovely surprise.' The girls clapped with excitement, fears forgotten. They loved going back to England. Rob and Fran had sold their house in Bagshot and bought a family home near Ruislip in Middlesex, to keep as a base for their trips home. Fran's mother lived there now with her large ginger cat, Marmalade. Her old boyfriend John had died of a sudden heart-attack and now that she had retired, she was more than happy to be looked after again by Fran and Rob. There were plenty of children around the same ages as Jess and Catrina in the small close of ten houses. That plus the cat, was a complete package for the little girls.

Catrina skipped off down the hall. 'Fuckie, fuckie, fuckie, we're going to see Grandma.'

Fran groaned, she shouldn't have sworn like that in front of the kids, they were like sponges. She tried to shut her mind off from the searing pain in her chest that threatened to immobilise her and forced herself to make arrangements for their departure.

'I never could trust that Rob. There was something about the shape of his mouth I didn't like.' Fran's mother was in full flow. Delighted for the chance, finally, to vent her spleen against her son-in-law. Their dislike and distrust of one another was mutual, although normally unspoken.

'Look Mum. I don't know what I am going to do just yet. Just give me a break. I need to clear my head. I can't think straight now. Make sure the girls don't overhear you complaining about their dad, it will just confuse them.' Rob had been bombarding her with phone calls since 'Suzannagate'. Begging, pleading with her not to leave him. He loved her, he loved his children. He would never be unfaithful again. On and on, he promised and cajoled, until she gave in and agreed to meet him in London to 'talk everything over.' Jess was asking every day to see her daddy.

He turned up with an enormous bunch of red roses. What a bloody cliché, Fran thought. What makes men think a bunch of flowers will put everything right again? They met in a café near Piccadilly Circus. Rob led her to a quiet spot at the back where they could talk in peace. He had tried to take her in his arms when he saw her, crushing his stupid roses against her back. She had pushed him away. All she wanted to do was to punch him. The rage and pain were bubbling up in her again.

'How long?' She glared at him, hating herself for asking.

Rob hesitated, looking down at his coffee cup. 'I met her two years ago, she was one of my squash students. She was very persistent. Kept coming on to me.'

'Right!' Fran snorted sarcastically. 'You just couldn't say no. Why can't you just be honest and say that you fancied her as well.'

He leaned across the table clasping her hands in a tight grip. 'OK I admit it, I was flattered, I was weak. But I promise you. I will never do anything like that again. It's over now anyway. Please, Fran, don't leave me. I need you. I love you. I love our girls.'

'It wouldn't be over if you hadn't sent me her letter by mistake, would it?' Fran wasn't going to let him off the hook that easily.

Rob insisted that he had been planning on bringing the affair to an end. The contract in Germany was nearly finished and he had signed another contract to work in the Middle East.

They talked on for an hour more although Fran did most of the talking. Rob just kept pleading and earnestly telling her he loved her. Eventually, she agreed to meet him in a local park in Ruislip the next morning so that he could see the girls before he flew back to Frankfurt.

'Daddy! Daddy!' The two little girls flung themselves at Rob. He lifted them both up, one under each arm and swung them round.

'Give Daddy a kiss.' He put them down and crouched down for the kisses. Fran had always disliked him asking the girls for kisses. They should feel free to kiss him if they wanted to, not because they had to. Fran remembered hating having to kiss her noisome grandpa, just because she had been told to. They both hung back a little, looking up at Fran. She just smiled at them. They both pecked him on the cheek and ran off to play on the swings.

Fran returned to Frankfurt and was there when Rob flew in from his last trip with Vultura Airlines. She packed up the house for their departure – on her own again. Rob had one last coaching session in Munich before they left, he said.

'Is Suzanna going to be there?' she asked suspiciously. Rob had been extra loving and considerate since she came back from London, but the distrust and hurt had not yet faded. Would it ever?

'No of course not. She has moved away. I don't know where she has gone. I promise you it is all over with her Fran. When we get to Jeddah we can make a fresh start. Put all this behind us. Everything will be better from now on.' He pulled her into his arms and she sighed a small sigh, deciding not to talk any more about the elephant in the room between them. But she felt that their fractured marriage was worth fighting for. The children loved Rob, even if he rarely got the fathering bit right. She was willing to try.

Iona questioned Fran about her decision to stick with Rob after the Suzanna episode.

'Are you sure you can trust him Fran? Once a womaniser, always a womaniser. It's in the blood, I know the type.'

'Oh, don't say that Iona, I've got to try. I'm doing it for the sake of the girls and hoping that I can get over what happened. He seems to be quite committed to us now. Anyway,' she said quickly changing the subject. 'What's happening with you and Hugh, are you still an item? And how's Keira?' she added anxiously, knowing that the youngster was spending more and more time with her father, Max and that Iona seemed unable to stop it happening.

'I've given up trying to keep Keira away from Max. She adores him and he spoils her rotten as you can imagine. She is turning into a petulant brat when she is with me these days. It's her life Fran, her journey. I must let it evolve and hope that he won't harm her in any way. She's very pretty, I think he likes showing her off to his friends, his little trophy daughter.'

Fran shuddered at the thought of Max Cohen having so much influence over Keira. She had been such a sensitive child and Max was transforming her into a little princess who had become demanding and rude when she did not get her own way. Every time Fran thought about Max, she remembered poor wee Harrison beaten to a pulp, probably on Max's orders. She couldn't prove it of course, but a Glasgow thug called Dougie Black had been charged with manslaughter and sentenced to twelve years. She just hoped that one day Max Cohen would do one shady deal too many and get caught in the act.

'Just don't give up on her Iona, she will always need to know that she has a safe haven with you. One day Max will let his respectable facade slip and she will see the darkness below the surface. Does she like Hugh? Do you see a lot of him?'

'I don't think Hugh quite knows how to handle her. He has never had children and is only interested in art. They tend to ignore one another when he comes here.'

'How do you feel about Hugh, is it serious?' Fran was hoping she would get a positive answer from Iona. She wanted her friend to find some peace in her turbulent life.

'Well he is nothing like Liam was, nobody could be, but we get on all right I suppose. He wants us to move in together, he has a house in Rutherglen near Keira's school. I'm thinking about it, this flat is too small for us now, but I'm not sure. Keira is capable of making his life very difficult. God knows, I have enough trouble trying to control her.'

'Let me know what you decide to do Iona. You never know, Keira might settle down a bit if she is in a proper home.' Fran had always thought the bohemian lifestyle that Iona led in the flat might have confused Keira. After Harrison had died, Iona always seemed to have some young writer or would-be artist hanging around the flat and she was still drinking too much. No wonder Keira preferred the company of her dad, who clearly adored and spoiled her. At least he had demonstrated consistency for her – so far.

Arabia

'*Allahu Akbar*.' The call to prayer was their first introduction to the Middle East. Fran's two young girls clutched her hands tightly as the eerie sound from the tannoys drowned out the chattering from the arrivals hall at The King Abdul Aziz International Airport in Jeddah, Saudi Arabia. They watched in amazement as hundreds of the faithful wearing *thobe*s, the long-sleeved floor length white tunics, or brown dhoti pants, worn with a knee-length loose shirt, emerged from all corners of the arrivals hall, fresh from their pre-prayer ablutions. With one fluid movement, they threw down their prayer rugs and prostrated themselves, facing Mecca the birthplace of their prophet, Muhammed. A sea of white and grey clad rears formed a solid wall. Fran wondered where all the faithful women were saying their prayers, but they were not visible. The prayer continued in a strange hypnotic rhythm and they watched fascinated as the men moved in unison, chanting the *rakats* or supplications; coming back onto their knees and prostrating themselves again, four times.

'What are all the men doing, Mummy?' Jess enquired curiously.

'Praying to Allah. Allah is God.' Fran added hastily, pre-empting Jess's next question. Jess always wanted explanations for everything. 'Allah, God, has slightly different rules here in Saudi Arabia, Jess, so we must follow the rules while we are living here.' Hoping that would serve for now, at least until they got through Immigration.

'But…' Jess started, looking puzzled. Her little nose wrinkling against the collective smell of hundreds of overheated bodies.

'Come this way Jess. I will tell you more about it when we get to our new home.' Fran gently led them all away, to stand in the queue for Immigration.

They had to wait until the prayers were finished before their passports could be stamped, allowing them into the Kingdom. Their luggage was searched thoroughly by an unsmiling Customs official who seemed to take particular pleasure in spilling the contents of Fran's carefully packed suitcases all over the counter. He gestured to Jess to hand over her big blue teddy bear that she always carried everywhere with her. Jess clutched her teddy tightly. 'Do I have to Mummy?'

'It's all right Jess, just let the man look at teddy and he will give it straight back to you.'

He handed the teddy back to Jess, but not before he had slit it all the way down the front of its body and had pulled out some of the stuffing. What was he looking for? Drugs?

Fran was furious, Jess was distraught cradling her mutilated teddy to her chest. Fran glared at him, but knew better than to make too much fuss. Rob had warned her to keep her temper under control going through Immigration. He gazed back at her coldly and waved her on dismissively. She quickly stuffed their clothes back into the suitcases, struggling to keep her anger from spilling over. Unable to comfort her little girl as she had to focus on moving them through Customs and Immigration as rapidly as possible.

'Let's go girls. Look, Daddy's over there.' Thankful to see Rob waiting for them on the other side of the barrier. Fran ushered the children through the pushing and shoving masses surging towards the exit. Jess was still sobbing as they went towards Rob, holding out her teddy for him to see.

'Daddy the nasty man cut teddy open,' she sobbed. Rob scooped her up into his arms.

'Mummy will sew him back up for you Jess. Let's get out of here and get home. Just wait till you see your new house.' He spoke to them all as he plonked Jess in the trolley and took charge of pushing her and their heavy cases out into the sunlight. Catrina, still silent, squeezed Fran's hand and she lifted her little girl and held her tightly. *I hope I haven't made a horrible mistake coming to this country with the children. If that's the attitude we are going to be experiencing from the Saudis, I'm not sure I will be able to put with it for long,* she thought. Fran felt anxious and uneasy. Not a very good first impression for her or the children. Rob led them through the crowds of mostly men (where were the women?) milling around outside the terminal. The heat hit them like a wall, the harsh sunlight bouncing reflections off the white buildings and white tarmac. They were drenched in sweat by the time Rob found his Jeep in the car park and bundled them all into the blessed cool from the air-conditioning unit. Fran watched in morbid fascination as all the cars on the freeway leading away from the airport, criss-crossed in front and behind them, driven like insane and suicidal dodgem cars. Rob was the only one driving in a straight line. Fran noticed two wrecks of expensive looking sports cars that had been crashed into lamp posts and abandoned.

'Look at that Rob! I'm sure that's a Porsche.'

'Yes, I know. I was told by one of the Saudi aircrew that they are usually driven by young, very wealthy boys, who just walk away from their wrecked cars – if they survive an accident like that. It's the will of Allah if they don't.' Rob added ironically. 'Keep looking and you'll see wrecked cars and speedboats mounted on pillars at the roadside. Maybe as a reminder to people to drive more carefully.' Rob slewed to a rapid halt as a Saudi man, clothed in a full-length white *thobe*, suddenly stepped into the road in front of them, imperiously holding up his hand to stop the traffic, so that his family could cross over four lanes of cars to the opposite side, where they all scuttled into the dark interior of a carpet shop. Miraculously, all four lanes of traffic succeeded in screeching to a halt, but it was like the start of a Grand Prix as soon as the family were safely across. Rob was last out of the starting blocks, for once, putting aside his competitiveness to drive his family home safely.

They had been allocated the huge, ground floor of a two-storey villa on a compound on the outskirts of Jeddah; newly opened for the expatriate families working for Saudi Arabian Airlines. It was like the League of Nations. Fran was delighted to discover that her neighbours included Americans, South Africans, French, Germans, Belgians and Scandinavians. Most of the men were either flight engineers or pilots like Rob and he was in his element living at close quarters with other aviators. He enjoyed nothing more than talking shop with the men on any aspect of flying or aircraft maintenance. Anything except deep and meaningful conversations with Fran. Possibly about why their relationship was struggling. Did he have any concept of what a huge commitment this was for her, she wondered? She was the Flying Dutchman, following hopefully in his wake, never found. The Middle East, Jeddah, a strict Muslim society where women were not allowed to drive or mix with men outside their own families. A recipe for disaster even in the most stable of relationships. At least it was a lovely life for the children she reminded herself.

'Mummy, Mummy! We've made friends with some of the children on the school bus. Can they come for tea please? We want to go to the swimming pool to meet them. Can we go now? Pleeeese?!' And so, her children's social life took off from day one. There were swimming pools in all four sections of the compound. Most of the aviators with families were housed in the same area. All the rooms were enormous with high ceilings, which helped to keep the rooms cooler. Fran hated the noise of the air conditioners, especially in the bedrooms and before too long, they had installed large ceiling fans, whose gentle whirring high above their heads, was a much pleasanter way of keeping cool indoors. The bathrooms and kitchens were tiled with beautiful ceramic tiles imported from Italy. No expense spared there. The other sections of the compound had one story bungalow-type houses or six-storey apartment buildings, all air-conditioned, all fully furnished. There wasn't a bit of greenery in sight when they first arrived. It was like living on a housing estate in the middle of an arid desert. Fran hated the bleak landscape, it felt so desolate, so far removed from the verdant fields and gardens of home. Eventually, droves of immigrant workers came and planted grass in the front gardens and bougainvillea climbers with their bright red and pink flowers which clambered up the doorways and softened the starkness of the white buildings.

It was mostly the British expatriates who cultivated their gardens themselves. Fran, naturally, was one of them. Her dad's influence again. It was so easy to grow exotic hibiscus shrubs and fragrant oleander bushes. All they needed to flourish was regular watering. Mona, Fran's excitable American next door neighbour, faithfully irrigated the weeds that pushed through the concrete. She had lived in an apartment in Arizona. For the women, establishing a social life, was a slightly slower process. Mona, was the first to arrange a coffee morning so they could all meet one another.

'It will be fun if we all share our craft skills, Fran. What can you do?' Mona stood on Fran's doorstep with her invitations already printed, to deliver to the women in their section of the compound. Fran couldn't even darn a sock properly.

'Um-m. I don't do any crafts actually.' She hated anything like that. Gaggles of women all blethering (as Fran's mum would have called it) and sizing one another up, was not her scene.

'Oh gee. Don't you?' Mona gazed at her through her thick, pebbled glasses, obviously puzzled. 'Well honey, just come along anyway. Maybe you could bake some cookies?' She added hopefully. Oh no, not cookies! Not ever, had she successfully baked cookies. What kind of wife and mother was she really? Maybe *that* was why her husband strayed? Had he been looking for a domestic goddess? Or a woman who was only allowed out of bed to get the coal in? She had heard that somewhere.

Probably one of Harrison's bon mots. It had made her laugh at the time.

She went along anyway, clutching a plate of flat brownies made from a packet mix. She thought, based on past disastrous attempts, that they were all right. Nobody ate them. Bizarrely, for Fran, Mona taught her how to weave macramé hanging plant holders and she got quite carried away with it. She could do a craft! Soon their villa was festooned with plant holders, but the little friendly geckos, tiny lizard-like creatures, took up residence amongst the foliage of the indoor plants. She was afraid to over-water the plants in case she drowned the geckos. The plants died and her passion for macramé died with them.

All the kids got head lice within the first few days of attending the International School. Fran got them too, so the house smelled pungent for a day or two from the nit shampoo. But, it did the trick. Mona dealt with the problem a little differently. Fran opened her door to check out where the acrid smell of burning was coming from. Mona was throwing towels and bedding onto a pyre made from the sofa and armchairs which she had dragged out of her house to the vacant piece of waste ground opposite. Bit extreme, but that did the job as well.

She made an international call to Iona, the only person in her world who would appreciate this story. The line was bad, crackly and buzzy, but Iona laughed wildly. This was just the sort of behavioural insanity that they both loved.

'How are things with Hugh and Keira and you?' she asked when their laughter subsided. Iona had finally moved in with Hugh.

'Hugh's fine, he encourages me to keep writing and painting but Keira…' Iona paused and Fran could hear the shift in her voice, even though the bad connection. 'She's a weekly boarder now at her school and goes to Max's most weekends. I don't see very much of her, unless I arrange to meet her on her own, sometimes at the weekends. She won't come here anymore; says she doesn't like Hugh.'

'What about half-term and holidays.' Fran asked, trying to imagine Iona's pain at the loss of Keira. Now that she was a mother herself, she understood better the bond between a mother and child.

'Hugh has agreed to go away for a few days during the holidays so that she can come here, or I will take her away on my own if need be. She has her own room here of course if she ever wants it.'

Fran could hear the sadness in Iona's voice but thought that Keira was calling the shots now. Max's influence was giving her too much control. She told Iona that she would come up to Glasgow on her first trip back home. 'I'll bring the girls with me if that's all right. I'm sure they would love to see Kiera again.'

'Yes, she would love to see them, and you too Fran. Keira often talks about you and remembers you reading her stories and putting her to bed when you visited us. I was never very good about all that sort of thing. I was drinking too much in those days. I didn't pay enough attention to her which is probably part of the reason she is so keen on being with Max.'

'None of us read the rulebook on raising kids Iona. You did your best for where you were in your life at that time. It's all we can do, and you're always there for her now. I worry too about the impact Rob's affair in Germany has had on my kids. They must have picked up on the tension between us then. Maybe us all living here together in Jeddah will be more peaceful hopefully. Try not to worry too much about Keira, Iona. I'll see you in a month or two.'

Fran was jogging most mornings with a couple of American women who lived on the compound. The pace was sedate enough so that conversation was not precluded. Otherwise, what was the point? That was more to Fran's liking, the women were interesting and easy to talk to. They put the world to rights. They all agreed that if women were in power, all would be well. She went out jogging with Rob once soon after they arrived, but he shot off at high speed, leaving her to trail behind him around the dusty compound. Not much fun. They joined the Hash House Harriers, but Fran only went once. Her new American jogging friends did not want to go running outside the security of their compound. But Fran thought she might meet some interesting people to have a chat with while they were jogging and she wanted the experience of running through the desert terrain in the safety of a group. The children were left in the charge of a handful of wives who weren't running themselves. There was a tent erected for shelter and plenty of refreshments and other kids to play with, so Fran was not too worried about leaving them.

'Mummy, Josie's mummy says there are leopards in the desert. Daddy, will you look after Mummy please?' Jess was anxious.

'Don't worry love. There are no leopards. We will be fine.' Rob distractedly patted Jess's head and quickly jogged after the runners gathering at the start point. Fran ran to catch up with him.

'Rob wait! What if there are leopards around?' Fran was feeling a bit worried too. But Rob was not listening. He was jostling with the runners at the front of the pack, determined to be first at the finishing line. Fran tried to keep up, but was soon left trailing behind as the pack of runners, including the wiry female triple H's, disappeared over the brow of a jagged outcrop of rocks. By the time she reached the top of the outcrop, they were way ahead. She would never catch up with them now. No chance of a friendly chat with that lot. The loneliness of the long-distance runner. She ran on, now feeling quite forsaken in the rocky terrain and wishing Rob had waited for her. There were chalk marks on the rocks on the trail to show which direction to take. She must have taken a wrong turn because she found herself running past a familiar-looking gnarled tree. She was lost! She felt panic creeping up. What if she couldn't find her way back.? She had no water with her. What if a leopard crossed her path? She thought she saw a big cat-like creature on a distant hill top. What if a tribe of Bedouin captured her and she never saw her children again? Come on Fran, she told herself sternly, surely Rob will come back and look for me? She ran on again, determined to stay calm and focussed, keeping a careful watch for the clues on the trail. Finally, just as the sun was beginning to dip below the horizon, the trail widened and she saw the finish line. The girls saw her first and came running.

'Mummy! Where were you? Daddy's been back for ages.' Jess and Catrina grabbed a hand each and walked back with her, clinging to her tightly. They had been getting worried. Rob was standing talking to some of the other runners. His back was turned. Like he said later, it had not occurred to him that a woman running alone in the desert might be in danger.

'Anyway,' he said defensively, I thought you would be able to keep up with some of the other women. I didn't know you hadn't got back.' He had been first over the finishing line.

When Rob wasn't flying, they went to the beach at the weekends. They rented a part-share in a large family beach-hut on a gated waterfront compound, used exclusively by the expatriates. Rob, always highly competitive, had taken up windsurfing and spent all their family days at the beach, racing in competitions on the Red Sea. At first Fran and the girls had watched fascinated, as he assembled the rig on the beach, pushed it into the shallow water, slipped his feet into the stirrups on the board, hauled up the huge sail and somehow caught the offshore wind. He would skilfully pull on the boom, tacking and gybing, turning the nose of his board away from and into the wind to be first at the start position for the race. The girls would jump up and down with excitement as they watched the competitors' colourful sails approaching. The windsurfers zig-zagged their way back to shore to avoid going over the banks of coral reefs which lay concealed just under the surface of the sea. Sometimes Rob's multi-coloured sailboard lead the way. There would be several races during the day. Rob entered every single one of them. The girls soon lost interest and would skip away to play with the other children, jumping in and out of the waves that kissed the sand and searching for crabs in the shallow water, as warm as a tepid bath. Fran stuck around for a while the first few times they went to the beach. Being supportive. But eventually it was just too boring standing at the water's edge watching the windsurfers waiting for yet another race to start. Seeing Rob disappear towards the horizon just felt like a metaphor for the state of their marriage. Rob was always leaving, returning, briefly touching base before disappearing again. Fran could feel the now familiar hollow emptiness that was pervading her being more and more these days. She stood barefoot at the edge of the water, watching the lapping waves pushing grains of sand between her toes. This, she thought, must be what loneliness feels like. Any connection she had known with Rob seemed to be stretching out further and further. Her optimism about their fresh start after the ghastly events in Germany was wearing thin. He was just so remote, like an island out at sea. Unreachable.

'Fran, we want you to set up an interview with Akram Bashara. We need another feel-good piece for the 'In Flight' magazine. That piece you wrote for us on The Falcon Breeding Centre was popular. See if you can do something similar on Bashara.' Joe Bartlett was the wiry, hyperactive editor of the *Arab Chronicle* and more recently, the 'In Flight' magazine for Saudia, the flag-carrying airline for Saudi Arabia. Fran had started off her career as a journalist with the newspaper, by submitting a few self-deprecating pieces about her own experience of expatriate life in the Kingdom and had been surprised and gratified when they were published. They were very lightweight, but the newspaper was short of English speaking writers. She silently thanked poor deceased Graham Gordon, her old buddy from the *Glasgow Express* for giving her the chance at writing for newspapers all those years ago and for giving her a few tips on journalese. The Al Faisal Falcon Breeding Centre story was her best to date. She had travelled with Rob and the girls, south to the Asir region, to interview the eccentric English falcon breeder who ran the Centre and had stayed there for two days on top of Al Suda mountain. The Centre was up near the top of the mountain and Fran had watched fascinated and awe-struck as the stunning creamy-feathered Saker falcons glided on the thermals above the clouds, returning to their perches at night. It was marvellous copy to write and the colour photographs supporting the story were amazing. She had been quite proud of that piece which had been published in the *Arab Chronicle* newspaper and the 'In Flight' magazine.

Akram Bashara was a wealthy Saudi businessman and known philanthropist. Joe Bartlett gave her a bit of background information on him. Bashara had funded the setting up of hospitals and orphanages in some of the poorest countries in the Middle East and had continued to support them with regular injections of cash from a trust fund set up by his enormous business empire established in the Middle East and overseas. Apparently, his father had acted as a broker between the Saudi Royal Family and the oil companies wanting to exploit the black gold waiting to be harvested in the desert regions. Bashara had taken over the already cash-rich business when his father died and had developed it further, negotiating other contracts outside the Kingdom. Fran had observed with distaste the excesses of the oil wealth amongst the rich Saudis, but it would not have been safe to write negatively about any of it – at least while she and her family were still living there. Knowing in advance that Akram Bashara, was using some of his vast personal wealth for good causes, cheered her enormously. If she had to write a sycophantic piece about him, there would be some truth and integrity about the writing. Too often, she had been forced to write articles about Saudi nationals, using hyperbole to describe some business achievement which had been born out of the exploitation of immigrant workers who were paid a pittance and treated like slaves in harsh working conditions.

Rob was away on yet another layover in London. He was always bidding for London flights, saying that he was bringing back spare parts for his and other people's windsurfers. Fran was miffed. There she was stuck in the desert with her kids, while he was swanning around at home enjoying all the Western freedoms that she had taken for granted, until she ended up in Jeddah. Why, even her houseboy, Ahmed, turned up in his car to clean her house. Fran had to make do with a bike. Catrina rode in a seat at the front and Jess perched on the back on a padded saddlebag, her rapidly growing legs almost scraping the ground as Fran laboriously pedalled the heavy bike. The school bus pick-up point was at the far end of the compound and they were always running late. How she hated that bike ride! She was always hot, sweaty and irritable by the time she got back to the villa. Thank God for the ceiling fans keeping the rooms wonderfully cool after the extreme humidity of the outside temperature. She kept the smallest bedroom at the back of the villa locked, never allowing Ahmed access. Behind that locked door, the homemade wine was bubbling and popping away in the large plastic containers. Anything more mature than one month was considered vintage. It always amused her that, in an alcohol-free country, the grape juice, sugar and packets of yeast were all side by side in the supermarkets, conveniently ready for the expatriates to cart off crates of the stuff for their home-brews. No opportunity lost amongst the canny Saudi shopkeepers. But heaven help anyone who was caught with alcohol on them. At any given time, some over-confident home-made wine or *siddiqi* (distilled alcohol made from fermented sugar water) maker from their compound would be languishing in jail for months before being deported; led straight to their aircraft in chains. No chance to go back to their homes or to say goodbye. She wouldn't dare to write up any of those stories for the Arab press!

Rob was becoming increasingly boorish and short-tempered when he was at home, particularly after a London layover. Often, he would go off windsurfing or playing squash as soon as he got through the door. Invariably, Fran needed him to drive her to the supermarket as their grocery supplies would have run low while Rob was away.

'You're turning into an Arab. I hate having to ask you to take me to shopping. You know damn well that I can't get off this bloody compound without you to drive me. I don't like going down town any more than you do, but we've got to eat. You're turning *me* into a shrew! None of the other husbands abandon their families the minute they get back off a trip.' She probably had uttered variations of that diatribe on many occasions, but Rob merely shrugged and promised that he would take them shopping later.

'I need to unwind, Fran.'

Sometimes he yelled back at her when the girls were out playing and couldn't hear them. Their relationship was at an all-time low. Some of the other wives referred to it as the Saudi curse. Many of them returned home after a year or two, unable to cope with the restrictions imposed on them by the strict Muslim laws, more so when their husbands were away flying. In theory, they had to have their husbands' permission to leave the compound and were not supposed to travel in a car with any man other than a family member. That went down well with the liberated Western women. At times the restrictions made it was hard to remember that women had enjoyed voting rights in the UK since 1928! There were many quiet and daring little acts of rebellion that kept the women from losing their identities completely. Including dressing up in men's clothing, sticking on a false moustache and driving the car home from a party. How Fran would have enjoyed telling stories like that in her regular newspaper column. They must keep until I get back to the U.K. when I can write what I want, she consoled herself. For now, her journalism would have to remain unchallenging and politically correct.

'Mr Bashara will see you now.' A male secretary, dressed in a spotless white *thobe* and red and white checked head dress, the *ghutra*, ushered Fran through the heavy oak doors into Akram Bashara's inner sanctum. It was already late afternoon. She had been met at Riyadh International Airport by a silent and somewhat surly driver in the Arrivals hall, who held up a white card with her name written in English and Arabic. He took her small overnight bag and her briefcase from her and without a word, indicated by hand gestures that she should follow him. She followed him trustingly, glad to get away from the curious stares of the crowds of men milling about aimlessly in the airport. What were they all doing there she wondered? It wasn't Hajj season yet. He drove her straight to the offices of the Bashara Foundation. An entire office block devoted to the running of this enterprise. Impressive. Bashara's office was surprisingly small, the space dominated by a large, pale oak desk, completely devoid of clutter, apart from a telephone and oddly, she noticed, a bottle of mineral water. A small coffee table and two comfortable looking cream leather armchairs had been placed in front of the large window, that gloried in panoramic views over Riyadh, the ever-growing capital city of Saudi Arabia. Fran had never met a multi-millionaire before, never mind a mega-wealthy philanthropic Saudi national. She was curious and a bit nervous, hoping that she had enough credibility as a journalist to make a good job of this assignment. At least her experience in her former life as a business woman in a predominantly man's world, should help her conduct this interview with some panache. Akram Bashara was sitting behind his desk talking in rapid Arabic into his phone. He gestured for Fran to take a seat, but as the only seat was one of the armchairs placed with their backs to his desk, she decided to remain standing. After a few seconds, with Fran feeling a little foolish to be standing, uncertain what to do. Mr Bashara finished his call and walked from behind his desk, his arm extended for a handshake.

'Good afternoon, Mr Bashara. Thank you for seeing me.' Fran chose to speak first. She was not going to let him think that she was a shrinking, subservient woman, like most of his own countrywomen, shrouded in black *abayas* and face veils, walking dutifully behind their husbands.

'Frances isn't it? Please, call me Akram.' His voice was deep and as smooth as melted chocolate. No trace of an Arabic accent. Just middle-class English. His handshake was warm and firm. For a moment, Fran felt the ghost of a similar sensation she had experienced a decade ago in Germany when she met Erik. She was almost the same height as Bashara, their eyes on a level. His were dark green, flecked with hazel. He wore the floor-length white *thobe*, long-sleeved and buttoned up at the neck, but his head was uncovered, his hair, a soft wavy, dark brown, falling absurdly over his forehead. Akram Bashara exuded confidence and a powerful animal magnetism, so tangible, she could almost taste it in the air between them. She had an unexpected urge to reach up and brush the wave of hair off his brow.

'I have read some of your articles in the *Chronicle*. Very interesting.' His eyes creased at the corners.

Oh no! Fran flushed in embarrassment. Not those trite articles about expatriates! He must wonder why I have been sent to interview him. Her self-confidence evaporated. Before she could reply, he added, 'I liked your piece on the Al Faisal Falcon Breeding Centre. Prince Faisal is very proud of his Saker falcons. I have been out in the desert hunting with him and his beautiful raptors many times.'

Fran breathed out. Thank goodness, maybe he would take her seriously as a journalist now. She smiled inwardly at the little theatre of name-dropping. Even multi-millionaires want to impress.

'Let's sit over here.' He placed a hand lightly on the small of her back to guide her to the chair. Electricity fizzled down her spine.

They sat opposite one another in the comfortable armchairs, the coffee table between them. Fran set up her tape recorder and began the interview. There was a discreet knock on the door and Akram's secretary came in, bearing a tray with a pot of Arabic chai which he poured out into the small clear glass cups with gold handles. Two bottles of mineral water and two larger glasses were also on the tray.

'Thank you, Malik.'

The secretary bowed slightly and left the room. Malik looked more like a warrior than a secretary, with his large hooked nose and fierce, beetling, bushy eyebrows, masking his deep-set black eyes. He was also unusually tall and burly. Fran wondered if he doubled up as Mr Bashara's bodyguard.

'Would you like some tea Frances?'

She had tasted the sickly-sweet Arabic chai before and would have preferred to decline. But she smiled politely. 'Yes thank you. Do call me Fran. I only get called Frances when I'm in trouble.' What was she saying? Why couldn't she stop herself uttering inappropriate banalities like that? Especially when she was trying to conduct a serious interview.

Thankfully Akram merely smiled back and handed her a glass of chai. She accepted the small glass, wondering how anybody drinking this stuff regularly, kept any teeth in their head. She noticed that Akram drank only the mineral water. He did have nice teeth.

Fran was struggling to concentrate on her interview questions listed on her notepad. Trying to claw back her dignity after her shaky start. Every time she looked up, Akram was gazing intently at her. She began to feel flustered. Her back still burning from his earlier, fleeting touch. Somehow, she got through all the questions and turned off the tape recorder. There was no doubt that he was passionate about the charitable work his foundation was doing. It would make a good story. She had a feeling that he might be passionate about other aspects of life too.

'Thank you,' – she hesitated – 'Akram,' – she said awkwardly. Saying his name for the first time sounded too intimate in this setting. 'I will send you a copy of the article before I submit it to my newspaper to make sure you are happy with it.'

'No need, I am very confident that you will write a perfectly accurate story. You know, you remind me of my first wife, Fran. She was very beautiful too. English. You are from Scotland, I believe. Such a soothing voice.' He spoke, almost wistfully.

His first wife? Fran wondered how many other wives there were. He added. 'Sadly, she could not have children, so we had to divorce. I have two sons with my second wife. She is

American, like my mother.' Ah, that explains the green eyes and the accent. Must have been educated in England, there was no trace of an American drawl.

'We have two daughters living with us in Jeddah. My husband flies for Saudia.' Fran joined in, just to level the playing field. They both stood up and Fran quickly lowered her head to hide the pulse that was beating visibly at her throat and busied herself packing away her tape recorder and notes into her briefcase.

Akram remained standing at the other side of the coffee table, she could feel him watching her.

'My wife is in America with the boys, visiting her parents. We are expecting another child in four months. We are hoping for a girl this time.' Both committed. 'Which hotel are you staying in? I take it you are not flying back to Jeddah tonight? Or do you have to get back to your husband and children?'

Fran had an open return ticket, just in case she had been delayed in Riyadh. She had arranged for one of the other British wives, a good friend, who lived on their compound, to meet her girls off the school bus and keep them overnight if required.

She made her choice. 'My husband is out of the Kingdom for another two days and I have arranged for my daughters to be looked after by a friend, so I don't need to fly back tonight. I haven't booked a room yet, but I will go to the Marriott. My editor has an account with them.' What was she committing herself to? She pushed aside her sudden doubts about this uncharacteristic decision, straightened her shoulders, raised her head to meet his gaze with what she hoped was cool confidence. Her knees however, trembled.

Fran was wearing a full-length, pale turquoise kaftan which suited her complexion and reflected a bluish light into her grey eyes. She was the slimmest and fittest she had ever been. Hours jogging round the compound and regular windsurfing lessons had firmed and toned her body. It was acceptable for Western women to be bareheaded, except during the holy month of Ramadan. Her dark hair waved softly over her shoulders. She was in her mid-thirties and in her prime. Except, that seemed to mean very little to her husband Rob. Invisible once more, at least to him. She yearned to feel the joy of breathless, mind-blowing sexual congress that she had only ever shared with one other man. Sadly, Rob could not ever give her that experience. Their lovemaking was perfunctory, mechanical, efficient, but devoid of excitement and longing. Akram's obvious interest in her had awakened a forgotten and deeply repressed need. She was shocked at the overpowering sensations flooding through her. She knew she was in dangerous territory, but her attraction to this man was overwhelming.

Akram walked over to his desk and pressed an intercom button. 'Malik, bring the car round to the front entrance, I will accompany Mrs Patterson to the Marriott Hotel.' He turned to Fran. 'One moment, I will phone and book a room for you.'

'Thank you. Can you please book it in the name of my editor's account? Mr Joe Bartlett.' Her voice shook a little.

Akram nodded and spoke rapidly into the phone in Arabic. His intense eyes, darkening now to a deeper hazel green, never left Fran's face. 'Come. Malik is waiting for us.'

Fran gathered up her briefcase and small overnight travel bag (what had she packed in there?) and followed Akram out into the still humid air of the Arabian dusk. The distinctive smell of the warm air carrying mixed aromas of spices from the nearby souk, gasoline fumes from the endless stream of horn-hooting cars and the musky smells from dozens of passers-by inflamed her senses further. Malik held the door open for Fran and she slid into the cool, leather comfort of the Mercedes, the heat and smells of the Riyadh night air replaced by the subtle and delicate floral scent of the car's interior. Akram followed and sat beside her, not touching, but there was almost a tangible vibration of sexual tension between them. Enough to light up the Arabian Peninsula. Fran hoped that Malik, driving impassively through the busy Al Wazarat district to the Marriott Hotel, could not feel it radiating through the smoked glass, separating him from his employer.

Fran headed for the check-in desk to collect her room key. Akram, stopped her, cupping her elbow firmly. 'No need, it is all taken care of.'

Fran's eyes widened in surprise, but without another word, Akram steered her towards a lift, punching in the sixth-floor button. He kept his hand, now with the lightest of pressure, on her elbow. Her heart fluttered like a captive bird as the lift glided upwards, rapidly and silently. The doors slid open, revealing the hushed, palatial corridor of the sixth floor, home of The Royal Suite.

'Come, explore. This is all yours for the night.' He seemed very boyishly pleased with himself, enjoying Fran's astonishment.

The suite was decadent beyond words and huge. Fran had never seen anything like it before. The only grand buildings she had been in in Saudi Arabia were the Foreign Embassies in Jeddah where she often went to interview some newly appointed cultural attaché or once, the British Ambassador. But none of those dignified Embassy interiors compared to this Royal Suite. Opulence abounded. Rich silk tapestries hung on the walls, gold-leaf embossed lamps and matching coffee tables were dotted around the vast lounge. Deep, luxuriously comfortable armchairs and sofas in the softest, matching cream and gold material (quite tasteful in a sea of otherwise overdone décor) were grouped in the centre of the lounge, facing a large TV cabinet. The bedroom was almost as big as the lounge with an enormous king-sized bed in the centre of the room, draped in white fur (fur!). The marbled en suite bathroom was as big as a bedroom. Double sinks and gold taps were reflected off the mirrors on every wall. The bath was the size of a small pond. Fran thought she could easily have shared the huge bath with all her family and a couple of neighbours. She walked to the huge floor-to-ceiling window in the bedroom and looked out in awe at the view. Akram was on the phone again. Millions of lights twinkled and blazed in every window of every building. No energy conservation in this city. From this vantage point she could see the made-up roads at the city boundaries, stretching into the empty desert, lights blazing night and day on both sides of the roads; waiting like the limbs of an octopus to embrace its prey of new buildings yet to be constructed. She had noticed the same bizarre phenomenon when they were approaching the runway at Jeddah airport and had enquired lightly of Rob if they ever confused the straight lit roads for the runways at the airport. He wasn't amused at this flippancy. He took his flying very seriously. She did not want to be thinking about Rob at this moment. Akram came across the room quietly, to stand behind her. She could feel the heat from his body.

'I've ordered some food for us,' he murmured into her ear, looking at the reflection of her eyes in the window.

Did this man do everything without checking in with her first she wondered. Us? He was obviously planning on staying. Her pulse rate escalated. How would she manage to eat with him in the room, when all she wanted to do was to tumble onto the massive king-sized bed with him? Clearly, he had more self-control than she did. The food arrived almost immediately, a huge trolley laden with savoury and sweet dishes. In the middle, an ice bucket with a bottle of Bollinger champagne. How did he manage that in a country where alcohol is forbidden? The Royal Suite had a separate lounge and dining area. The waiter set out all the dishes on a low table surrounded by large plump cushions patterned with stylised peacocks displaying their magnificent tails in iridescent colours of emerald green, blue and turquoise. At a nod from Akram, the waiter opened the champagne bottle with a discreet pop and poured out two glasses before replacing the bottle, wrapped in a pristine white starched napkin, in the ice bucket. Akram waved him away and he backed out of the room as quietly as he had entered, without uttering a word, or looking directly at Fran.

'Come and eat, you must be hungry after your long day. I am very hungry too.' He smiled at her before leading her to the cushions. 'Will you be comfortable eating at this level Fran? Perhaps we should have sat at the table.' He stood, uncertain for a moment, waiting for her to answer.

'No, this is perfect! Thank you for arranging all of this Akram, it's wonderful, but I'm not sure if my expenses' budget will cover everything though.' She just had to make sure, although she knew what he would say. She sank down as gracefully as she could onto the cushions and he sat cross-legged opposite her. Such a leveller, sitting on the floor to eat.

Her handed her a glass of champagne. 'Let us drink to the success of your story about my Foundation. There will be many contributions from Saudi Nationals who will want to be associated with the charity because of reading your article. That is worth more to me than all the gold in Arabia.' He laughingly paraphrased the cliché. They carefully touched the rims of the ornate crystal champagne glasses together and drank.

'That is so kind of you. I will write the best article I am capable of for you,' she promised him, wondering if she could avoid telling her editor that she had an expenses-free night in the Royal Suite of the Marriott. The champagne bubbles replaced the concerns about such matters as Akram guided her through the names and origins of the many dishes of food laid before them.

The food was delicious and she was willing to taste most of them with one or two goat and lamb exceptions. Bowls of rosewater and napkins were placed at her elbow so she could rinse her fingers between courses. Akram translated the Arabic names for the dishes into English for her in his rich, velvety voice. Extraordinary how seductive ordinary yogurt and cucumber salad sounds when pronounced in throaty Arabic, *Laban bi Khyiaar,* or another one she thought might have been chicken. *Hammam Mahshi,* stuffed pigeon. Pigeon! Fran wished she hadn't been told that one. Another one to avoid. Akram just laughed, not remotely offended by her reactions to some of his country's traditional delicacies. She was happier with the *Samak fi as Siniyah,* a wonderful fusion of fish and spicy vegetables. She watched as Akram sampled each one of the many dishes he described to her with undiminishing enjoyment. He was like her old friend Polly from Germany, she with the insatiable appetite, But, also like Polly, he was not carrying any excess weight in defiance of the amount of food he was getting through. She could see the lean contours of his body through the slim-fitting *thobe* he was wearing. Akram encouraged Fran to try some of the desserts which he had moved onto now. Pudding heaven! She couldn't resist tasting a few of them. Fresh tropical fruit, mangoes and papayas, the only ones she recognised, were beautifully presented in sliced harmony, alongside the delicious *Mutabbag Hilou,* rich pastries folded over with banana and syrup. The bottle of champagne was soon emptied and Fran feeling replete, allowed herself to relax back onto the incredibly comfortable cushions. Akram too, stretched out his legs with a sigh of contentment and propped his back against the cushions as well. They talked easily about their families. He asked a lot of questions about her background and seemed genuinely interested in who she was and what had brought her and Rob to Jeddah. It was extraordinarily friendly for a while. Just two people getting to know one another. Then, an indefinable exchange of glances, grey eyes on green and the mood shifted.

'Shall we have *Gahwa,* coffee? There is a pot here if you want. Unless it keeps you awake?' He looked steadily at Fran, a slight smile twitching the corners of his mouth. Oh, that mouth! Full and generous. He was incredibly attractive. She was lost.

'I suppose I had better then,' said Fran, pouring out two cups of the strong Turkish coffee for them.

They finished the coffee and Fran excused herself to go to the bathroom. It was quite hard to rise gracefully from the cushions. She looked at her reflection in the mirror. Her eyes were wide and luminous, shining with a fever that she could no longer contain. When she came through the door, Akram was standing looking out of the window into the blackness of the night sky, broken up only by the constellations of stars. When he saw her reflection in the glass, he turned around. 'Come over here Fran and look at the view. The night is clear and pure.'

Hypnotised, Fran walked towards him knowing that she would no longer have the strength to walk away from what was to come. He stepped behind her and stood very close to her as they looked out at the stars. 'So beautiful,' he murmured. Was he meaning the stars? She took the tiniest of steps backwards until she could feel the fabric of his white *thobe* brushing against her kaftan. They stood together like that for what felt like an eternity, every pulse spot in her body beating wildly. She could hear his breath shorten, but he made no move to put his arms around her. Slowly she turned, he did not move. 'Are you sure Fran?'

She looked at him wordlessly for a second and inclined her head. Only then did he pull her body close in to his. Their first kiss was long and deep, firing up an unquenchable primal longing. He led her over to the bed where they feverishly helped one another out of their clothes. The intensity of their lovemaking took them both by surprise. Afterwards they lay still, breathless, arms wrapped around each other, unable to break their embrace. Akram looked into her eyes and said; 'My God Fran, what have you done to me? You have taken my breath away.' She smiled at the age-old cliché, but she too felt the same. Not since Erik, had any man made her feel this way. Although her connection with Erik was soul to soul. What she had just shared with Akram she had to admit, was based on sheer magnetic mutual lust.

'Not too sure Akram, but that was extraordinary.' Then to lighten the mood. "Shall we try that amazing shower before you go?'

The hot water from the huge walk-in marble shower room fought to find a passageway between them. Their bodies, slick and warm from the jasmine-scented shower gel, joined together again in blissful union. He did not leave.

Fran was overwhelmed. The charge of physical attraction between them did not abate that night. Akram at last, announced that he had to go. Dawn was just breaking as he took his leave.

'I should have met you years ago Fran. You are so beautiful. I could drown in your eyes.' He murmured in her ear, cradling her head on his chest, before slipping out of the vast, sheet-crumpled bed. He stepped into his white *thobe*, retrieved from the tangle of discarded clothes on the floor beside the bed. He turned at the door. 'I'll call you.'

There was an unspoken understanding that this relationship would stay in the realms of the purely physical. There would be no possibility of anything else developing. Their lives were playing out on separate platforms.

Her story on Akram Bashara's charitable foundation was very well received by the newspaper and was subsequently published in the 'In Flight' magazine. She kept a copy of the magazine article and often looked at his photograph, a close-up of head and shoulders, his green eyes looking straight at the camera; her stomach lurching with longing as she remembered their long night of passion in Riyadh. It was weeks before he contacted her. 'Fran, I have business in Jeddah, could I see you? You should know that your article has attracted some very large donations from several Saudi businessmen. I am so pleased that you interviewed me.'

I did slightly more than interview you she thought wryly after they had arranged to meet. Rob was away on a trip and the girls were at school. He came to the house, carelessly parking right outside the door of their villa. With hindsight, she shuddered at the risks they took on those occasions. He was so well known, so recognisable; also, so powerful, which might have protected them if they *had* been found out. After all, they stoned women to death for adultery in this country she reminded herself. It was always the woman's fault apparently. But she was smitten and could not resist him. They never had more than a couple of hours together, but although their hasty lovemaking lacked the intensity of their first, long night in Riyadh, he made her feel as if she were the most important woman in the world to him when they were together. Their secret, infrequent, passionate couplings over the following years kept her sane, restoring her belief in her femininity, so damaged by Rob's infidelity. The irony of the double-standard was not lost on her. She had to ignore it. She just did not feel guilty. She used to dread Rob coming home from a trip, he was such a curmudgeon these days. Yet, she was beginning to hate it when he was away and she was imprisoned on the compound, unable to get around without him. She admitted to herself that the infrequent meetings with Akram helped her to tolerate her life. But the gaps between his visits were too long. How her adrenalin coursed when he called her to arrange a meeting. Sometimes she missed the opportunity to see him because Rob was at home or one of the girls was off sick from school. Her disappointment at missing him would leave her deeply frustrated and hating the sight of Rob, if it was him being at home that had blocked her chance of seeing Akram. Her life in between seeing him was devoid of joy and excitement and she realised that she was developing an obsessive addiction to him. Not very healthy.

Her girls were happy, but they were maturing into their pre-teen years. 'Mum! Mum! An Arab man tried to get Catrina and me into his car, but we ran away!' Jess and Catrina were breathless from running and flushed with the drama of what had just happened.

'Where is he now! Was he on the compound?' Fran's fierce tiger mother emerged. She was quite prepared to run after him and rip his head off if she could.

'He's gone Mum. He drove off the compound. He was in a white Mercedes,' said Catrina helpfully, less fazed than Jess.

Great, thought Fran, ninety percent of the Saudis drove white Mercedes cars. They had recently been moved out of their villa into one of the bungalows. The villas had been converted into offices for the airline. There were too many young Arab men cruising around, leering at the women in the compound. That was the tipping point for Fran.

'I'm going back to England with the girls Rob. You can stay on if you want, but I've had enough of this place' (and you, she added silently). They had been living in Saudi Arabia for six years. Rob behaved like an ill-tempered, uncommunicative moron most of the time. She was very unhappy. They were always arguing. Sometimes unavoidably, the girls overheard them. It was damaging for them. She had to get away.

'You're just going to clear off with my children and leave me living here by myself? Don't think you can take my girls away from me that easily. I could get custody of them if I wanted,' Rob spluttered in a rage. He *was* turning into an Arab.

'What are you on about? I'm not asking you for a divorce! We just need some space from one another. Anyway, you spend half your time off in London as it is. What's all that about? Have you got another girlfriend?' She spat out, all her suppressed, jealous rage bubbling up once again. It was the custody comment that did it. As if he could raise two pre-teen girls. He had hardly spent any time with them since they were born. Stupid man. Rob stalked off without further comment.

'Are you and Dad getting a divorce?' Jess had asked her worriedly, after overhearing some of that heated exchange. Catrina had become very withdrawn and didn't want to spend any time with them when they tried to go out together as a family. She preferred to hang out with her Greek friend Marty, over on another part of the compound. Fran felt that she was losing touch with her youngest daughter. Guilty too, that her constant fighting with Rob was pushing both her children away.

'No Jess, don't worry. It's just this place. It's not healthy any more for all of us. It's time for us to go back to England. You will see just as much of Dad as you do living here.'

Home Again

Fran left a big chunk of what had been a major part of her life back in the Middle East. Her children had enjoyed a carefree childhood spending many hours after school, playing happily in the security of the compound, splashing about in the huge swimming pools in the recreation areas. They had many friends from several different countries and almost every weekend, they were taken to the beach where expatriate families from different compounds would gather together to enjoy water sports in the balmy waters of the Red Sea and socialise throughout the day with shared picnics and copious quantities of homemade wine.

The weather from September through to June was wonderful, especially at the seaside with the onshore breeze keeping the temperature perfect. Sometimes, one of Fran's friends, a Belgian couple with two children of their own, would take them out on their speedboat to the three-mile coral reef where they would snorkel just over the edge of the reef. Even just floating over the edge of the reef they could see through the clear water, the shoals of colourful clown fish, parrot fish and many other species of Red Sea fish and extraordinary, brightly coloured coral shapes, burning forever images into their minds. Stunning. Rob never came out on the boat with them, he was always windsurfing. That aspect of life in Jeddah for expatriate families was idyllic.

Fran regretted taking her children away from all of that back to densely populated Middlesex, where they were miles away from the sea and the joyful freedom of the beach and the swimming pools. But they were moving into their teenage years. It was time to move on. For all of them. But the future was uncertain. Would the girls settle back home? They would be starting again at new schools, not having any friends. All their education had been in the American system. This was going to be very different for them. What would she do? She might be able to carry on with her journalism, but breaking into writing for British newspapers could be difficult. Joe Bartlett her editor in Jeddah, was quite interested in Fran submitting articles about life in the U.K. that might be of interest to their readers, which at least was a start.

'I will be in the U.K. on business fairly regularly Fran. I always go to the Saudi Arabian Embassy to meet up with Saudi businessmen there. Can I call you at home?'Akram was holding her close, seemingly unwilling to let her go after she told him she was leaving Jeddah for good.

'Yes of course. It's just that Rob might be around more often now and might answer the phone. If that happens, I will tell him that I am writing another article about you.'

That last meeting in Jeddah with Akram, just weeks before she left, was quite difficult for her. Despite what he had said, she suspected that she would fall off his radar as soon as she left the country. She felt she should have drawn a line under their relationship there and then. But the physical attraction between them remained powerful, she could not give him up just yet. He told her that day that his wife was expecting their fourth child, so there was absolutely no future for them. But she had always known that, right from the beginning. She felt guilty. What would the poor woman feel if she knew her husband was a philanderer? Maybe she did know already? Her sense of guilt dissolved during their last ecstatic hour together on Arabian soil. She was drugged with desire for him.

They had been back home for a few weeks and Fran had been out most of the day shopping with the girls buying them uniforms for their new school. They had to wear ties and blazers. After the casual comfortable shorts and T-shirts they had worn to go to school in Jeddah, they were appalled at the stiff material they would have to tolerate now.

'You got a call from someone called Bashara. Wants you to call him at the Saudi Arabian Embassy. Is that the wealthy Arab you wrote about before? What does he want? You need to watch these guys. You can't trust them.' Rob was looking at her quite intently, the irony of what he was saying totally lost on him.

Fran could feel her face heating up and quickly replied. 'I expect Joe Bartlett, my old editor from Jeddah has given Bashara my number. Probably wants me to do another interview with him. I'll call him tomorrow.' She so wanted to mention the pot and kettle, but managed to restrain herself and drifted casually into the kitchen to start dinner.

Rob left early for the airport, he had to go back to Jeddah to pick up his next flight schedule. He had bought an old run-around car that he would leave parked in the short-term car park. It saved Fran having to drop him off and pick him up after flights. Both girls were feeling nervous about starting their new school, so although they could have walked, Fran drove them the half mile, reassuring them that after today, they would feel a lot happier and would probably want to walk to school with their new friends from their street. As soon as she got through the door, she picked up the note that Rob had scribbled the Embassy number on. Her heart was hammering with nerves as she dialled.

'*As-Salaam-Alaikum.*' The polite voice enquired. 'How may I help you?'

'Good morning, my name is Frances Patterson. I have a message to contact Mr Akram Bashara. May I speak with him please?'

'One moment please.' He spoke again almost immediately. 'Mr Bashara has left a number for you to contact him. Please write this down.'

Fran scribbled down the number, it was a mobile. She thanked the operator and hung up.

She took a moment or two to calm herself down before dialing his number. Hoping it would be a voice recorder so she could leave some sort of neutral message for him. Just in case this was just about another interview.

'Hello Fran. How are you?' His familiar, warm voice washed over her. How did he know it was her calling him? Her number must have come up on his screen.

She had to swallow nervously before answering him. 'Hi Akram, I'm fine thank you. Are you over on business?' She realised her fingers were painfully crossed.

'Yes, but I am returning to Jeddah this evening. The *Arab Chronicle* has requested another follow-on article about the recent structures of new schools and hospitals in the Yemen which of course, are being funded by my charitable foundation. I would like you to write the article Fran. Are you free today? I am in the Marriott Hotel on the Bath Road if you could meet me there? I have one more meeting here this morning, but I should be free by twelve. I will order lunch for us.'

So, it really was over. He just wanted another interview about his charitable work. Disappointment flooded through her but she pulled her chaotic feeling together and replied quite coolly. 'Yes, I can be there Akram. Shall I meet you in the foyer?'

'No come to my room. We can eat there.'

'I need to be back by 4 p.m. My daughters are at their first day in their new school. I want to be there for them.'

It was important to establish that her family commitments were a priority.

'Of course, then we must not waste any time. I will see you later.' He gave her his room number and hung up before she could reply.

This fantasy about Akram has got to stop. You're a forty-one-year-old married woman with two kids and a husband. It was justified in Jeddah, things between me and Rob were so bad; but he is trying his best now that we are back in England. I think he has more respect for me now that I have my independence back. Thinking he might be losing his family shook him up. Life's easier for me now. I needed Akram in Jeddah. He kept me sane. The thoughts ran rapidly through her head as she pulled jeans and trousers from the wardrobe and a kaleidoscope of coloured tops and shirts out of drawers. What to wear? If this was a formal interview she should look smart. In the end, she wore her tight black jeans and a white silk blouse and as a concession to smartness, pinned her hair back in a loose chignon. She had not cut it for months and it was skimming her shoulders. The gentler climate of England had improved the condition of her hair and her skin had paled from tan to warm ivory. She made her eyes up carefully (he always complimented her on her eyes she remembered). She wore her short black linen designer jacket and flat black pumps. With a last hasty glance in the full-length mirror in the hallway, she stuffed her notepad and tape recorder into her black leather shoulder bag and headed off to the Marriott ready to do her interview.

He was in Western clothing. The first time she had ever seen him dressed in anything other than a full-length white *thobe*. He wore denim jeans and an open-necked white linen shirt. Devastatingly attractive. He held the door wide for her to come in.

'Hello Akram.' She managed to sound normal. 'Good to see you again,' and leaned in to kiss his cheek.

'Fran,' he murmured in his deep brown velvet voice and kissed her cheeks three times in the traditional Arabic greeting. 'You look wonderful'. He held her by the shoulders and stood her at arm's length appraising her from head to foot. 'You are one sexy lady in those black jeans. Let me take your jacket.'

This was going well. How was she to maintain a cool exterior when he was already making the blood course manically through her veins just by the proximity of him? The subtle citrus and sandalwood scent from his skin triggered memories she did not need right now.

'Are you hungry. I ordered food for us.' He pointed at a platter of sandwiches. 'Not quite as interesting as the food we shared in the Marriott in Riyadh.' The creases at the corners of his green eyes deepened as he smiled at her. Was he remembering everything else they shared that first night in a very different hotel room five years before?

'No thanks, I'm not hungry, but you carry on. I'll just have some water.' Her mouth was dry with anxiety. 'I'll get my tape recorder and notebook ready for the interview.'

'I am hungry, but not for these awful sandwiches.' He came over and sat beside her on the sofa. 'Fran, I have missed you. Missed seeing your eyes close when I kiss you.' He reached behind her head and pulled out the pin holding her hair in its loose chignon. As her hair tumbled around her shoulders, he grasped a handful at the back of her head and gently brought her face towards his. 'This is when you close your eyes Fran.'

'Akram, I'm supposed to be interviewing you,' she managed to say before his mouth silenced hers and her whole being dissolved. She closed her eyes.

'Oh my God it's three-thirty, I have to go.' Fran panicked and threw on her clothes. Their lovemaking had been as intense as always, but there had been a different quality to it this time. There was a gentleness and a sense of deep connection between them that had not been apparent in Saudi Arabia. Akram had been quiet for the last while, just holding her and stroking her hair.

'Fran, I have something to tell you. My situation has changed since I last saw you. I will be spending most of the year in New York from now on. My wife wants to have our children educated in America and to be near her family. Riyadh is proving too difficult for her and the children to live there any longer. She did not convert and does not want the children brought up as Muslims. I may not be back in the U.K. for a while.' Akram came over to her and held her close. 'I don't want to cause any problems for you and your family. Shall I call you again when I came back?'

This was it – closure. She fought off the wave of profound sadness and longing, buried her face in his neck and in a muffled whisper said, 'I don't think so. I am trying to salvage my marriage and this – us – it is too unsettling. Goodbye Akram, I will never forget you or how you made me feel.' They shared one final bittersweet embrace and she left.

As she raced back home, the tears threatened to blind her as she drove. She had regained her composure by the time the girls came hurtling through the door demanding food and anxious to share their experiences of their first day at the new school.

The scent of his aftershave lingered on her black linen jacket for a long time. It was months before she could bear to have it dry-cleaned. Her heart ached for longer. She told Joe Bartlett, her editor in Jeddah that she had missed the opportunity to interview Akram Bashara in London because of her family commitments. The requests for articles stopped after that.

Retribution

By the time, Iona's letter arrived, she had already had the mastectomy and was having chemotherapy. Why in God's name hadn't she let Fran know sooner? This was so typical of Iona to go through something like this without asking for help. Fran started making arrangement to fly up to Glasgow straight away. They had bought her mother a flat nearby. It was not working with them all living together in the same house. Rob and her mum were always at loggerheads over something. Much to Rob's disgust, Fran arranged for her mother to come back and stay in the house to help look after the girls. Rob did not seem to have any problem with her going and accepted rather grumpily, that her mother needed to be there as he would be away flying some of the time.

'Well I didn't want to bother you with it. There's not much anyone can do really. Anyway, you've got your own family to take care of.' Iona was back home and had just finished a course of chemotherapy. Her unruly blond curls had already fallen out. She looked too frail in the brightly coloured gypsy scarf tied defiantly around her head. Her eyes were huge in the angular planes of her face, with dark circles bruising the skin under them. It ripped Fran's heart out to see her friend like this.

'I can stay for as long as you need me Iona. I've sorted the girls out with Rob and Mum, they can all muddle along together. They'll be fine.'

Iona sighed and leaned back in the chair. 'OK Fran, thanks. I recognise that determined voice, so I won't try to dissuade you. Hugh does his best, but he's not very comfortable with illness, or me looking like this. To be honest I could do with some support. The chemo treatments make me so sick. Thank the Lord, I've just had the last session.' Her eyes closed. She looked exhausted.

Fran got to know Hugh quite well over the following days while Iona slowly regained her strength. He was a pleasant soul, but very relieved that Fran had taken over looking after Iona, allowing him to retreat once more to his study to write his theatre and art critic's columns for his newspaper.

'Have you seen much of Keira recently? She finally decided to ask Iona, as there had been no message from her daughter in the days since Fran had arrived. Keira had grown into a tall, stunningly beautiful young girl although wild and spoiled. Her father Max indulged her every whim. He had allowed her to leave her exclusive private school before sitting her Highers, to become a fashion model. Iona had not been happy about it, but since Max had taken over raising Keira, she had very little control or input into her daughter's life.

'I knew the little turd would ruin her.' Iona had complained over the phone to Fran several months before she was diagnosed with breast cancer. 'She'll end up anorexic and probably start using drugs. But once she was under his influence, I couldn't get her back. She likes the lifestyle too much. He bought her a Mini Cooper the minute she turned seventeen. She's already written it off and had it replaced. The insurance is probably more than I make from sales of my poetry books.' Fran had listened sympathetically to Iona's rant, but she had to agree. The turd was indeed spoiling his and Iona's beautiful daughter. She was now even more of a prized trophy for Max to show off to his friends. Iona had sent her a picture of Max and Keira coming out of a theatre in Edinburgh during the Fringe Festival. He was clutching her arm possessively, grinning like a Cheshire cat at the photographers. Keira looked at the camera with studied insouciance, but was truly beautiful. She stood at least half a head taller than her father, her dark eyes heavily made up, no lipstick needed for her naturally pink lips and her glorious mane of dark curls flowing down her back. She was wearing a short black leather skirt that showed off her endless legs, a black tank top and a short white leather jacket slung carelessly over one shoulder. She had been signed up by a modelling agency after that picture had been published in the gossip column of the newspaper.

'Iona? Has Keira been to see you? Fran repeated the question, not sure if Iona had heard her. She was sitting at her painting easel, not moving, just gazing out of the window at the birds and squirrels competing for the nuts in the bird feeder.

'She doesn't know about this.' Iona placed her hand over the flat place on the left side of her chest. She kept her gaze averted from Fran but her voice wobbled a little.

'Oh Iona, you should tell her, she needs to know. I'm sure she'll come over as soon as she hears. She will be devastated that you didn't tell her before.' Fran placed her hand gently on Iona's shoulder.

'I don't know about that; I haven't seen her for months. She has been so caught up with everything since she started modelling...' Iona's voice trailed off, she sounded so tired and defeated.

'She's just carried away with it all Iona, but she still cares, still loves you I'm sure. Is she still living at Max's place?'

'Not sure, I expect so.'

The next morning Fran made sure that Iona was comfortable and told Hugh to give her lunch. 'I have some shopping to do in town.' she told them both. 'I won't be too long. Can I borrow your car Iona?'

'Sure. I won't be needing it for a while.' Iona turned onto her side in bed, clearly not ready to get up and face the day.

Fran's pulse quickened as she pulled into Max's driveway. His house was set back from the road, one of an exclusive development of large Victorian villas built around the golf course in Lenzie. There was a black Jaguar and a Jeep parked on the curved gravel driveway. No Mini Cooper. She parked Iona's car facing the wide gateway and walked towards the heavy wooden front door. She thought the chances of finding Keira at home would be slim, but she had another, riskier reason to see Max Cohen. It was mid-morning. She rang the doorbell and waited uneasily as footsteps approached from the hallway. She heard a chain being pulled aside before the front door swung open. A large woman swathed in a wrap-around white apron glared suspiciously at Fran. 'Yes?'

'Is Mr Cohen or Keira at home please?' she asked in her firm, interviewing voice, looking straight at the unfriendly face of the guardian blocking the doorway.

'Who wants to know?'

'I'm Fran Patterson, a friend of Keira's mother. Mr Cohen knows me.'

'Wait there.'

Fran obeyed, wisely deciding that she would not risk the woman's ire. Wouldn't want to meet her in a dark alley she thought. The big woman stomped back along the hall and pulled the front door wider to let Fran through. 'Follow me.' She pushed the door shut with a bang and marched off again down the hallway, leaving Fran to follow. Didn't slide the chain back into place. She flung open a solid oak door, one of several other closed doors leading off the hall, which revealed a book-lined study. She departed without a word. A bit short on the social graces.

Max Cohen was sitting on the edge of a large, dark mahogany desk, swinging his leg, a glass of whiskey in one hand. He looked dishevelled, unshaven and with black circles under his dark brown eyes. It was 10 a.m.

Fran got in first. 'Hello Max, looks like you've had a long night. Poker?'

He ignored that and took a long swig of his whiskey. 'What do you want Fran? I've got a round of golf arranged for eleven o'clock.'

Fran hoped he had a large handicap to help him get a round in anywhere near par, the state he was in. He needed a shower and a change of clothes. She had a sudden image of him in a ridiculous pair of plus-fours and a yellow sweater all topped off with a flat cap. It helped her to steady her nerves.

'This won't take long. Is Keira here? I need to get a message to her urgently. It's about Iona.'

Max slipped off the edge of his desk and took an unsteady step toward Fran. 'What about Iona? What's the stupid bitch done now? Why does she need to see Keira?'

'Max, Iona's had breast cancer. She has had a mastectomy. Keira doesn't know about it and Iona does not know that I came here to find Keira. She should come and see her mum. Is she still living with you?'

'Nah. She's gone and shacked up with some ponce photographer from the model agency. I only see her now when she wants money,' Max said bitterly, adding, 'So Iona's lost a tit. Pity, she had a great pair. Still, I don't expect that milksop art critic she lives with would even notice.'

Fran's bile rose at the harshness of Max's words. He really was a little shit. She gave him a disgusted glare and turned to leave. 'By the way Max, I heard that Dougie Black has contacted the newspaper. He wants to sell his story. He's getting out of Barlinnie prison next month and says that you paid him to beat up Harrison.' She watched Max's sardonic expression freeze for a second, his eyes widening, glittering dangerously, his mouth contorting into an ugly snarl as he moved menacingly towards her.

'That little shite Harrison deserved all he got, but nobody will ever be able to pin that on me. Dougie Black's a liar. Now you fuck off out of here and don't come back or you will regret it.' His face was inches from Fran's and she felt a frisson of fear and revulsion as his sour whiskey breath and evil energy washed over her.

Fran turned quickly and headed for the door. 'God knows what Iona ever saw in you,' she managed to throw at him before he slammed the heavy oak door behind her. She ran along the hallway and got out through the front door before the big woman appeared again. She had turned on the engine and was heading out the drive, tyres churning up the gravel, before she reached into her jacket pocket and switched off the small recorder that she had kept from her journalism days.

She was almost in the centre of Glasgow before her heart slowed back to a normal pace. She wasn't cut out for daring and dangerous stunts like her encounter with Max. But now she had valuable evidence, even though he had not actually confessed to being directly involved in Harrison's murder.

She found the modelling agency in Royal Crescent that had hired Keira. The receptionist wouldn't give her Keira's phone number, but promised to pass on a message to her when Fran explained that Keira's mother was ill. She noticed that Keira's photograph, gazing with sultry dark eyes, directly into the camera, was displayed prominently on the wall with the other agency models. She was strikingly beautiful. She reminded Fran even more of Liam now rather than Max. Strange. Fran spent another hour or two wandering around the stores in Glasgow to give herself time to calm down after her perilous exchange with Max. Corruption leaves its mark. He positively exuded evil, it seeped from his pores.

She bought a few items from the clothes stores for her girls and herself and got back to Iona and Hugh's house. A red Mini Cooper was parked in the driveway. Fran was shocked and amazed that Keira had made it to the house so quickly, the receptionist must have called her straight away. The engine of Keira's car was still warm, so she must have got here just ahead of Fran. Fran felt very uncomfortable, she had hoped to tell Iona first that she had tried to contact Keira. Iona would probably be mad with her for interfering. She let herself in and walked nervously towards the living room where a low murmur of voices drifted through the closed door. Fran opened it quietly and immediately, tears sprung into her eyes. Keira was lying half sprawled over her mother, her head buried into Iona's neck.

'Oh Mum. I'm so sorry. I should have been here.' Her body shook with sobs and her beautiful face was streaked with mascara. Iona was stroking the mane of her daughter's black curls and soothing her quietly with words of reassurance. Iona looked up at Fran standing uncertainly in the doorway. She shook her head slightly at Fran, trying to look stern, but her eyes too were bright with tears, or was it just the light?

Mother and daughter sat together on the sofa, talking for ages, Iona smiling and laughing softly at some of Keira's tales from her modelling experiences. Fran bustled around happily in the kitchen making a meal for them all. Iona was coming to life with her beloved daughter around her again. Later, when Iona had gone to bed early as she usually did, exhausted with the effort of the day, Keira sat by her bed, holding her sleeping mother's hand. Unwilling to break the contact with her.

After another week, Fran felt that it was safe to leave Iona with Hugh and Keira to go back home. Hugh and Keira tolerated one another well enough for Iona's sake, Fran suspected. Keira's presence was the best tonic for Iona, she was much brighter and managed to stay up a bit longer in the evenings, chatting to her daughter. Keira had been booked for a catalogue modelling assignment for country clothing, but it was being shot in Scotland, so she would still be able to spend time with Iona.

Fran had a quiet word with Hugh and let him listen to the recording she had of Max's reaction.

'I haven't heard anything about Dougie Black wanting to sell his story to us. Is it true?' Hugh looked puzzled.

'No, it's not. I just wanted to get a reaction from Max. I am sure he paid Dougie Black to beat Harrison up. I was hoping he would give himself away. He nearly did, you should have seen his face! He was incandescent with rage and possibly fear. It was hard to tell.'

'We can't use this Fran, it's inadmissible and a sort of entrapment.' Hugh frowned. 'I wish we could get justice for Harrison though, everyone at the *Express* thinks that Max might have been behind the attack, but there is no real proof.'

'Keep the tape anyway Hugh, I just really wanted to prove to myself that Max was involved. It is a sort of justice for Harrison. Probably all he will ever get. Don't worry Iona with it though. Now that she and Keira are close again, I don't want to stir up trouble for them.'

'Thanks a lot for contacting Keira, Fran. Iona is much happier now that they are back in touch and I think it will help her recovery. Not that she would ever admit that. You know what she's like.' Hugh smiled, Iona was well-known for keeping her feelings under wraps. 'There might even be a bit of progress between me and Keira,' he added. 'She asked me if I minded if she stayed here occasionally while her mum is recovering. She refused to come here before, out of loyalty to Max I suppose.'

'I'll come up as often as I can Hugh, but Rob is considering another overseas flying contract based in Alaska, we might be going with him, but possibly living in Seattle. I know Iona will get through this. She's tough and she's got you and Keira now to support her.'

A few weeks later, Hugh phoned Fran to tell her that a body had been pulled out of the River Kelvin at Partick, a suburb of Glasgow. The corpse was later identified as Dougie Black, newly released from Barlinnie Prison. The coroner's report said that his blood-alcohol levels were very high but there was also a contusion on the back of his head consistent with a hard punch. A police investigation was under way.

'Fran, if it's all right with you, I'm going to let a detective pal of mine listen to your tape. It will be off the record, but it might be enough at least to have Max Cohen questioned about Dougie Black's death. He's a dangerous bastard. I want to see him put away. Not just for Harrison, but to protect Iona and Keira.' He paused. 'And you, Fran, you're on his radar now.'

Fran shivered. Had she indirectly caused Dougie Black's death? What if Max had arranged for Dougie to end up in the Kelvin because of her? She had been so driven to extract a confession from Max, she had not considered the possible consequences. Now she too might be in danger from Max if the police could not find any definite link between him and Dougie Black.

She realised that she would have to stay away from Glasgow and Iona while Max was being investigated. How would Keira feel if her father was implicated? What a mess their lives were in! At least Iona and Keira were reunited, but Iona had a long battle for survival ahead of her and Keira might have to cope with the fallout of discovering her father was a criminal. Fran's mind went into overdrive. *And what have I gone and created for myself? Possibly on the hit-list of a ruthless thug? My marriage is a disaster zone. Rob is so disassociated from me and the girls. Totally self-absorbed. Does his own thing without ever considering our needs. Catrina's behaviour is spinning out of control and Jess is unhappy at her school. Maybe a move to Seattle might be good for all of us? Although typical of Rob, he announces that he has accepted another overseas contract and just expects us to follow him. Still, better to try and keep the family unit together I suppose. The girls need a father even if he is totally hands-off with helping to raise them. Might as well be a single mother for all the help he has been.* Fran's mind grew weary of her internal monologue; it was time for another change of direction. They all deserved a chance of a better family life. The girls would love living in Seattle.

Eternally optimistic that, if Rob could spend more time with his family in Seattle, rather than living alone in a bachelor pad in Jeddah, he would be more cheerful and engage more with them, Fran set about organising another move for them. They rented a three-storey home in the Seattle suburb of Kirkland, near the shores of Lake Washington. Seattle's reputation for being wet was true enough, but it seemed to Fran that even on the dampest of days, it would dry up before sunset and they would be treated to glorious skies slashed with red, pink and orange-streaked clouds mirrored in the waters of the Lake. Whenever possible, Fran would walk down to the Lake at sunset where at the end of the pier, she could look south to the iconic, permanently snow-capped Mount Rainier, rising majestically above Tacoma and Seattle, the tallest mountain in the Cascades. Fran learned that it had last erupted spectacularly a century before. Beautiful but potentially deadly, the mountain held an endless fascination for Fran. She felt connected with its glacial, solid exterior concealing the slowly building cauldron of pressure at its heart, preparing to burst forth at any moment. But hopefully not while they were living nearby.

Rob did seem to be more content in Kirkland. Seattle was such a beautiful city, tucked away in the north-west corner of the U.S., nudging against the Canadian border, but with its own unique vibe and climate, unlike any other part of the U.S. that Fran had ever visited. It seemed to spread its gentle, easy-paced way of life over them all–for a while. They explored the famous Pike Place Market, the oldest farmers' market in the region, situated right on the shores of Elliott Bay on the Puget Sound and took home the freshest seafood and vegetables in the world it seemed to Fran. Rob treated them to a meal in the revolving restaurant in the Space Needle with its stunning views over the whole of Seattle; but Fran probably enjoyed that experience the least of all as her fear of heights kept her pinned back against the wall of the circular observation platform. She watched enviously as Rob, Jess and Catrina leant over the rail to take in the views. More to Fran's liking was the soul connection she felt at a Native American tribe pow-wow on Bainbridge Island. The thudding drumbeat and the chants had her blood stirring, even more so than the skirl of the bagpipes at the Edinburgh Tattoo. It could have been the perfect experience for them as a family. Jess was in her element and very happy at her first year in High School with her new group of fresh-faced young friends. But Catrina's friends all turned out to be troubled kids with difficult home lives, who hung around in the basement bedroom where Catrina had chosen to live.

Why are parents always the last to find out? Catrina's behaviour deteriorated and she became morose, rude and uncooperative. Fran assumed she was having trouble adjusting to life in her new school as she had to finish her last year at

Middle School when all the kids had already formed close-knit bonds. Catrina was left on the fringe with the dysfunctional kids. Although Fran did not realise that until it was too late and her daughter was using LSD, paying for it with dollars stolen from Fran's purse. Fran had always been vague about how much money was in her purse. Especially dollars which felt like Monopoly money to her. It took Fran too long to make the connection between puzzlement over the missing money and her daughter's behaviour. She tried her hardest to pull Catrina back from the brink, Rob's solution was to get her out running. No chance, she simply refused and Rob retreated into the inner recesses of his mind, not communicating about Catrina with Fran. Once again he was pushing his company for London trips out of Alaska. Fran was desperate to get Catrina away. Her personality had completely changed and she was severely depressed. Life in Seattle ceased to be a pleasure and became instead, a nightmare for Fran. How could she salvage her daughter's sanity without any support? Jess wanted to graduate from High School before she was willing to come back home. There was no other way, she had to leave Jess for six months in Seattle with Rob and commute back and forth. Catrina stayed with friends in Middlesex and went to the local high school. Both girls needed her, Rob seemed detached again. She was torn.

Disintegration

The same London number kept appearing on the B.T. bill. Some of the calls were less than a minute, but many were forty or fifty minutes long. Fran searched for earlier B.T. phone bills but there were none. Her skin crawled, she could feel a pulse beating in her neck, her stomach cramped and her breath came in shallow bursts. Intuition screaming a malevolent truth.

'Iona, can you do something for me please? Can you phone this London number and let me know if a woman answers? I think Rob is involved with someone again.' Fran's voice cracked as she read out the number.'

'Oh no. What a shit he is to be sure. I take it you don't recognise the number?'

'No I don't Iona, but there are so many calls, it can only be Rob. He is away on a trip until the end of the week. I don't know what made me look at the bill. I don't normally bother. Rob usually pays by standing order every month. He has been acting weird since we came back from Seattle, all impatient and constantly doing battle with the airline scheduler for more London layovers. They want him flying out of Alaska of course. I can't bring myself to call, I feel sick.'

'Look, I'll get back to you after I've called. Do you want me to say anything?'

'God no! Just hang up if it's a woman's voice. Thanks, Iona.'

Iona called back ten minutes later. 'I got an answering

machine Fran. It was a woman's voice. She said her name. Precious? Does that mean anything to you?'

Fran's mouth was dry. 'No, it doesn't. Who would call themselves Precious? What a stupid bloody name.'

'Fran, there's more.' Iona added quietly. 'I just hung up without saying anything but she called me back straight away. I just said hello, no name of course.'

'Who is this?' she asked. 'Why did you ring my number and just hang up?'

'Sounds a bit paranoid to me Fran. I just said quickly, sorry wrong number and hung up. I'm afraid it all sounds a bit suss. What will you do?'

'Challenge him about it when he comes back from this trip. I don't think I can handle any more lies and deceits around Rob. I've had enough. I gave him a second chance after the German episode. He just can't do staying faithful.' Fran tried to steady her voice and stay in control, but her whole body was trembling.

'To be sure, I don't have the best track record myself in the affairs department,' said Iona. 'But I warned Hugh at the beginning what I was like, but now of course, it's hardly an issue,' she added.

Fran had an image of her friend placing her hand over the empty place where her left breast used to be and reminded herself once more that all life's challenges were relative.

'Don't worry about all of that right now Iona. Thanks for helping me. I'll find a way through it. What's happening at your end. Has Keira calmed down a bit now?' Fran asked anxiously, recalling how upset Iona had been when her reconciliation with Keira had blown up in her face about year ago, when Fran was still living in Seattle. She could not forget that she was partly to blame for it all and often broke out in an uncomfortable cold sweat when she thought about what had happened and that she had been the catalyst. As far as she was aware Hugh, Iona's husband, had not told Iona about the secret tape recording she had made of Max Cohen almost admitting that he had something to do with arranging a revenge beating for Harrison.

When Dougie Black was found guilty of Harrison's manslaughter and ended up drowned in the River Kelvin a few days after being released from prison, Hugh had a quiet word with a contact in the police force, implying that Max Cohen knew Dougie Black and that it might be worth asking him a few questions. Although they could not find any direct evidence to link Max with Dougie's death, it gave the police an opportunity to investigate Max's business affairs. The detective in charge of the enquiry now had an opening to follow up on an old complaint about Max's dodgy business dealings, with some fresh evidence supplied by Hugh. Hugh had kept an old journal of Harrison's where he had jotted down comments and observations that he could use in his satirical cartoons that he had been so famous for at the *Express* newspaper. Hugh had read quite a few references about Max Cohen and his alleged attempts at bribery of a planning officer in the City Council Housing and Development department. All unsubstantiated as Harrison wasn't around to confirm any of it, but the police now had a valid reason to interview the named planning officer who had since retired to a seaside bungalow in Troon with his wife. His wife had died recently, and the poor old chap was more than pleased to have some attention and support from the nice policewoman who came to interview him and stayed for tea and digestive biscuits. He well remembered that Max Cohen had offered him a 'fair amount' of cash to push through a planning application to convert a warehouse into a block of luxury flats in the west of Glasgow. He was more than happy to sign a statement and give evidence against Max Cohen if called upon to do so.

Further police enquiries turned up more evidence of Max's corrupt business dealings and he was arrested and charged. The case was a sensation, as it blew open a hornets' nest of tax-evasion, bribery and manipulation of planning consent applications given to Max Cohen by two Council officials. It had all been going on for years. One planning officer had left and gone to live in Marbella and the other one, a woman, was still working for the Council. She and Max were also having an affair. The story was all over the press and media for weeks. All three were remanded in custody until the trial.

Keira had been beside herself with rage and humiliation and totally blamed Iona and Hugh for betraying her dad. Iona contacted Fran after Max's arrest. Fran was still commuting back and forth to Seattle before they all settled back in the house in Middlesex.

'Jesus Fran, you should have heard her! She said Max told her that it was my fault he had been arrested and that Hugh and I had set him up somehow. I told her not to be an eejit that Max must have done something serious. But she just screamed and yelled at me and stormed out. I haven't seen her since. I've lost my girl again Fran.' Iona's voice was flat.

'I'm so sorry. Keira only sees her dad through rose-tinted glasses. If she knew half of what he was capable of and what he had done, she would be horrified I'm sure.' Fran said, not sure at all that Keira would care about what her dad had done. She adored him. 'Hopefully she'll calm down.'

'I won't be holding my breath. His trial starts soon, no idea how long it will last. I phoned up Keira's modelling agency but she is away on a long location photo-shoot in Germany. Just as well she is out of the way, the press guys would hound her if she turned up at his trial. She's been attracting the wrong sort of press coverage herself recently. They are calling her 'Glasgow's Sensational Wild Child', always being photographed staggering out of nightclubs at 2 a.m. I'm worried she'll go too far with all this rebellion act. I think she's like me, got an addictive personality.'

'Try not to let it get to you too much. If he gets sent to prison, she might realise that he really is a criminal.' Fran had crossed her fingers, she needed Max Cohen to be taken out of action. She hadn't been back to Glasgow since he threatened her. Now she was back in England, she should go and see Iona. But if she was honest with herself, she was quite afraid of seeing Max again. It was hard to get the image of his contorted, enraged, hate-filled features out of her mind at her last encounter with him.

He had almost ruined Keira by completely spoiling her. Indulging her every demand for clothes, jewellery and cars and going out of his way to do the exact opposite of what Iona had wanted her for daughter. Fran was also worried that all this stress would set Iona back and that she might start drinking heavily again. She knew that Iona had just started writing again, not poetry, she said her muse had deserted her since her cancer surgery, but she was working on a novel, her first.

'I'll try and get up to see you as soon as I can,' Fran promised.

'I think you might have a few problems to sort out first at home Fran.'

'Too right, I might be coming up on a one-way ticket with a big suitcase and two daughters.' Fran laughed, but her stomach was still in a knot.

Max Cohen pleaded not guilty, but the jury convicted him on the overwhelming evidence against him. He got eight years. The other two conspirators pleaded guilty at their much shorter trials and were each given four-year sentences. Fran slept better the night after Max went to prison than she had for a long time.

Confessions

'So, you're at it again! Who is it this time? Some bimbo from the airlines?' Fran launched right into Rob as he stepped through the front door. She was clutching the phone bill and waved it wildly in his face. Her voice had risen to a hysterical pitch. It quite took her by surprise. She had intended to approach this quite differently; calmly, coldly, detached. She had thought that the wound from Rob's affair with the German Fraulein from years before had healed. Seems that it was merely covered by the thinnest of plasters. In an instant, she was right back in the pain of a heart-pounding, adrenalin-fuelled, jealous rage. She wanted to claw at his face, punch his nose and kick his shins. More. She wanted to kill him.

'No! You're wrong. She – she's just a friend. I promise you. I met her on a flight back from Tokyo. She's a counsellor. We got talking about Catrina …'

Fran spluttered, enraged. 'I don't believe you! Why would you keep her a secret if she is just a friend? If you were worried about Catrina why wouldn't you talk to me about her? When all that drug stuff was going on with Catrina in Seattle you completely shut down. I needed your support too Rob. You just weren't there for me either. You never discuss anything important with me!' She ran out of breath trying to stop the angry tears choking her nose.

Catrina had stopped using drugs now, but her depression had taken a firm hold. She couldn't cope and had dropped out of university. Fran was still desperately worried about her, but Rob rarely wanted to talk about it. Except it seemed, with some random woman he had met on a plane.

'She told me someone from Scotland had called and hung up on her. Was that you Fran, or did you get Iona to call for you?' Rob sounded quite defensive and annoyed.

'What!' Fran yelled. 'She's paranoid and warning you to make up a good story. That's very reassuring. So, come on, tell me what your precious friend wants you to say about you two?'

Rob looked startled. 'How did you know her name was Precious?'

'I didn't, but you have just confirmed it. Iona called that number and her answer machine said to leave a message for Precious. What kind of counsellor would give herself such a stupid childish name like Precious?' Fran was hyperventilating. 'This is it Rob, we're finished. You are lying again; I can't do this anymore. Always on edge with you, never being able to fully trust you, especially after what happened in Germany.' She could not look at him. His handsome features which had always attracted her, seemed closed in. His deep brown eyes were hooded now and blank. She turned to walk out the door.

'Fran. Please, don't just go like that. I can't bear to lose you. There's nothing going on between Precious and me. Honestly. She is just a friend. I'll prove it to you. I'll get her to talk to you, tell you herself that we are just friends.' Rob had stepped in front of her barring her way. He reached out and pulled her in close to his body. 'Please darling, you must trust me. It's you I love and our girls. Give me a chance to convince you.'

How she wanted to believe him. The familiar feel and warm smell of his solid muscular frame took her back to a place and time when she was secure with him. When she loved his masculinity, his decisiveness. When he rescued her from the emotional tyranny of her mother and had promised that he would love her and cherish their lives together until the ends of time. No wait, that was me that said that last bit she remembered. But she desperately wanted to think that he might, just might, be telling the truth this time.

'All right,' she sighed and just for a moment let her body relax against him and managed to shut out the screeching doubts clamouring and knocking inside her head.

'Darling. I've got Precious on the phone. She wants to talk to you, to reassure you that she and I are just friends.' Rob tried to hand the phone to Fran who was just getting dressed. She had not even had her morning cup of tea. Not the best time. Her mouth instantly dried up with nerves. She quickly gulped down the glass of water on the bedside locker. She had refused to share a bed with Rob last night. He was obviously panicking. But 8 a.m.? Who would want this conversation first thing? She shot a furious look at Rob, but had no choice but to take the phone he was holding out to her. She waved him away and shut the bedroom door.

'Hello. I gather you want to talk to me.' She kept her voice firm but her heart was hammering against her ribs and her mouth dried up again. She drained the last mouthful of water from the glass.

The voice was soft and quiet, very well spoken with just a trace of accent that Fran could not quite place. 'Mrs Patterson, I need you to know that Rob and I are just friends. He is more like a father figure to me and he needed someone to talk to about your daughter, Catrina. He is very worried about her and he talks about his family all the time.'

It sounded like a well-rehearsed speech, but Fran let her talk without interrupting. When she finished, Fran, feeling cynical, said. 'I might not have been so suspicious if he had told me about all the phone calls to you and if he didn't already have a history of being unfaithful. He had a long affair with someone some years ago. It's hard to trust him.'

She heard a sharp intake of breath. Silence for a second. Then. 'I'm so sorry that you were worried. I told Rob that he should tell you about our conversations. I can understand why you were suspicious, but Mrs Patterson, I assure you…'

'For goodness sake, call me Fran,' she interrupted. 'As you know so much about me and my family already, Mrs Patterson is a bit unnecessary.' Her voice was sharper than she intended with an edge of sarcasm. 'Since you have taken the trouble to talk to me about it, I suppose I must believe what you say. I don't mind if Rob wants to phone you, we all need friends, but only if he is open and honest about it from now on.'

'Thank you, Fran. Rob truly loves you. He would never leave you. Goodbye.'

Fran exhaled deeply and sat cradling the phone, unable to fully process what had just happened. Surely the women would not have had the nerve to make that call if she was having an affair with Rob? More like a father figure to her. What was that supposed to mean? Probably young and beautiful too.

Some young flirty guy at a recent party had told Fran that fifty was the new forty as he tried a quick grope and told her she was gorgeous. She had felt quite flattered at the time. But now suddenly, approaching fifty and knowing that Rob was confiding in some younger woman, made her feel washed up and threatened. She wasn't ready to let it go. She pulled the bedroom door open, Rob was pacing nervously up and down the hall. Fran wondered if he had heard any of the conversation.

'Well. Do you believe me now?' He was still sounding defensive and was looking at a point just above Fran's head. She could see that even through his tanned skin, his cheeks were flushed.

'I suppose I'll have to believe you Rob but I just don't understand why you had to be so secretive about her. When did you meet her?'

'When we were living in Seattle and we were going through that really difficult time with Catrina. I got talking to her on a flight out of Tokyo when I was a passenger and she was sitting next to me. I ended up telling her about my family and how worried we were about Cat...' his voice trailed off.

'That was two years ago! You never thought to mention her to me before now?'

'Because I knew you would jump to the wrong conclusion and I just needed someone to talk to about everything.' Rob sounded defensive again.

Fran's chest tightened painfully. He had no idea that those words were just as hurtful as if he had admitted to an affair. Rob would never open up to her, to explain his feelings. He was a closed book, always retreating into himself or disappearing off to the gym or squash court whenever she tried to have a meaningful conversation with him. Yet here he was, apparently involved in a long phone friendship with another woman whom he *could* talk to.

'What's she like? Is she young? She has an accent, where is she from?' Fran couldn't help herself, she had to know what was so special about this friend who could make her taciturn husband garrulous.

'Does it matter?' Rob tried to put his arms around Fran. She pushed him away.

'Yes, it does matter. Tell me. Is she Asian, I can't quite place the accent?'

'She is about thirty-five and she is originally from Uganda. Her family were Ugandan Asians and had to get out the country when Idi Amin started his purge. They fled to Germany but her mother died soon after. Her father married again to a German woman.'

Fran had an immediate image of a beautiful, olive-skinned, petite woman with long silky black hair and big, doe brown eyes gazing up adoringly at her handsome husband. She felt sick.

'OK. If you must have someone to talk to other than me about our private family affairs, then the least you can do is to be transparent about it from now on. I still have several male friends from my working days, but you know about them. I always tell you when I meet people when you are away.' Fran still felt sick but decided that this was the best strategy if she was going to come close to believing him about his relationship with this woman. He did not have too many friends anyway outside of aviation, maybe an outlet with this person who claimed to be a counsellor would be good for him. But, she could not be comfortable with this odd relationship.

He phoned her a few times when Fran was there, but she was oddly respectful of his privacy and didn't eavesdrop. Which would have been difficult anyway, as he always disappeared into the dining room to speak to her. He had a mobile phone too, but she never saw the bills from Vodaphone.

'Iona, do you mind if I bring Catrina up to Glasgow with me this trip?' She's not in a very good space. Quite depressed. I don't want to leave her on her own. Jess is away at university, staying in digs. I need to get away too. I've just found out that Rob *does* have a secret phone friend. That Precious woman you called for me. It's a long story, hope you can cope with me unloading on you?'

'Sure, but it sounds ominous Fran. Catrina can have Keira's room. She has only been here once since Max went to prison and that was only to dump some of her things she rescued from his house before it was sold. I haven't seen her for weeks.'

Fran could hear the pain in Iona's voice. Clearly Keira, was still blaming her mum for reporting her dad to the police. I've got to put that right Fran thought to herself, it's me she should be blaming. It's my fault. But she couldn't help being pleased that Max was locked up and in a roundabout way, finally paying for his probable part in the death of Harrison.

Iona was looking better, although she still had dark shadows contrasting with the startling blue of her eyes. She had gained a bit of weight and now there were two rounded shapes under her top where before, she had refused to wear a prosthetic breast.

'How's the book coming along?' asked Fran as Iona made them a drink. Catrina was gazing intently at photographs of Keira on the sideboard from when she was a toddler with unruly dark curls, through to the latest ones of her modelling a range of outdoor wear. Even in walking books, heavy trousers and waterproof jacket, she still looked incredibly beautiful, leaning casually against a wind-blown rowan tree with her long dark curls flowing out behind her.

'It's nearly finished, on the final draft now. My publisher wants it by next month so that we can plan a book launch to coincide with the Cameron Mitchell Book Fair in Edinburgh next autumn. I've had a bit of a writer's block since all this carry-on with Max's trial and Keira's dramas.' Iona blew out her cheeks. 'Never mind, maybe I'll get re-energised now that you are here Fran.'

'I hope we don't get in your way staying here. Iona, do you mind if I give Keira a call to see if she will meet up in town with me and Catrina? I think Cat would enjoy chatting to another young person. It might cheer her up.'

'You can try if you like. I don't know if she is still staying with that photographer from the agency. Max couldn't stand him. He was jealous of anyone who showed an interest in Keira. Control freak, so he is.'

'He won't have much control over anyone for a while now, will he?'

'He still managed to turn Keira against me even after he was arrested.' Iona furiously scribbled down Keira's phone number.

'Keira, it's Fran. I'm up in Glasgow with Catrina for a few days. We'd love to see you; are you free any time in the next couple of days?'

'Oh, hi Fran. Yes, sure, that would be great. I'm free tomorrow morning. Do you know Mario's Place in Argyle St? I could meet you there at eleven.'

Keira sounded pleased to hear from Fran, they always got on well. She had a little smile to herself. Keira sounded terribly well-spoken for a Glasgow girl. The benefits of an expensive private education, polished off by mixing with an eclectic group of people from the modelling agency she supposed.

'Great. We'll see you tomorrow then.'

'Are you staying with Mum?' Keira asked quickly.

'Yes of course, I always do. She's busy trying to get her book finished.' She did not want Keira to think that this was a set-up and that Iona might be coming along too. She needed to find an opportunity to speak to Keira alone and explain her part in Max's downfall. To take the blame away from Iona. She held her breath, wondering if Keira might change her mind.

There was a short silence then, 'OK.' she added breezily. Relieved? 'See you tomorrow.'

Very quickly, Catrina and Keira were behaving like the best of friends. Heads together, giggling at some shared joke. Fran was delighted to see her daughter light up in Keira's company. They both had a quirky sense of humour. It reminded Fran of the way she and Iona used to carry on when they were young and finding absurd things to laugh about. Fran was still hoping for a chance to have a quiet word with Keira on her own, but the opportunity had not presented itself yet.

'Cara! Here you are. Call me later, we have work to do this afternoon.' The tall, extremely attractive dark-haired, olive-skinned young man placed proprietorial hands on Keira's shoulders and kissed the top of her head. His eyes however were focussed on Catrina. 'Who are these two beautiful ladies?' he enquired, his heavy accent, liquid gold. Fran gave him brownie points for at least including her in his appraisal.

'Fran and Catrina, meet my boyfriend, Angelo. He is a photographer with the agency. He does most of my photo shoots.' she added, leaning her head back against him for a moment.

I never saw anyone who looked less like an angel thought Fran as she extended her hand to the Adonis with the camera, noticing the appreciative gleam in his brown eyes as he gazed intently at Catrina.

'*Ciao!*' purred Angelo, shaking Fran's hand briefly before taking Catrina's hand in both of his. '*Bellissima!* You should be a model,' he murmured to Catrina. 'You have the most beautiful bone structure and those eyes! The colour of amber.'

Fran glanced quickly at Keira, wondering how she was reacting to her boyfriend's blatant flirting, but she seemed indifferent, merely looking across at Angelo with mild amusement as he fawned over Catrina.

Catrina on the other hand was looking flustered, but Fran could see what Angelo meant. Her large eyes were the most unusual colour of amber, flecked with green and framed with dark arched eyebrows and long black lashes. She had inherited her father's high cheekbones and Fran's wide, generous mouth and her rich chestnut hair waved softly around her shoulders. But surely modelling would be the last thing Catrina would want to do? She had just dropped out of university and was considering going travelling to India with a girlfriend. She wanted to 'find' herself.

'Seriously, if you are interested, I can take some photos of you for a portfolio. My camera will love you, I can tell. Let Keira know and we can arrange it. I must go now. *Arrividerci belle donne!*' With another lingering kiss for Keira, he was gone.

'Angelo is right Cat, you are beautiful and you could be a model, you are tall and slim enough. It is hard work but the money is good. I can show you how to pose and you can borrow some of my clothes if you want Angelo to take some pictures of you. I'll chaperone you, Angelo likes women too much!' she added with a laugh.

'I don't think I could be a model. I hate dressing up. Where's the loo here?' Catrina stood up abruptly and sloped off to the toilet. Looking at her retreating back in her ripped jeans and Doc Martin boots, Fran could not imagine her troubled daughter modelling designer clothes and being made up to the nines. Not her style.

'Keira, I need to tell you something important quickly, while we are alone.' Fran placed a hand over Keira's in an unconscious conciliatory gesture. 'Your dad, Max. It was me who. triggered the investigation that led to his arrest. Not your mum, please don't blame her.'

Keira look strangely at Fran.' What do you mean? You were in Seattle for two years.'

'I know, but years ago, Harrison, you remember Harrison don't you?'

Keira nodded. 'Of course, I loved Harrison.'

'Well,' Fran continued rapidly 'Harrison threatened to expose your dad for bribing a planning officer over a property development deal when you were a baby. Harrison was attacked and died from his injuries a few years later, when he was living with your mum and you in Byres Rd. A man called Dougie Black was blamed and went to prison. I'm sorry Keira, but I always thought your dad had ordered that beating in revenge against Harrison.'

Keira's eyes never left Fran's face, but she pulled her hand away.

'The last time I was in Glasgow, after your mum's operation, I went to see Max and told him that Dougie Black had contacted the *Express*, wanting to sell his story when he was released from prison. I told him that Dougie was implicating your dad. Keira, he almost confessed, saying that Harrison got what he deserved and that nobody could pin anything on him. He threw me out, but I had taped the conversation. I handed the tape over to someone in the *Express* and that is what triggered the investigation into Max's corrupt property deals.' Fran spoke in torrents, wanting to let Keira understand why she had exposed her father. She did not mention that it was Hugh she had given the tape to, that wouldn't help her cause at this point.

'Dougie Black was the man drowned in the Kelvin. Do you think my dad had something to do with that too?'

'I really don't know, Keira, but if he did, then I am also partly responsible for that, because I lied to your dad about Dougie Black threatening to expose him. I just made that up to get a reaction from him. I am just going to have to live with that, but I can't bear to see your mum suffering. She needs you back in her life. It's me you should be mad with.'

'I am mad with you, Fran. My dad might have been a bit of a wheeler-dealer, but he would never be involved in having someone killed. I don't think I can ever forgive you for your part in sending him to prison.' Keira spoke loudly enough for half the people in the café to hear her. 'Tell Cat to give me a call if she wants to meet up. I'm going.' She stood up immediately, pushing her chair back and without looking again at Fran, walked quickly out into the street and disappeared.

Fran breathed out. Well at least she had let Iona off the hook even if she now was persona non-grata with Keira. Hopefully Keira would reconnect with her mother. Fran knew she would be paying the price of losing Keira's high regard for her, but it was worth it for Iona's sake.

Two old biddies who were sitting at the nearest table were agog with interest. One woman leaned over and patted Fran's arm. 'Never you mind hen. They young yins are aw the same. They watch too much telly these days. Nae respect for the auld yins. Sounds like that dad of hers deserved all he got.' She got up and she and her companion, nodding in sage agreement, wandered away without needing or expecting a reply from Fran.

Fran smiled ruefully. Only in Glasgow were such unsolicited opinions handed out with total unconscious equanimity.

Catrina was surprised and a bit put out that Keira had left without saying goodbye, but cheered up when Fran passed on the message about getting in touch if she wanted too. At least she's not cutting Catrina out of her life she thought and they left before anyone else in the café had an opinion to share.

Over a few glasses of red wine and a whiskey or two for Iona, Fran poured out her story about Rob's latest betrayal. OK, so apparently, they weren't having an affair they had claimed, but the whole secretive thing just felt wrong to Fran. Iona added helpfully, that most men never had relationships with women without trying to get into their knickers at some point in the proceedings. Still, they both agreed that the Precious woman at least had enough bottle to phone up and deny everything, so perhaps, just give them the benefit of the doubt. As Iona pointed out, Fran led a comfortable life and Rob was away a lot. Now that the girls were grown up, she could reinvent herself if she wanted. They talked around the topic for a long time, until finally, Fran decided that as soon as she went back home she would enquire about retraining as a massage therapist.

Something she had been interested in for years but never had the opportunity to pursue, as they had been trailing after Rob and his overseas contracts. Jess seemed quite stable and was enjoying her final year of her degree course, but Catrina was still a worry. She insisted that she wasn't using drugs any more, but she was very unstable and had not been able to keep a job for long since she dropped out of university. All she wanted to do was to travel to India. Fran worried about her constantly, her bouts of depression were debilitating at times.

Now that she had told Keira what she had done to Max, and probably permanently, had lost her connection with Keira, Fran knew that she would need to come clean with Iona too. Did she run the risk of Iona's wrath and maybe damaging their friendship as well? But, she had kept this secret for too long. She took a deep breath and another long swig of her glass of Pinot Noir.

'I have something to confess Iona, it's about Max…' Before she could say more, Iona interrupted.

'It's all right Fran. I know about the tape. Hugh told me. He can't keep anything to himself for long.'

Fran felt her cheeks flame. 'Why didn't you tell Keira what I had done? She might not have reacted so badly against you if she had known it was me.'

'There was no point in both of us being blamed. Remember that it was Hugh who passed your tape to the police, so she would still have hated me for not stopping Hugh. Not that I knew about it until after Max was arrested.'

'Would you have stopped him if you had known?' Fran asked hesitantly.

'No, he's a crook. I know him Fran, he is a mean bastard and would have been determined to take revenge on Harrison. I'm glad he got a prison sentence, although Keira is devastated. I think she knows that her father is bent, but just doesn't want to admit it. She has had him on a pedestal since she met him.'

'What will she do now that Max's allowance for her has stopped.' Fran was both very relieved and touched that her friend seemed untroubled. Iona had kept the tape recording a secret from Keira to protect Fran's relationship. That was extremely noble of her to accept the blame-and Keira's wrath.

'She'll be fine. Max set up a trust fund for her when he got access to her years ago, and she is old enough to draw money out of it now. She wants to be an actress and was talking about enrolling in the Royal Scottish Academy for Music and Drama in Renfrew Street the last time I spoke to her. Mind you that was months ago now, it all might have changed.'

'She seemed pretty close with her photographer friend Angelo this morning and they had a photo shoot arranged for this afternoon, so she is obviously still with the agency. Trouble is, after I told her what I had done, she cut me dead, so I won't be able to talk with her again any time soon. Although she is still friends with Catrina, so we might find out from her what is going on.'

Catrina phoned about midnight to say that she was staying overnight at Keira's place. She had gone back out that evening to meet up with Keira and Angelo and some other friends 'to have a few drinks and then on to a nightclub.' Fran's stomach knotted a bit with anxiety, hoping that her girl would stay safe and not be tempted to take drugs or drink too much. For heaven's sake, relax she told herself. Catrina is old enough to look after herself now. It's good that she is having a social life.

Fran could tell that Iona was pleased that Catrina and Keira were together and seemingly forming a friendship. It was helping to keep Keira in the fold and maybe she might eventually get over her rage against her mother? Fran didn't hold out much hope for her broken relationship though. Still, it was a small price to pay if it helped reunite Iona with her daughter.

Catrina arrived back at Iona's house late the next day looking tired but more relaxed and chilled than Fran had seen her in a long time.

'Mum, Angelo took lots of photographs of me and wants to show them to the modelling agency. He and Keira think I could be a model, but I don't think anything will come of it.

Anyway, I still want to travel to India.' Catrina tried to sound all nonchalant, but Fran could tell that she was faking her disinterest.

Looking at her scruffy daughter in her ripped jeans and unkempt hair, (at least the Doc Marten boots had been discarded in the hall) Fran silently agreed that probably nothing would come of it.

'Well let's wait and see if they get in touch with you and then you can decide if you want to follow it up or not.' Maybe photographic modelling would be marginally less dangerous than trekking around India Fran thought. Why couldn't her daughter take up something safe and predictable like teaching or nursing? Bad idea, on reflection. That just wasn't Cat, another volatile and free-spirited soul, just like Iona had been at that age.

Rob was phoning her almost every day when she was in Glasgow. Obviously terrified that she might not come back.

'Darling when are you coming home? We need to talk. I miss you. I have a two-week trip via Japan and the U.S. scheduled. I really want to see you before I leave.' He sounded a bit desperate.

'Of course I'm coming back Rob, but I can tell you that I am still feeling uncomfortable about your so-called friendship. I just wish you had been honest about it.'

'I promise I will be from now on. I can't lose you.' Echoes of an ancient pledge.

Why did it all have to be so difficult? It all took so much energy and Fran felt totally weary of the effort involved. It was time for her to move on with *her* life and pursue a career path before she was too old to do anything constructive. Since her girls had been born, she accepted that she had sublimated all her natural drive and ambition for a career and had sunk her energy into motherhood and trying to keep the family unit intact by following Rob around the world.

Seeing Iona just getting on with writing her book and painting, despite all the negative crap she had dealt with recently, gave Fran the incentive she needed to make some decisions. She had to accept now that there was little prospect of Rob's self-centred ways ever changing. God knows she had waited patiently enough. Could she have done things differently? Would it have made any impact on Rob's behaviour? Probably not. Did she dislike living with him enough to leave him and her relatively comfortable life? Honestly, she didn't think so. Not a good time for a mid-life crisis. After all, they had shared some good times. Not many, but enough not to justify unravelling their marriage and family. She tried to push to the back of her mind, the unsettling thoughts that Rob's bizarre friendship with this Precious woman had stirred up and decided just to get on with it. It was a choice. They went home.

'Rob, I have decided that I want to retain as a massage therapist, but it will be at least a year before I can start treating clients.' Fran and Rob had just shared a 'landing drink' before going out for a meal at their favourite Italian restaurant. They always ate out on the first night when Rob returned from a long-haul trip. Fran quite enjoyed these evenings. Rob was relaxed and unwinding from his long flight home. She was pleased to see him. Always experiencing fresh hope about their relationship and basking in the pleasure of looking at his handsome features over the candlelit table. Anticipating the intense, but largely silent coupling that would follow at bedtime. Perhaps a deeper level of communication? Optimism triumphing over experience.

Rob just shrugged. 'Why don't you go back into the recruiting business? You made a lot of money doing that. Don't know why you had to give it all up.'

She felt her gut tighten in irritation. Not that old chestnut again! Jesus, would he ever let that go? He had never forgiven her for giving up her lucrative business to devote herself to being a mother. She took a deep breath. This was not the time for another verbal slinging match. She needed him to cooperate with her plans. It would cost quite a bit to get trained, although she was eligible for an Individual Learning Account from the Government.

'Yes, I know. It was a shame, but I think it was the right decision for us then. I'm glad that I was able to be there for our girls and that's down to you Rob, being willing to support us all these years.' She held his hand and smiled impishly at him. 'You can be my guinea pig for my massage practise if you like.' She hated herself for being so obviously manipulative, but knew how Rob would respond.

Rob's expression changed. 'That could be fun. Do you want to start practising now?' He lunged at her and pulled her body in hard against him. Fran wondered if they would get their usual table when they turned up late at the restaurant.

Millennium Moments

It was just after the Millennium. 'Hi Fran. What a coincidence. James bumped into Rob in Richmond yesterday. He saw him in Tesco's buying a box of chocolates.' Fran's stomach lurched as her friend elaborated on the chances of the two men meeting in Richmond when they both lived in Middlesex. Rob's phone friend, Precious, lived in Richmond apparently. However, he hadn't spoken about Precious for ages and she had not heard him on the phone to her either. Fran had almost forgotten about her.

And here was me thinking that our life had settled into a tolerable place she thought as the adrenaline coursed through her veins making her heart beat painfully against her chest.

It had taken her a few years to build up her repertoire of holistic treatments. She had managed her own successful practice in her local town for a while and then after gaining a postgraduate teaching certificate, started a training school for therapists. She was as fulfilled as she could be, doing a job she loved. The girls were reasonably fine, Jess working as an Occupational Therapist and Catrina, after travelling through India for a year and 'finding her true self', was living in Glasgow with Keira and doing some freelance photographic modelling and God knows what else. She and Rob had been managing to get along when he was at home. He was easier to live with now that the girls had left home. Less competition for her time and attention.

She had been away for a day or two running a training course in Kettering, Rob was at home more often now as he was flying for a U.K.-based air freight company. They were often both away from home from time to time and usually checked in with one another. But, there had been no mention of the domiciliary visit to Precious.

'Here we go again.' Fran spoke out loud at her pale reflection in the mirror after she hung up the phone. She wondered what the story would be this time.

'I didn't mention it because I knew you would react like this.' Rob tried to walk away from her as she confronted him, her voice approaching fever-pitch. 'I was putting a new unit in her kitchen, that was all. There is nothing going on between us Fran. I swear to you.'

'Give me a break. I'm not stupid!' Fran pushed him hard in his chest as he turned toward her and tried to pull her into his arms.

'Darling please, she's got cancer. Precious has cancer. I just wanted to help her.'

Fran's rage evaporated. 'Oh, I'm sorry to hear that Rob, but why in heaven's name did you not just tell me? With our history, I'm obviously going to think the worst. Where's the cancer?'

'It was the cervix, but she's had surgery and hopefully she'll make a good recovery. But she was scared Fran. She doesn't have any close friends or family to support her. She told me to tell you that I was helping her out so that you wouldn't feel threatened after the last time with the phone call thing. I should have told you. I'm sorry. I love you Fran. Please believe me.' Rob held her shoulders and gazed into her face. His dark brown eyes glistened with unshed tears. Tears for her or for Precious?

'OK Rob. I believe you, but you must not lie to me again about this. I've had enough deceit. This marriage won't survive otherwise.' She walked away.

California Dreaming

'They want to make a film from my book Fran! I had a call this mornin'. I can't believe it.' Iona's usual breathy voice was crackling with excitement. They want me to fly out to Hollywood next week to work on the script. I'm taking Keira with me too.'

'Oh my, Iona, that's incredible! Congratulations. How long will you be gone? Fran felt a mixture of delight for Iona's success and stomach-churning pain at the prospect of her friend leaving the country.

'Don't know exactly, but it could be a while. Fran if you come up to see Cat, will you drop in on Hugh? He's not been too well recently, it's angina and he doesn't want to be travelling for now.'

'Of course I will.' Fran experienced a stab of anxiety realising that Catrina, without Keira on the scene, might be feeling abandoned. The two girls had grown close in the last few years sharing a flat in the west end of Glasgow. Angelo had been replaced by a series of young aspiring actors on the same acting course at the R.S.A in Glasgow. Keira had been offered small parts in one or two British movies filmed at Pinewood Studios. The lure of Hollywood was too compelling to ignore.

Maybe Catrina would come back down south now. She had done some modelling for fashion clothing catalogues, but was spending a lot of time with a Glasgow band called 'Intake', who were trying to break into the music scene. Their music was a fusion of folk, rock and ballads, all penned by two of the band members. Catrina had offered them some of her own songs and was thrilled when they recorded a couple on their latest album.

Fran was overwhelmed with her mixed emotions when Iona finally hung up. She was not too surprised that a contract to make a film of Iona's book had been signed. Her debut novel had shot to the top of the bestseller list for psychological thrillers within six months of publication. Almost unprecedented for a new author, but it was a riveting tale of love and rivalry, set in rural Ireland and in the business heartland of Glasgow. Iona had clearly drawn on some of her experiences with Liam, the love of her life and the corrupt Max Cohen.

What would happen to their friendship now she wondered? She had a feeling that once in California, Iona and Keira would get caught up in the lifestyle there and not want to come back. Iona had not travelled much before now. Life in the U.S.A. could be very seductive as Fran well knew. I hope we don't lose touch she thought, I don't know how I will cope without our regular visits and phone calls. She keeps me sane. Nobody makes me laugh as much as she does. Poor Rob, so easy on the eye, but with a sense of humour as barren as the Gobi Desert.

'I've resigned Fran I have had enough of flying a dodgy plane and living out of a suitcase in third-rate hotels.' Rob made his unexpected announcement after returning from a particularly long flight. His aircraft had been grounded in China because the struggling freight company had to fly out a replacement part for the ageing 747. He had been grumbling about this company for a while which he had joined when he was close to retirement age for aviators. Unlike the flag carriers he had always flown with, this freight company cut costs at every opportunity and the owner frequently didn't pay his airport maintenance bills on time, which often caused delays.

'How are we going to manage without your salary Rob?' He had made a huge decision without talking it through with her. Yet again, she experienced that helpless rage around him and his inability to communicate with her. This could be life-changing for them. She was deeply concerned.

'Don't worry Fran,' he said confidently, 'I've been talking to some people I met a while ago at an air show in Singapore and I am going to set up as a broker selling executive jets. I have made some good contacts. We'll be fine, the commissions for brokering a sale are very good. Huge actually.'

Trouble was, he was under her feet all the time, glued to the phone or his computer. Although, Fran couldn't help being impressed by his commitment and knowledge. He could talk about all things involved in aviation in mind-numbing detail.

By default, Fran learned all the specifications for the executive jets his wealthy clients were either wanting to sell or upgrade to. She was soon as familiar as Rob was, with the selling points of Bombadiers, Cessnas, Dassaults, Gulfstream or the Hawker Range private jets. He made more useful contacts at the large aircraft exhibitions in Geneva, Paris and Farnborough, but no sales were ever made and soon they were living on their bank overdraft and credit cards. Rob had not taken into full account the huge amounts of upfront money required to market the aircraft effectively. Or indeed how competitive the market was.

He continued to work obsessively at his business, convinced that the big sales were just about to be made, but the months rolled into almost two years without an income. At least nothing that Fran was aware of. Time and time again the strict requirements for the sales of the aircraft imposed by the U.K. C.A.A or E.A.S.A, held up the transaction and Rob lost the business.

Fran had been as supportive as she could be, but they were drowning in debt. She certainly was not earning enough money to cover all their bills. Rob barely spoke to her about anything other than his business. She was glad to get away to run her training courses and have some interaction with enthusiastic adults. How she wished that Rob would accept his situation and get another job. She was getting angry and stressed, he was so damn stubborn, wouldn't give up on his dream of making a fortune. They had to re-mortgage. Fixed rate, interest only repayment for two years, but still barely affordable.

'Have a break Fran. Come to California for a few days. I'm dying to show you where we live. You need to see this apartment and the view. It's out of this world!' Before Fran had a chance to answer, Iona added. 'I'll pay for your airline ticket. It's not a problem. They are paying me obscene amounts of money over here!'

Fran was thrilled at the chance to get away for a few days from the intense atmosphere at home. Rob was growing desperate and frustrated as yet another sale fell through. He was short-tempered and difficult. He still wanted to make love to her regularly, which she was struggling with more and more. Did he not understand that the last thing she felt like doing was being close in bed with him at night when she had not had a pleasant word out of him all day?

'Also, got some amazing news.' Iona rushed on after Fran had accepted her kind offer. 'Keira's been offered a small talking part in the movie they're making of my book! She's over the moon about it.'

Fran laughed. 'A touch of nepotism there Iona?'

'Of course! I'm pally with the producer. But seriously, she did well at the audition. You should hear her Californian accent. Got it off to a T.'

'Fantastic. I'll hear all about it when I arrive. Thanks for asking Catrina to move in with Hugh, she says she gets on better with him than she does with her own dad.'

'Glad it's working out for them. I can't persuade Hugh to come out to Hollywood. Says the superficiality would drive him insane. He also says Catrina is easy to live with, particularly as she isn't at home a lot! Still, I'm glad he's got some company. He seems to be very tired these days. He's on pills for his heart. Maybe that's what doing it.'

Fran checked in with Catrina and Jess after she had booked her flight to California. Jess promised to visit her dad with her new boyfriend if she could and Catrina told her that she was now singing with her band 'Intake' and that they had gigs booked in Edinburgh, Dundee and Perth. Fran had been amazed at how talented Catrina was at writing lyrics and coming up with the basic tune for her songs. Duncan, the lead guitarist was a talented, trained musician and he did the arrangements for Cat's songs. They obviously were in a relationship, but Catrina as usual did not have much to give away about that. Still she seemed to be happier than she had been for years. Jess had been dating her chap for a few weeks now and seemed very keen on him. At least her girls seemed to be getting on all right with their lives. Rob wasn't too thrilled that she was leaving, but didn't try to dissuade her either. She couldn't wait to get away.

New Reality

'Fran, Rob has collapsed in the garden!' Their next-door neighbour was banging and shouting at the front door. Fran rushed out. Rob was lying on his back gasping and choking. His face distorted, his eyes rolled back. His limbs scrabbling uselessly at the grass. She knew at once that he had had a stroke.

'Call an ambulance!' she screamed at the neighbour, who was still standing at the door, white faced and shaking. Fran bent over Rob trying to pull him over into the recovery position. How the hell does that work? She could not remember, but did her best to turn his body so that she could clear his airway. 'Rob! Rob! Can you hear me? The ambulance is coming; you are going to be fine.' He tried to say something but it came out as a guttural mumble. The ambulance arrived and within minutes they were off to the hospital. Blue lights flashing. Sirens screaming.

'Your husband has suffered a serious insult to his brain.' The medic's quaint term for a stroke or a seizure. 'The MRI scan shows a large area of damage to the cerebellum. Part of the visual cortex has been destroyed, so he will be irreversibly visually compromised. He may never fully recover his balance impairments either, although some improvements can go on for up to ten years or more.' He added optimistically, staring intently at his notes.

Surely he can't be talking about Rob? He's so strong and fit. He will make a good recovery from this. I've learned a lot about how the body functions. I'll help him get over this. There must be a way. Fran convinced herself that the doctor was exaggerating. Giving her the worst-case scenario. They often do that, don't they?

Rob lay unconscious for ten days after his stroke. Fran stayed for hours at his bedside, stunned and unable to comprehend what was happening. Why won't he wake up?

'Rob come on. Open your eyes, please wake up.' she implored him softly, willing him to come to, conscious of the patients in the opposite beds watching her. Nothing else for them to do.

Nil by mouth. She watched in horror as his handsome, rugged features shrivelled and hollowed, the bruise from the hastily inserted cannula spreading over the back of his hand. At other times, all she could do was to lay her head on his bed, and let the desperate tears flow. Helpless and exhausted.

Her daughters visited. Catrina flew down from Glasgow and she and Jess kept vigil with her for a while, comforting her and trying to come to terms with their own confusions and distress at seeing their dad inert and absent. None of them sure if he would ever wake up again. What if he *didn't* recover? Or worse if he did recover and was completely disabled? She had seen people who had survived serious strokes. Some were blind, had lost the power of speech or were wheelchair bound. This couldn't be happening. He must recover from this. I won't let him become an invalid. It was the stroke consultant who finally dragged him back to awareness.

'Mr Patterson. Rob. Open your eyes,' he commanded in a loud authoritative voice.

Rob's eyes fluttered open and he grunted unintelligibly. For the first few days, he was unable to talk or move and it was obvious that he was almost blind. And still, they wouldn't give him anything by mouth in case his swallow reflex wasn't working. Watching him lick his cracked lips and needing a drink was too much for Fran. She gave him a tiny mouthful of yoghurt and he swallowed it easily. She told the nurse and they came and carried out a swallow test and after that, when he could eat and drink, his face filled out a bit, although he was still terribly gaunt. I wonder how long they would have left him on IV fluids if I hadn't intervened, thought Fran.

His rehabilitation went on for weeks in the stroke ward in hospital and Fran spent hours with him, trying out various alternative treatment which she had read would stimulate new neural pathways in his brain. She had seen the MRI scan. There weren't too many neural pathways left to stimulate. Just acres of white, dead brain cells. He had seemed quite optimistic at first. Light years away from acceptance of what had happened. Convinced that his eyesight and his balance would return to normal. They did not. He came home

'Rob, you need to accept that your eyesight is probably as good as it will get. It's time to come to terms with everything. You've had a stroke. It could be worse.' It got worse.

'There's no point going there/doing that. I can't see anything!' That became Rob's angry mantra for anything Fran suggested to get him out of the house. He raged and sulked, his anger and disbelief over his lost eyesight festering. A canker, eating away at his soul. Fran did her best to keep him motivated. Desperately wanting him to make the best of his new situation. Their situation.

She had to wind down her business as Rob couldn't look after himself now. Jess was back at home temporarily. Her relationship had failed and she took the opportunity to be at home to help Fran with Rob. Jess put on her Occupational Therapist's hat and tried to get him to be a bit independent and at least learn to make a cup of tea and a sandwich for himself. But he refused to try and had to have everything done for him. Using his bad eyesight as his excuse for not trying to help himself.

He got an electric wheelchair, but wouldn't go out in it unless Fran or Jess walked along beside him. They tried to take him on outings in the car but always had to take a fold-up manual wheelchair with them as he could not walk very far. At least he can still go to the loo by himself, I couldn't stand it if I end up having to clean him up. Fran consoled herself with the small positives. But, he refuses to sit down in the shower. Insists on standing, hanging on precariously to the newly installed grab handles. He takes forever under the shower, can't leave him in case he falls. And the drying process, talk about obsessive compulsive! Insists on having in between each toe dried, but can't do it himself. Drives me mad. It all takes so long. I wonder if he will ever improve a bit, but it has been four months now and nothing seems to be any better. Thank goodness Jess is here. Not sure if I could cope without her and still manage to keep working.

Fran was in Dublin running a therapists' training course when Rob called.

He sounded distressed. 'It's Precious, she's dead. She died. It was the cancer, it spread…' His voice trailed off.

'Oh, I'm so sorry to hear that, Rob. I had no idea she was so ill. You didn't tell me.' Fran tried to sound sympathetic, but the existence of Precious had been a troublesome shadow since the day she had phoned to deny any affair with Rob-twelve years previously. Had it been that long? At least she could stop thinking and wondering and still feeling suspicious every time Rob contacted Precious. She had not heard Rob on the phone with the woman for a long time. Not that it mattered now anyway. Rob was hardly in any state to be straying from his marital bed. She did wonder though, who had contacted him to tell him that Precious had died? He had told Fran that Precious did not have any family or many friends. But someone must have known about her connection with Rob. Jess phoned.

'Mum, Dad asked me to take him to the funeral. We're in Richmond waiting to go into the service.'

'Jess, you're joking! He can hardly walk. Why would he want to go all that way to a funeral? I can't get him out of the house normally.' Fran was incandescent. What was he thinking? He had no business asking Jess to take him to this funeral. He had not mentioned to Fran that he wanted to go.

'Sorry Mum. I thought you should know.' Jess sounded stressed.

'Don't worry, Jess. He should never have asked you. We'll talk about it when you get home. Just drive carefully. My flight from Dublin leaves soon. I should be home before you.' Fran hung up, shaking with rage. What a selfish bastard he was. Jess was a soft touch. He knew that she would not refuse him, just as clearly as he knew that Fran would never have been prepared to drag them both to *this* funeral. Some friend. This time she listened to her intuition. She knew now exactly why he had wanted to go so badly.

'So you *did* have an affair with Precious then?' Fran waited until they were in bed before confronting him. Jess had gone to stay with a friend for a few days. They had not talked any more about the events of the funeral when Jess arrived home with him. They were both exhausted and Jess left almost immediately. Enough drama for one day. Silence. 'Well?'

'Yes. But it only lasted a short time and it has been over for years.'

'How long is a short time?' Fran hissed through her teeth, aware that what felt like a red mist was blinding her vision. Now she understood bind rage – and why people got killed during it.

'I don't remember – a couple of years, but I've always loved you Fran. You know that, don't you?'

'No I don't. I don't believe you either. First the German girl and now this. You just can't help yourself, can you? Makes me wonder how many other affairs you've had. You are a serial womaniser. I wish now I had left you years ago. Before you had your stupid stroke.'

'Please darling. Please don't leave me. I need you.' His voice broke. Tears. Stroke does that. Brings the emotions to the surface.

Fran flung herself out of bed. Turning at the bedroom door. 'I can't leave you now. Can I? But this marriage is finished. Don't worry, I'll still take care of you. I don't have any choice.' She left the bedroom and slept downstairs. She could hear him crying. She felt cold and numb, drained of further emotion.

A few weeks later he had a massive seizure and descended into confusion and paranoia. He was in hospital for three weeks, totally delusional. Convinced that the nursing staff were trying to poison him and refusing his medication. Fran was stunned at the complete personality change in him. He was behaving like a madman. Had she caused him to have a seizure by being so harsh with him after he confessed to the affair with Precious? The thought tormented her. How was she to look after him now?

'Mum, it was awful.' Jess broke down sobbing. Fran, Jess and Catrina had just come back from visiting Rob in hospital. He was completely off his head, thinking that they were plotting to kill him. They were clones of their real selves. It was very unsettling. They were having a glass of wine or two and Fran had opened the topic of Rob's infidelities and her unresolved anger about him forcing Jess to take him to the woman's funeral. It seemed pointless now trying to pretend. But there was more. 'Dad threw himself over her coffin at the end of the service and wept uncontrollably. I was completely shocked. When I managed to get him out of the church and back into the car, I asked him what that was all about. He finally told me that their affair started in Germany when he was working for Vultura Airlines. Her real name is Suzanna. She was a flight attendant…'

'Precious is Suzanna? That was twenty-nine years ago!' Fran gasped in disbelief. 'Does that mean…?'

'Yes Mum, it does. He was leading a double-life. She followed him to Saudia. It was so obvious at the wake that her friends and family knew him well. They were all consoling him as if he had lost a partner. Even her father came over and hugged him.' Jess completely broke down in tears. 'Oh Mum, it was so humiliating. One of Suzanna's friends, an ex-Saudia flight attendant, said she remembered me and Catrina when we were little girls! They all must have known that Dad had a family, that he was still married to you. I'm so sorry, but he made me promise not to tell you.'

Fran was numb. Her history had been shot to pieces. Her whole marriage had been a joke, a hurtful deceit. Every memory tainted. All those trips to London that Rob was always desperate to arrange when they were living in the Middle East and Seattle. All to spend time with his mistress. His other life. He was well named, a robber of truth. How could he have betrayed his family for so long and then, the final insult, making his daughter a party to the whole sordid mess? Fran felt that she would never forgive him for that act alone. She had long given up on trying to feel love for Rob, but she thought that they had a reasonable working relationship. Not much worse than most of the other middle-aged couples she knew. She had settled for mediocrity. She got total blow-out.

Three weeks later, the hospital wanted to discharge him. He was taking his medication at last and was more lucid.

'Will you be able to manage looking after your husband at home Mrs Patterson?' A rhetorical question really, as the Care Assessment manager continued, almost without drawing breath. 'We can arrange for carers to come in to help you with him and the Occupational Therapist will come in and assess the environment and suggest measures to make his home (his home?) safer for him. You may be eligible for a grant to convert your downstairs shower room into a wet room for him.' She spoke cheerfully but firmly, fixing Fran with an unwavering stare. Was she expecting Fran to throw up her hands and say she couldn't manage to look after him? Had she any idea what Fran was sacrificing with this new arrangement, so neatly setting itself in stone with every word the woman uttered? Fran nodded her head in mute, defeated agreement. There was nowhere to run. It was goodbye to her interesting career, her freedom, any hope of a more peaceful future with Rob. Her life as she knew it, like Starship Enterprise, was going into orbit. Never to return.

It got even worse. He could not talk coherently about anything after his seizure. Fran had to confront him about the double-life thing when he was fit enough to understand her. She couldn't not really. Could she? She screeched at him for quite a sustained period. Twenty-nine years of lies and betrayal!

It was quite cathartic. But it did not change her reality. She was stuck with him. The unpaid carer. The seizures continued, treated but not controlled. Frying millions of brain cells every time. She had to watch him regress gradually, into an angry, childish, demented curmudgeon.

His care needs went through the roof. Fran converted the front sitting room into a bedroom for him. For his benefit, of course. But, she could never have shared a bed with him again. A carer came in once a day in the morning for thirty minutes to help him shower and dress which did help a bit. The rest of the day and night was Fran's watch. Relentless, peppered with manic, stress-filled epileptic episodes. Powerful whole body convulsions only brought under control at first, when the paramedics arrived.

Fran lost count of the ambulance rides she went on with Rob. Or the hours she sat in A&E with him, waiting for him to be transferred to a medical ward. He was always unconscious, knocked out by the powerful anti-seizure medications administered by the paramedics or the hospital doctors, so she had to be there to give them his medical history. They should know it off by heart by now she thought to herself after the fifth visit in as many months. She was sure that the same doctors as before were asking her about Rob, but she might have been hallucinating. It was always in the wee small hours of the morning when Rob had his seizures. Not one for a more convenient nine-to-five emergency.

After three years of this, they finally got a suitable dose of the anti-epilepsy medication that controlled his condition, cutting the frequency of seizures to once every two to three months. He recovered better too and Fran could avoid the hospital trips and managed him at home. Exhausting, but better than spending hours sitting in A&E followed by the daily visiting in the ward while he recovered enough to be sent home again. Except that after every seizure he would be quite manic and extremely verbally aggressive for several days until his brain activity quietened down. Until the next one.

Payoff

Iona was still living in California when her husband Hugh died in the Western Infirmary hospital in Glasgow. Catrina had come home and found him slumped, unconscious at his desk and had called for an ambulance. Iona had flown back immediately when Catrina phoned her and they were both at his bedside when he quietly stopped breathing. He had not regained consciousness fully and Iona told Fran how guilty she felt about that. Hugh had stubbornly refused to come out to California and Iona had only flown back to see him a handful of times in three years. Too late for regrets. Fran tried to console her by pointing out that Hugh and she had made their choices about their long-distance relationship. Hugh remained loyal and supportive of her – from a distance. It had worked quite well for them. Hugh was a quiet, cerebral chap with a weak heart. Iona's frenetically paced lifestyle in California would not have suited him. Iona mourned for him in her own unique way; toasting his passing with a few glasses of forty-year-old Glenfiddich malt whiskey. Hugh would have approved. He had been a whiskey connoisseur.

She had been asked to stay on by the studio and join a scriptwriting team for a new cable channel detective series. The main character was a middle-aged Irish man with a jaundiced take on life. They thought Iona would understand his character!

Keira had fully embraced the California way of life and had a part in the detective series as the glamorous assistant in the forensic labs. She had moved out of Iona's apartment and was living with one of the buff, bronzed actors from the show. Mercifully not the guy with the lead part, the disillusioned Irish detective. Iona told Fran that she had a fling with him herself for a few weeks, not long after she was asked to work with the script writers.

'I thought he was always just about to catch a cold the first few times I saw him. He was always sniffing, then I saw him inhaling a line of coke one night at my place when he stayed over. That was it for me Fran, I had visions of his nostrils flaring apart with nothing to hold them together.'

Fran laughed at the other end of one of their many overseas calls. Iona was incorrigible.

Fran arranged for Rob to go into respite care for a week and flew up to Glasgow to be with Iona and Catrina who was still staying in the house, or at least kept a lot of her stuff in a bedroom. Most of the time she was away on tour with her band, 'Intake.'

It was a miracle that she had come home to find Hugh, he could have died alone in the house. She was the lead singer with the band now and they were very popular with the Scottish crowds, but hadn't made much impact elsewhere. Keira couldn't get away; she was in the middle of filming. She and Hugh had never had a good relationship anyway.

It was a few days after the funeral. 'Not a bad turnout, considering he left the *Express* years ago,' said Iona, surprised at the number of people from the newspaper who turned up to pay their respects.

Fran silently thought that many of them came out of curiosity to have a look at Iona, she was after all, something of a celebrity these days and some of the older reporters remembered her, and Fran too as it happened, from their early years as gallous young things in the Press Bar in Albion St.

The mark of the passing years sat lightly on Iona's intriguing features. The blond curls had been tamed into a sleek bob framing her still smooth face. Only faint lines around her large blue eyes with their captured hint of pain, betrayed the lingering sadness of her losses. She remained statuesque and slender, no obvious signs of the copious amounts of whiskey that her liver had processed over the years. She had undergone pioneering reconstructive surgery in California with a top plastic surgeon and now had a pert pair of breasts that belied her age.

Fran thought ruefully about the ongoing battle she had with her own figure. Only hours working out at the gym and depriving herself of the chocolate her sweet tooth craved, kept her body in reasonable shape. She did love a glass or two of red wine, she had read that it was full of antioxidants so, why worry? She had long given up trying to control the greyness which showed up in such stark contrast against her dark brown hair (her crowning glory, as Rob had once said many years ago). After years of gradually lightening it with blond streaks, she finally gave in and let it grow out to silver. But it was still thick and lustrous. The facial lines were beginning to creep around her eyes and mouth, but she reckoned she had earned every one of them over the years. If she didn't scrutinise herself too closely in the bathroom mirror (why do bathroom mirrors always lie?) she thought she was still holding on to some semblance of her younger self. And why did it matter anyway? Her husband had stopped noticing or commenting on her appearance a long time ago, and now of course, he was so self-absorbed in his shrinking world that he probably wouldn't have cared if she walked around naked. She supposed it was sitting beside her still glamorous friend that made her feel so self-aware; a bit fed-up and envious of Iona's wealth and freedom.

There was a loud knock at the front door. The two women looked at one another in surprise. It was getting on in the evening, the light was fading quickly from the late summer sky. Iona walked to the door, still clutching her glass of whiskey.

'Bit late for visitors.' Fran said and followed Iona to the door.

'Max! What the hell are you doin' here?'

Instinctively and protectively, Fran stepped up alongside Iona, although her legs turned to jelly and her mouth dried up at the sight of her nemesis standing on the doorstep. Max had aged during his incarceration. The black shiny hair was now almost white and his dark eyes were sunken into hollowed orbs. His skin was sallow and his once sensuous mouth had thinned into a tight, compressed line.

'Let me in Iona. I need your help. You owe me.' The two women moved closer together and barred his way.

'Whatever you want Max, you can tell me here. You're not coming in.' Iona had reached behind her and was squeezing Fran's hand tightly.

'Come on Iona.' Max's voice turned wheedling and cajoling. 'I've read all about you and Keira's success in Hollywood, you must be loaded. Look, I've got nothing left. All my assets have been frozen. I'm a changed man Iona. I just want a peaceful life. There's nothing left for me in Glasgow now. I think moving to Israel and living in a kibbutz for a while would do me.'

If she hadn't felt so anxious about the real intentions of the malevolent man in front of them, Fran would have laughed at the absurdity of the high-living Max Cohen living the simple life in a kibbutz. Although she had to admit that he looked more like a hobo than the slick, wheeler-dealer of old. Was he still planning revenge against her for her part in his arrest she wondered? He was now glaring at her with undisguised loathing, obviously seeing her again made him forget his mission. Fran shivered and returned Iona's hand squeeze.

'All right Max. I'll buy your airline ticket for you and meet you at the airport with some cash to keep you going for a while. How soon can you leave? But,' she added quickly, 'only if you promise not to try and get in touch with me or Keira again'.

'You have my word. However, Keira is my daughter. If she wants to see me, you can't stop her. Can you?' Max stared challengingly at Iona. 'Depends how much it's worth to you for me to disappear for good.'

Fran heard Iona's intake of breath. 'Find out what flight you can get tomorrow from Glasgow to Israel or where you need to change and I will meet you at the airport. Is that a deal?'

'Aye. You got yourself a deal.' He turned to go. 'By the way, I am going via Panama. I need an open ticket.' He squared his shoulders and walked away.

'Panama!' they said in unison.

'No prizes for guessing why he wants to go there first. Wonder how much he's got stashed away offshore.' Iona continued, shutting the front door with a bang and draining her whiskey glass. 'We'll never be free of him you know. Keira will seek him out for sure. She keeps asking me when he is coming out of prison. I suppose I must tell her where he is.'

Fran stayed on for a few more days after Iona had met Max at the airport and sent him on his way. She never did tell Fran how much she had paid Max to get rid of him, but she told Fran that she would be selling the house, apologising that Catrina would soon have to find somewhere else to live.

'I have to get back to my job now Fran, but I want you to promise that you will come out and visit me as soon as you can.' Iona was restlessly pacing the room, the night before they both returned to their respective realities. Clearly, the encounter with Max had shaken her up and Fran wondered how much he had set her back financially. Fran had been hoping that she might have been considering coming home soon, but maybe she could not afford to now. Max had her in chains.

Poverty is all relative though, Fran considered. It will be a while before I can afford to put Rob into respite care again, even with help from Social Services. Will I ever get to go to California to visit Iona? But I don't envy Iona's situation. Max Cohen is like a pernicious disease in her life. What future influence will he have over Keira and will he keep coming after her and Keira for more money?

Caring

'And now Fran. What do you do?' She had just joined a new book club and they were going around the table introducing themselves. Eight pairs of eyes looked expectantly at her, waiting for her reply.

She had been the last to speak and had already learned that the group included a lady doctor specialising in paediatrics, a retired schoolteacher who was still doing supply teaching, a woman who ran her own catering company and the one token male who was a retired Royal Air Force Squadron Leader and was now an Air Training Corps instructor. For a few insane seconds, she considered blurting out 'Dominatrix' just to see the reactions.

'I am a full-time carer for my husband these days.' Fran had watched the light of interest in their faces die out. She was going to elaborate a little about what she used to do, but the group leader cut in quickly.

'Right. Now we all know what we do in our "real lives",' she paused, wiggling two heavily ringed fingers from each hand like animated rabbit's ears, 'let's get on with our chosen book title to be read and reviewed for our next meeting. That's the first Tuesday of next month.'

At the end of the meeting most of the group members chatted animatedly. Fran glanced at her watch realising she needed to get back home quickly – just in case. Two hours was the maximum amount of time that she ever felt comfortable leaving Rob unattended – on a good day. The doctor lady had been leaving too. Fran couldn't remember her name.

'See you all next month,' she announced, for them both, in her confident medic's voice, so Fran waved and murmured goodbye as well. The others looked around briefly, a collective 'Bye, see you next month,' salutation followed them as they headed for the library door.

'How long have you been caring for your husband?'

'Eight years now.'

'Oh dear, that's tough. Sorry, must dash, but hope to see you next month.' With an almost imperceptible brush of Fran's arm, she hurried away.

'To the day.' Fran added.

Fran clutched her copy of *Midnight's Children*, wondering how she was going to have the time, energy or interest to plough through it over the next four weeks. She had been hoping the book club might have provided a bit of light relief, *50 Shades* perhaps? She should read it. Everybody else had. She would download it tonight. Anything to avoid *Midnight's Children*. The possibility of some social contact away from the house had been appealing too. That obviously wasn't going to happen in a hurry.

'Eight solid years with no respite.' she muttered under her breath. The familiar, heavy sensation settled over her like a mantle as she turned the key in the front door.

'Is that you, Fran?' the querulous voice hit her full on in her solar plexus. 'Can you empty this… this.' He could never remember what his catheter bag was called.

'Give me a minute, I just got in!' What was the point? He was as immediately needy and as single-minded as a child. 'Just slightly worse than you were eight years ago *before* your stroke.' Fran had taken to talking quietly to herself; an alternative to yelling at him.

She sat downstairs with a cup of tea after sorting him out. A guilty sandwich bought from Marks & Spencer on the way home saved her the tedium of cooking him a meal, just for today.

He was unusually quiet at that moment, so Fran rested her head back on the sofa, enjoying the peace while it lasted. Carer. She hated that word. That was how the world defined her now, who she had been, her identity almost, had been taken from her. Most of her waking moments revolved around concerns about his health and well-being. She was a nonperson, a mere conduit for his needs. At that moment eight years ago, when he had collapsed spectacularly in the garden with half his brain being obliterated by a blood clot, so too, had Fran's identity starting deserting her.

She thought of all the aspects of her 'pre-stroke' life that might have ignited a spark of interest in her from the book club group. She could have mentioned her successful recruiting business from years ago, her therapy work (she still did the occasional massage for friends) her corporate stress management business. Perhaps even her stab at journalism while living in the Middle East. There were some juicy tales to share from that era of her past life! But, that is just what it all was and where now, it needed to stay, in the past. This was her reality now; she was in bondage as full-time carer to a man whose brain was destroyed beyond repair. Beyond forgiveness? How much longer? *I don't know how much more of this I can take.* The social worker said she would recommend that Rob be assessed for residential nursing care, but that was weeks ago. She had heard nothing.

She dwelt again on the passing of the years, punctuated by his regular seizures, every one destroying more cognition. He had shouted very loudly and quite aggressively most of the previous night, the fourth in a row. His prostate had ballooned two months earlier, blocking the exit. He didn't want anyone but her to empty his catheter bag, every two hours, day and night. He couldn't manage it himself, he said.

Her thoughts continued remorselessly, rolling through her mind like tumble stones, piling up in the back of her throat. *You wouldn't keep an animal alive like this. There is no quality to his life. There is no quality to* my *life. Arrogant bastard refused to take warfarin when he had that mini-stroke nine years ago. Thought he knew better than the doctors. All this could have been avoided. My marriage has been a total sham and now I am trapped forever.*

Her chest felt tight, her heart constricted, beating behind her eyes. 'I am so tired – of it all.' Her eyes closed.

'Fran! Fran! Help! Help!'

Fran's eyes flew open, her heart hammering, breathless with panic. She ran up the stairs and into his room.

'What is it now? I was sleeping!' As if that was relevant.

'Can you empty this for me?' He pointed his shaking hand at the bag strapped to his leg.

'For God's sake, there's nothing in it. I just emptied it ten minutes ago!' Her voice sounded unearthly, hovering in the air above her head. He slumped back on the bed, his eyes closed, feigning sleep, avoiding the tirade.

She could not take much more of this. She could not. It wouldn't take much to shut him up. Maybe she could poison him, or suffocate him with a pillow? What would people think if they knew she was feeling so murderous. *I don't care anymore.* She would phone Iona, she gets me. She always did.

Dimly, in the distance, she heard the insistent ringing of the phone. The noise amplifying until it filled her head. She heard the answer machine clicking in.

'Mrs Patterson? This is Steve Wilson, the manager of the Nightingale Care Home. I'm pleased to tell you that a dementia support room has become available for your husband. If you still want to take it, we will need to arrange a home visit for a care assessment for him. Can you call me back please?'

A Kind of Freedom

It was so strange having the house to herself – and so much time. Now, she had so many options. She had her life back (except for the twice weekly visits to see Rob). Fran luxuriated in sleeping. So much lost sleep to catch up on. Do you ever catch it up she wondered? Or is it like saving money in a bank, dipping into your sleep bank whenever you were short? What would she do with all her spare time? Perhaps she might manage that long-awaited trip to see Iona in California, or another old expatriate friend from Saudi Arabia, now living in Switzerland? Join the National Trust, the gym, a walking group, go to concerts and the theatre?

Then reality kicked in. She had managed their finances quite well with their two pensions and Rob's Attendance Allowance. As soon as he went into the nursing home, she had to pay nearly all his pension to the Trust that owned the home to top up the portion paid for by Social Services. She would need to generate some extra income somehow. They had no savings. So much for retirement she thought grimly. The only other option was to downsize again or move out of the area. But they had lived in this area for years, she had a few good friends, a support network, familiarity, she wanted to stay. She was too old to be employed, it would have to be massage work. Maybe she could still do that from home? She had a spare room. Yes! That was the answer. Good job I'm still quite fit.

Rob's essence was fading from the house. She had redecorated his room and had the carpets cleaned. It smelt fresh. Different. Why then did she feel so bereft? Her grief she realised, was not for his leaving, but for what might have been. For a life they could have shared. A fantasy life that she had wanted and hung on for. A life that was never going to play out the way she had dreamed of. Love and the companionship of a partner with a long, shared history. Living out their golden years together...

She remembered the only time he had cried, a few years before he quit flying. They were in bed together and she had suddenly realised that his neck had creases, the first time she had noticed them.

She started singing, 'Darling we are growing older/silver threads among the gold.' He wept, a rare event, and she made love to him very tenderly that night. Feeling connected with him for once. She wondered now if the words had struck a guilty cord in his conscience. Her own tears of self-pity welled up.

That night she dreamt she was being held and loved, a wonderful mixture of passion and tenderness, but her mind would not create a clear image of her lover. She woke up in a state, her heart pounding in the old tell-tale rhythm. Cell memory. A pensioner with a pulse in overdrive because of a shadowy remembrance.

She did not think she would ever want to share her life with a man again, even if Rob were to die before her. She had spent too much time on her own. Loneliness had gradually morphed into acceptance and satisfaction from doing things her own way and in her own time. But sometimes she longed to feel a pair of strong arms around her; protective and caring. She remembered with gratitude, the men who had made her feel that way, for two brief episodes in her life, back in the day.

Better to have loved and lost than never to have loved at all. She had often repeated that saying to herself over the years when the voids in her relationship with Rob overwhelmed her. Rob had tried in his way – but he could not make it work for them. Whatever love and loyalty he had felt for her had been diluted for years with another woman.

'Did you love her? Suzanna?' She had asked him not long after he moved into the nursing home and she came across Suzanna's photograph on the funeral programme tucked away in Rob's bedside locker at home. Yes, she was beautiful, dark, sultry, but with a deep sadness reflected in her large brown eyes. She too had waited half a lifetime for Rob to make a commitment to her which he never did. She must have loved him very much to have put up with the lies and deceit gluing their relationship.

'Yes, I did love her, but I loved you too Fran. I couldn't lose you or the girls.' His voice was weak, tremulous.

'But Rob, you should have let me go. Given me a chance to create another life for myself. She would have been a better partner for you than me. You could never communicate with me, but obviously, you could with her. You would still have had contact with the girls. They loved you. Still do despite everything. You are their father. You should have made a choice. You were selfish and ruined the lives of two women because you were too weak to let go of either of us.' Maybe I was too weak as well she thought.

Rob just closed his eyes and turned his head away. He had no more to say. Fran was not sure that he could even remember half of it. Just recently he was forgetting names, his siblings, his grandchildren and sometimes even his son from his first marriage. Possibly pointless bringing it all up again now, but Fran realised that she had never actually said anything like that to Rob before. It was a sort of closure, at least for her.

'Fran. Sorry to wake you. It's Trisha from Nightingale. Can you come in? We think Robert's had another stroke.' (they always called him Robert, he protested at first, but gave up). 'The ambulance is on its way.'

Fran drove through the night at breakneck speed. No police cars around thank God. Her heart was in overdrive again, echoing the earlier experience. But fuelled this time by some cortisol-enhanced, nameless fear. He had only been in the nursing home for a few months, but had been hospitalised twice. Once with a urinary tract infection (damn catheter was a bug trap) which made him have a seizure and go out of control. Manic and unmanageable. The second time, he had fallen and fractured his hip. Silly old fool, trying to do some exercises he had said. The only part of his old self that was still occasionally active. Some part of his destroyed brain still clinging on to his internal landscape of what had once defined who he was; his obsession with fitness. His dementia took a nosedive after that. Accepting at last that he was beyond reach or reason, Fran began to feel compassion and something approaching true pity for him. Was it forgiveness? He was such a broken man. He would not want to live like this if he had any say in the matter. He spent most of his days curled up in his bed, sleeping away what was left of his reality. She got to the Nightingale just as the ambulance was pulling up to the door. Saturday night, they were busy.

'OK, love. Let's see what going on with your husband.' Fran felt reassured by the company of the efficient paramedics. She stopped shaking. She had been grateful for their professionalism and support several times when Rob was still living at home. The last few seizures he had had were horrendous. She had not been able to get near enough to him to give him the buccal midazolam, the oral medication that brought the seizure under control. He would push her out the way. Still very strong for a man who spent most of his life in bed.

When they got to his room, the carer and the nurse were leaning over him. 'He stopped breathing, just this minute.' The nurse was agitated. 'We don't have a defibrillator here.'

The paramedics took over. 'Does he have a D.N.R. in place?' the shorter one asked Fran.

'Yes. I think so.' Fran answered, distracted. She could not take her eyes off Rob's face, waxy and so very still. His mouth contorted, white spittle on his lips. She glanced quickly at the nurse who nodded in agreement. She had just discussed and agreed the D.N.R. issue with Rob's nursing home G.P. the previous week.

'His heart has stopped.' The paramedic with the stethoscope looked up at Fran. 'Do you want us to try and resuscitate him?'

She took hold of Rob's hand. The skin was soft, dry and very hot. She lifted it and placed it against her cheek. She felt the tiniest flutter. The merest fraction of pressure from his fingers. She kissed his palm.

'Yes,' said Fran.

'Don't worry Fran. We'll look after Robert very well while you are away. Just relax and have a wonderful holiday. You're going on a transatlantic cruise with a friend I hear?'

Enduring friendship. Iona, the one constant in her turbulent life. Irreverent, courageous and surviving. It was a while since they had met up, but Fran knew they would immediately fall into their usual pattern of daft exchanges, lightly wearing their troubles, sharing life's absurdities, as they always had.

'Yes, thanks Trisha. I am, at long last, with my friend Iona. We have been trying to arrange it for years. We are going on a seven-night cruise to New York, exploring there for a few days and flying over to California to stay at Iona's apartment for a week before I fly back on my own. Hear that Rob? Trisha and the others will look after you until I get back.' Fran bent over the frail shape of her husband curled up in his bed facing her. His dark eyes fixed onto her face. He clutched her hand.

'Don't leave me Fran. I love you.'

'I won't ever leave you Rob. I'll be back soon.' She kissed his forehead. He smiled, sighed and closed his eyes.

Reflections

'He will probably outlive me you know. When you think that he has survived a serious stroke, seizures, pneumonia and cardiac failure twice – plus endless urinary tract infections, all in the last ten years. He must have a constitution like an ox.' Fran closed her eyes against the sparkle from the lapping Atlantic waves. They were on their private balcony of Iona's Britannia Suite on Cunard's *Queen Mary 2*.

'Then you need to make sure that you live what's left of your time to the full. I don't know how you managed to look after him at home for as long as you did Fran. I couldn't have done it. You should have left him after the first episode in Germany. It might have been hard at first, but you were young then. You could have had a whole different life with somebody else. You are just too forgiving Fran.' Iona stretched languidly on the padded sun-lounger, her blonde, shoulder-length hair bleached almost as pale as Fran's hair, tied back into a careless, silver ponytail. 'Maybe I should have come back to look after Hugh when his heart started to fail, but I was too caught up in my script writing career in Hollywood. I suppose I was selfish.'

'That was a different situation Iona. You were already living and working in California and Hugh didn't want to come out. You had an understanding with Hugh about that. Perhaps I *should* have left after I found out about Rob's affair the first time, but the children were so young and I had no home to go back to at that time. And, he seemed so genuinely sincere about never being unfaithful again. I so wanted to believe him. I thought I owed it to all of us to forgive him and keep going. Then he had his stroke before I found out for sure about his double-life with Suzanna and after that, it was too late to leave him. Although to be honest, I did not dream that he would still be alive after all this time…

'Self-centred to the end Fran. He sure has put you through the mill. And you're still doing your best for him. You're a saint so you are.' Iona's speech was slurring slightly.

'I'm no saint believe me. I took a great delight in telling him about my fling with Akram after that ridiculous phone call from Suzanna denying that they were having an affair, which my instinct was telling me was a lie. It was sheer spite, I wanted to punish him. Make him feel something of the pain he put me through. Do you know what he said to me?'

'Don't blame you, he deserved it. What did he say?' Iona sounded interested.

'I quote,' said Fran 'How could you have slept with an Arab? You could have caught a disease. Don't understand why it had to be him.' Fran laughed. 'Unbelievable!'

'Amazing, the wonderful rationale of the cuckold.' said Iona

'I know it got to him though. He referred to it a few times over the years. Maybe he felt justified in carrying on with Suzanna after I told him that.'

'I doubt it, he would have carried on anyway, guaranteed.'

'If I'm honest, I'm still not sorry that I told him about Akram, but I gave that relationship up because I wanted to give my marriage a chance to recover. What a joke! Knowing Akram's reputation as I know now, he would have kept on seeing me if I had pushed it. Even though he was spending so much time in America. I think he quite enjoyed the risks. I heard on the grapevine that he got divorced. Wonder where he is now? I can tell you that my heart would flip like a teenager if I ever saw him again. He's probably with someone else. Not the type of man to live without a woman in his life.'

Iona patted Fran's arm. 'For sure, bloody men. At least my time with Max gave me an education and of course Keira. I can at least be grateful to him for that blessing. Although he did his best to ruin my relationship with her. Little turd that he is.'

Fran was on a roll now 'I suppose I always hoped that Rob and I would mellow into old age and at least enjoy some sort of companionship. Maybe take up golf, or something we could do together. Although knowing Rob, he would have been too competitive to want to play at my level.' Fran laughed again. 'He just didn't get any nurturing as a child and according to what I've read, that is probably why he is the way he is. Always looking for love. Very Freudian,' she added lamely.

'Yea, right,' Iona snorted. 'Max's mother was a harmless wee soul. Thought the sun shone out of her son's arse and look how he turned out. He was born a bastard. Some people just are.' There was no point arguing with Iona when she delivered such sweeping, incontrovertible statements.

'Whatever, but I think now that my anger about what he did has almost burned itself out. I just feel sorrow for him now. He is such an empty shell. It would be so much kinder for him if he would just let go.' Fran stared reflectively into her drink. Talking it all through again with Iona was beginning to feel quite cathartic. However, she realised that the pain of the betrayal still lurked just beneath the surface, always waiting to catch her out, like a troll waiting under the bridge.

'What about your girls? Do you hope that they might want to look after you when the time comes?' Iona asked.

'Good lord no! After my experience of coping with my clinging mother, that's the last thing I would expect of them. Mum never did manage to connect with me, even just before she died, she was not the nurturing type, just needed to be looked after. Anyway, Catrina has decided to stay in Scotland with her kids. Did I tell you she had split up with Duncan?'

Iona nodded. 'Yes, you did. Your memory is getting as bad as mine!'

'I know, I should keep a diary to remind me what I've done. But Catrina has made a lot of friends and Duncan has the children every other weekend.' Fran continued. 'She still writes songs for the band and has started a counselling course. I will be able to see her more often now that Rob is in the nursing home. Jess and David are thinking of emigrating to Australia. I'll miss them and the boys, but, I would never try to influence their decisions. They will have a better life over there. They both love the climate and the lifestyle. I'll find a way to go and visit them. If Rob goes before me, I could always stay with them for a month or two. But just for now, I can't go anywhere for too long.' She took another long sip of her drink to hide the sudden tightening in her throat, unexpectedly feeling trapped and resentful. 'What about you Iona? Are you ever going to come back home?' Fran asked tentatively. She had not seen much of Iona after Hugh's funeral and the unwelcome encounter with Max soon afterwards. They spoke regularly on the phone, but Fran had been too caught up with looking after Rob to take time out to visit Iona in California.

'I would like to come back at least during the summer months, but I'm spoiled now with the Californian lifestyle and the wonderful weather. I hate feeling cold! I have to pinch myself sometimes when I look back at how quickly I fell into all of this.' She spread her arms wide, embracing the luxury of their cabin and the vast expanse of Atlantic Ocean overlooked from their balcony. 'However, I have been offered the possibility of co-writing a new British comedy drama which could mean spending several months a year at home. I'm seriously considering it as I haven't done much writing recently. I don't need the money these days as the royalties from my book and the film just keep rolling in. But it would be good to spend some time near you, Fran, especially during the summer months! Keira doesn't show any signs of settling down anywhere with anyone. She just seems to bounce from one disastrous relationship to another. She's very serious about her acting career though and I hardly see her now.'

'I hope you do accept Iona, it would be marvellous to see more of you. You could stay with me until you decided if you wanted a place of your own or not. I was thinking of taking in a lodger, or signing up for that Airbnb thing. But I won't do that if you want the room. Plenty of massages on the house if you want.'

'Thanks Fran. Despite everything, I get lonely in California. The Americans don't quite 'get' me. I will decide after our holiday. I don't want anything getting in the way of this.' Iona clinked glasses with Fran 'Although, to be honest, I would give it all up in a heartbeat if I could have one more day with Liam. Nothing in my life compares to the love I shared with him.' Iona continued, turning the small horse brass over in her hand, the only memento of her life with Liam that she had kept by her over the years. 'I will never get over losing him.'

Fran's heart squeezed painfully for her friend's enduring loss and for her own sudden feeling of emptiness. She laid her hand on Iona's arm. They were in danger of becoming maudlin.

'At least you still have Keira and she is still in the same country as you' Fran added brightly, hoping to lift the mood.

'Fran, Keira got in touch with Max. He was on Facebook of all things and sent her a 'friends request'! He was making it easy for her to find him. He is not allowed into the U.S.A. because of his criminal record, but she was a week late coming back from Europe after filming of the movie was finished. She was all hostile with me at first when I asked her where she had been. Then she got very defensive and admitted that she had been to Panama to visit Max. She wants to go again. She says he has changed and that he is not very well. Needs to pay someone to look after him.'

'So, he never made it to the kibbutz after all?'

'Of course not! He never had any intention of going there. All he was interested in was extorting money from me and now it seems, from Keira. The sleazy toad. I thought I had finally paid him off. He has cost me a fortune, but I know Keira has given him money now too. Probably to keep him quiet. She wouldn't want the studio bosses to know that her father is a criminal. He will never let her go now. Poor girl, she still can't see through him. He still knows how to charm and manipulate her and he will probably try to turn her against me again.' Iona stabbed furiously at the dish of olives on the table between them.

'I'm sorry to hear that Iona, hopefully Keira will realise that he is just a con-man. He has not changed, has he? What a pair we are, both of us stuck with two very different men we can't shake off.' Fran bit hard into a green olive.

'Well, you know what Fran? From now on we must just 'seize the day' and stop waiting and hoping for them to fall off their respective perches. You must come out to California regularly and have holidays with me. I'll take care of it. I have a huge collection of air miles you can use up.' She added, suddenly cheerful again and squeezing Fran's arm hard, 'I miss you girl. I miss the fun we had back in the day. I can't believe it's over sixty years since I first met you. Life sure got in the way for both of us'.

'It certainly did, but as Shakespeare quite rightly said, *Love is not love which alters when it alteration finds.*' quoted Fran sleepily, taking another sip from her gin and tonic.

'*It is what it is,*' responded Iona philosophically, morosely drinking deeply from her whiskey cocktail, especially invented for her by their personal steward, the lovely Antonio.

"Yes indeed, *there it is.' Amadeus,* my favourite movie of all time,' added Fran, not to be outdone.

What is '*it*' anyway?' Iona asked, as Antonio magically appeared and expertly replenished their drinks before disappearing quietly.

'You know, shit. Shit happens.' Fran sank back onto her sun-lounger, examining her arms, tanning nicely after three days on board. She probably should dilute the next gin with a lot more tonic.

'Who said that? Sigmund Freud or Carl Jung?'

Fran spluttered into her drink. 'Forrest Gump.'

'Oh yes. So it was.'

The grace notes of their laughter echoed across the ocean, before dissolving and blending into the churning waves. The first clap of thunder, followed by a bolt of forked lightning and the sudden, fat raindrops, sent them scuttling unsteadily into the palatial interior of Iona's cabin suite. Both had managed the transition without spilling their drinks and they collapsed into the comfortable armchairs, still laughing about their alcohol-fuelled attempt to explain the meaning of life.

Below decks, the Petty Officer in the Communications room answered a call on the ship to shore telephone.

'Please request that your passenger, Mrs Frances Patterson, calls the Nightingale Nursing Home urgently.'

The End

Acknowledgments:

Many thanks to artist and friend, Libby Evans who designed the book cover. Also to my friends and fellow writers from my creative writing class who patiently read various draft versions and encouraged me to continue. To my teacher, Jan Moran Neil who taught me the craft of writing and to Diane and Anne whose extraordinary lifelong friendship and experiences inspired me to write this story.